Peter Cheyney and The Murder Room

>>> This title is part of The Murder Room, our series dedicated to making available out-of-print or hard-to-find titles by classic crime writers.

Crime fiction has always held up a mirror to society. The Victorians were fascinated by sensational murder and the emerging science of detection; now we are obsessed with the forensic detail of violent death. And no other genre has so captivated and enthralled readers.

Vast troves of classic crime writing have for a long time been unavailable to all but the most dedicated frequenters of second-hand bookshops. The advent of digital publishing means that we are now able to bring you the backlists of a huge range of titles by classic and contemporary crime writers, some of which have been out of print for decades.

From the genteel amateur private eyes of the Golden Age and the femmes fatales of pulp fiction, to the morally ambiguous hard-boiled detectives of mid twentieth-century America and their descendants who walk our twenty-first century streets, The Murder Room has it all. >>>

The Murder Room
Where Criminal Minds Meet

themurderroom.com

Peter Cheyney (1896–1951)

Reginald Evelyn Peter Southouse Cheyney was born in Whitechapel in the East End of London. After serving as a lieutenant during the First World War, he worked as a police reporter and freelance investigator until he found success with his first Lemmy Caution novel. In his lifetime Cheyney was a prolific and wildly successful author, selling, in 1946 alone, over 1.5 million copies of his books. His work was also enormously popular in France, and inspired Jean-Luc Godard's character of the same name in his dystopian sci-fi film *Alphaville*. The master of British noir, in Lemmy Caution Peter Cheyney created the blueprint for the tough-talking, hard-drinking pulp fiction detective.

By Peter Cheyney

Lemmy Caution Novels
This Man Is Dangerous (1937)
Poison Ivy (1937)
Dames Don't Care (1937)
Can Ladies Kill? (1938)
Don't Get Me Wrong (1939)
You'd Be Surprised (1940)
Your Deal, My Lovely (1941)
Never a Dull Moment (1942)
You Can Always Duck (1942)
I'll Say She Does (1946)

Slim Callaghan Novels
The Urgent Hangman (1938)
Dangerous Curves (1939)
You Can't Keep the Change
  (1940)
It Couldn't Matter Less (1941)
Sorry You've Been Troubled
  (1942)
They Never Say When (1944)

Uneasy Terms (1946)
Dance Without Music (1947)
Calling Mr Callaghan (1953)

The 'Dark' Series
Dark Duet (1942)
  aka *The Counterspy Murders*
The Stars Are Dark (1943)
  aka *The London Spy Murders*
The Dark Street (1944)
  aka *The Dark Street Murders*
Sinister Errand (1945)
  aka *Sinister Murder*
Dark Hero (1946)
  aka *The Case of the Dark Hero*
Dark Interlude (1947)
  aka *The Terrible Night*
Dark Wanton (1948)
  aka *Case of the Dark Wanton*
Dark Bahama (1950)
  aka *I'll Bring Her Back*

Dark Bahama

Peter Cheyney

An Orion book

Copyright © Peter Cheyney 1950

The right of Peter Cheyney to be identified as the author of this work has been
asserted in accordance with the Copyright, Designs and Patents Act 1988.

This edition published by
The Orion Publishing Group Ltd
Orion House
5 Upper St Martin's Lane
London WC2H 9EA

An Hachette UK company
A CIP catalogue record for this book is available from the British Library

ISBN 978 1 4719 0187 4

www.orionbooks.co.uk

To Walter Whisker

Nut-brown baby, you got rovin' eyes.
You don' say nothin' but yo' sure is wise.
You don' say nothin' with dem honey lips
But yo' sure say plenty when you swing dem hips.
Ah feel de knife in ma breeches when yo' swing dem hips
At dem high-yaller bastards off de sailin' ships.

CHAPTER ONE

FOURTEEN MILES off the tail end of Andros Island in the Bahamas lies the island called Dark Bahama—which, says the guide book, is a natural paradise.

Day and night the golden sand beaches, the calm inlets, the palms, the cats-tail trees, are bathed in sunlight and moonshine—especially moonshine. It is always summer except when a half-hurricane strikes in the season and the drunks have another excuse for nerve troubles.

Many people—people not looking for trouble—have discovered that they can find plenty of it in a place where the atmosphere is filled with sunlight and happiness, moonlight and love, calypso melodies, hard liquor and what-will-you.

Love, light and laughter live on Dark Bahama, and if these lovely attributes are gently interrupted by the soft sea-winds sighing in the palm trees and between the jacaranda groves, it may well be that the same sweet sounds are no louder than the cries of those ladies and gentlemen who have discovered that some minds are impervious to the beauties of nature and that it sometimes pays to watch your step even in a natural paradise like Dark Bahama.

Of course things are not like they were in the good old prohibition days when anybody with a sixty-foot motor-boat and enough money to take aboard a cargo of hooch at Jamaica could make a fortune *if* they were smart enough to run past the U.S. Coastguard cutters that lay, like sharks waiting for a bite, off the Miami coast.

Dark Bahama is a small island. Thirty-six miles by eleven, it is a slice of heaven in a summer sea. A place of sweet rest and what-have-you-got-baby.

And you can always buy what you want if you want it, and if nobody else is a trifle more interested in having it too.

If you see what I mean.

II

A small wind was blowing when Mervyn Jacques— a coloured gentleman with plenty of what-it-takes where dark lady lovers were concerned—came out of the Green Cat saloon, walked down to the quay, boarded his fishing motor-boat, sat in the stern and lighted a cigarette.

Jacques was of middle height. As negroes go, he was good looking. He wore a pair of rope-soled shoes, dark blue, gaberdine pants and a thin silk shirt. He moved like a cat and you could see the muscles ripple under his thin shirt. On his black, curly hair he wore a red skull cap with a long peak. He sat there, smoking his cigarette, drawing deep breaths of tobacco smoke into his lungs. After a while he threw the cigarette stub over the side. He began to sing "*Nut-brown Baby*." He had a quiet, rather soothing, tenor voice. He liked singing. It made him feel happy.

> "*Nut-brown baby, you got rovin' eyes.*
> *You don' say nothin' but yo' sure is wise. . . .*"

Jacques turned his head when he heard Mellin's footsteps on the quay ; Mellin was tall ; thin. He was a white man with a sun-browned skin.

He said : "Hi, Skip. . . ." He jumped into the stern ; stepped up on to the narrow passage-way that

ran past the pole-supported awning ; went forrard.
he called out : " Where's the customer, Skipper ? "

Jacques lighted another cigarette. He said : " You
tell me ! When ah think of all the goddam time ah
stick around here waiting for that no-good bastard. . . ."

Mellin said : " He'll be along."

Jacques heard the click as the ship's lights went on.
He said : " Hey, Mellin, you get some whisky out,
see ? Ah reckon when he comes aboard he's gonna
have a skinful and he'll want more. Ah reckon he'll
start bawlin' for whisky."

Mellin said : " You seen the straps on that fishing
seat ? "

" Ah seen 'em," said Jacques. " What's the matter
with dem straps ? "

" They're sorta frayed. Another thing, those straps
was all right two days ago. Maybe somebody's been
messing around with this boat."

Jacques shrugged his shoulders. " Ah'm not gettin'
excited."

Mellin said in a surly voice : " If it's O.K. by you,
it's O.K. by me. What do I care ? "

" That's right, boy. Don't you care about anythin'.
Ah don' care about anythin', an' ah'm the skipper. So
what do you have to care ? "

Mellin, who was right forrard, leaned on the canopy,
looking over the top towards the quay.

He said : " Boy, here he comes. Jeez . . . an' is he
high. . . ! "

Jacques got up. He walked between the two steel-
girdered fishing seats in the stern of the boat. He
jumped up on to the stern.

He called out : " Hi, Mister Sandford . . . ah'm
glad to see you . . . thought maybe you wasn't
comin' with us."

Sandford lurched on to the boat. He was big, burly,
over six feet tall. He jumped at the stern slope ; fell

into the cockpit. Jacques, moving like a cat, caught him before he hit the floor.

He said : " You take it easy, boss. You take it easy. . . . Look, let me give you a little straightener. . . ."

" Goddam you, nobody has to tell me to take it easy." Sandford's voice was thick. " And what the hell are we waiting for ? Let's get the hell out of here."

Jacques said softly : " Yo're the boss, Mister Sandford." He hollared : " Hey, Mellin. You got that blood aboard ? "

Mellin said : " Yeah. . . . I got it forrard here . . . four buckets."

Sandford said : " What the hell's all the talk about ? Do we have to stay here all night ? "

He sat down on the board seat that ran round the cockpit. He took a flask from his pocket ; unscrewed the stopper ; took a long swig.

Jacques said : " Here we go, boss." He moved forward in the cockpit ; switched on. He let the engine run, came back to the stern and cast off. The boat began to move, slowly at first, then gathering speed. A mile off the island Jacques took her in a half-circle, round the bottom of Andros Island. He headed in the direction of Cat Island.

Sandford was trying to light a cigarette. Over his shoulder Jacques watched him trying to get his lighter somewhere near the end of the cigarette. After several attempts he succeeded. He leaned back, drawing on the cigarette, trying to pull himself together.

Jacques began to whistle softly to himself.

Sandford said : " For crissake ! . . . Why don't you get yourself another tune. Every goddam time I come near you you're whistling or singing ' *Nut-brown baby.*' "

Jacques said : " Sorry, boss . . . sorta like that old song. It's got somethin', you know, Mister Sandford."

The moon came out from behind a cloud. The sea was quiet, but the air was hot and there was a restlessness about. Mellin, making some coffee forrard, thought it was one of those uncomfortable things. The heat was occasionally relieved by a sharp breath of cool wind. Mellin thought when the wind came it felt like an ice-box, and when it wasn't there the night was like an oven. You sweated or chilled, but most of the time you sweated.

He brought the coffee. Sandford drank it in great gulps.

Jacques said : " Mister Sandford don't want no coffee. He just had some whisky. What the hell he want with coffee ? "

Sandford seemed a little better. He asked : " Where're we going ? I want a big one to-night— a real one, see ? "

Jacques said softly : " Ah know exactly how you're feelin', Mister Sandford. Ah know. . . . We'll get one. They been around here to-day—amber heads an' all sorts." He busied himself preparing the line. When it was ready Sandford lurched into the fishing seat. He heaved himself into the chair and sat back.

Jacques said : " You play it quietly, Mister Sandford, an' you'll sure get a big one, ah promise you." He went back to the wheel ; cut the engine. Now the boat was moving slowly in a wide circle. Mellin was still standing forrard leaning on the canopy.

Jacques said : " You put the blood overboard, boy. We'll play around it."

" O.K.," said Mellin.

Sandford, sitting in the stern, watched the scene drunkenly ; heard the splash as the buckets of blood went overboard.

Jacques kept the boat moving slowly in a wide circle. Mellin put his head under the canopy. He said : " He's sitting in the port seat—the one I told you about."

Jacques said in a low, quiet voice : " Go fry an egg,

you goddam punk. What you worryin' about . . . hey ?
Why the hell don' you keep that goddam trap shut ?
You make me tired. . . . Yes, sir . . . an' how ! "

Now the moon came out of a cloud. For a few
minutes it was bright. The moon lay across the calm
waters like a silver dagger. Jacques began to narrow
the circle the boat was making, in the centre of which
Mellin had thrown the blood. The boat circled easily.
There was little sound. Then the moon went behind a
cloud. The sea was dark again.

Quietly, Jacques began to whistle, almost under his
breath : " *Nut-brown baby* . . ." Mellin was forrard.
He sat with his back to the bow, looking over the
canopy watching the stern. He saw the shark's fin.

He yelled : " Here she comes ! . . . Here she comes,
Mr. Sandford. . . ."

The shark's fin showed fifty yards astern of the boat.
Jacques cut the speed to nothing. He stood, one hand
on the wheel, half-turned, watching Sandford.

The shark dived ; took the hook.

Sandford said : " Jeez . . . a big one. . . ." He leaned
forward in the seat. Then, as the line jerked, he went
out of the seat ; shot across the stern. He knelt in
the stern sheets, his face stupid. He tried to get to his
knees.

The line jerked again. Sandford went over the stern
into the sea. A split second later Jacques, the cigarette
stub still hanging from the corner of his mouth, saw
the fin and the twist of the tail as the shark turned.

Mellin said hoarsely : " For God's sake . . ." He
ran towards the stern ; knelt, hanging over, looking
into the water.

There was a fearful shriek, a flurry of foam, then
quietness.

Mellin, white-faced, turned. He saw that Jacques
was lighting a fresh cigarette. He moved towards the
negro.

He said : " Well, it's got him. He didn't even get the belt done up. If he had it wouldn't have been any goddam good to him." He was sweating.

Jacques looked at him in the half-light. The moon came out from the clouds. Jacques looked over his shoulder at the sea. It was calm and moonlit.

He said : " What d'you always get so goddam excited about ? It ain't the first time a shark got a fisherman, is it—'specially when he's high an' don' know what he's doin' ? See what I mean ? "

Mallin said : " Yeah, I ain't worrying. It's not my boat."

Jacques said : " You won' never have no boat. No, sir . . . you won' never have no boat, boy, because you get so goddam excited. An accident can happen— can't it ? Ah reckon it's no good us stickin' around here. We can't do nothin'. Maybe we'll put back." He went on : " You get yourself a cup of coffee, Mellin. Ah'm mighty sorry about this . . . mighty sorry ! Mister Sandford was a great guy . . . ev'body like Mister Sandford."

Mellin said : " Maybe . . . except when he was drunk . . . and he was *always* drunk."

Jacques said : " That's a silly thing to say. Ah reckon Mister Sandford wasn't drunk to-night. No, sir . . . he was sober all right. Ah never seen him so sober. See, Mellin ? "

Mellin said slowly : " Yeah . . . yeah. . . . I guess he was sober."

Jacques smiled. He showed his even, white teeth. " You good boy, Mellin. You never know . . . maybe you keep your nose clean an' one day you'll get a boat —a boat like this. A swell boat, see ? "

Mellin said : " I'm going to have some coffee."

Jacques jumped on to the narrow passage-way that ran round the boat. He took off his left canvas shoe. He put his foot under the canopy and took the wheel between his black toes. He stood there, hanging on to the side of the canopy, steering the boat towards the lights of Dark Bahama.

He began to croon. He sang softly : " *Nut-brown baby, you got rovin' eyes. . . .*"

CHAPTER TWO

I

VALLON CAME out of the lift; began to walk towards the offices of Chennault Investigations. He looked at his strap-watch. It was ten o'clock—too soon for Madeleine to have left the theatre. He walked down the corridor past the telephone operators' room; the night staff room. He unlocked the door of his office; switched on the lights; took off his hat; sat at his desk. He lighted a cigarette; put his feet up on the desk.

After a while he moved the house telephone towards him with one foot; reached forward; picked up the transmitter. He said to the girl on the switchboard: "Is Mr. Marvin in?"

"No, Mr. Vallon. He went out about half an hour ago. He said he'd be back soon after eleven."

Vallon asked: "Anything else?"

"Yes, there is. I'd have called you before but I didn't know you were back. There is a lady in the waiting-room. She wants to see you."

Vallon asked: "Who is she, Mavis?"

"I don't know," said the girl. "When I told her that you weren't here but were coming back she said she'd wait. I asked her her name. She said she didn't want to give it."

"All right," said Vallon. "Send her in, Mavis."

He took his feet off the desk.

The side door leading from Vallon's office to the staff offices opened. Johns, one of the night staff, ushered a woman into the room. He went away, closing the door quietly behind him.

Vallon got up. He said : "Well, for God's sake . . . Thelma . . . ! Wonders will never cease."

She stood in the middle of the floor. He thought she made a superb picture. She was tall, slim, supple, curved in all the right places. Her blue-black hair made a vivid foil for her camellia-coloured skin and scarlet lips. She wore a close-fitting, black crêpe cocktail frock, trimmed all over with tiny jet tassels. Over it she wore a mink cloak. Her stockings were sheer, her tiny feet encased in high-heeled, black satin sandals. She wore long, pale-pink gloves, a close-fitting feather hat to match.

She said : " Well, sweet ? . . ."

He came round the desk. He stood looking at her. He said : " Has anybody ever told you that you look good enough to eat, Thelma ? "

She nodded. Her dark eyes were sparkling. " Somebody did once. *You* did. That was before you became quite so important as you are now—the proprietor of Chennault Investigations—the man who took a run-out powder on me."

Vallon laughed. She thought she liked the look of him when he laughed. His quiet eyes shone wickedly, and when his lips parted you could see his strong white teeth, the clear-cut line of his jaw.

He said : " Why don't you sit down and have a cigarette ? " He pushed a large leather armchair in front of his desk. She sat down. He gave her a cigarette ; lighted it.

" So I took a run-out powder on you, did I ? That's a slander."

She smiled up at him. She said in her soft, low voice : " It's almost true, Johnny. If you hadn't been in such a hurry to go off and marry some woman I think there might have been some future for us."

Vallon shook his head. He sat down on the edge of the desk looking at her. He said : " That's what you say now, and it's a long time ago, Thelma. Maybe you've forgotten that you took a run-out powder on me and got yourself married before I did."

She smiled ; shrugged her shoulders prettily. " What are a few years between friends, Johnny ? By the way, how is Mrs. Vallon ? " She leaned forward a little. " You're not telling me that you've been faithful to one woman for more than a few months, are you ? "

Vallon said : " You bet ! . . . When I've found a good thing I stick to it."

She raised her eyebrows. " So she's all that good, is she ? "

" Better than that." Vallon got up ; walked round the desk ; sat down in his chair. " I never expected to see you, and certainly not at this time of night. It's only by chance I'm here. I was filling in time before I went to the theatre to meet my wife."

She said : " I see. . . ."

There was a little silence. They sat looking at each other.

Suddenly Vallon asked abruptly : " What's this in aid of, Thelma ? Is this a social call or is it business ? "

She got up. She began to walk round the room. Vallon thought that she certainly knew how to move. She was as graceful as a cat. She turned and stood on the far side of the room, leaning against the wall. She looked remarkably effective like that. He thought that everything about her was very effective. She knew how to talk, how to carry herself, how to do everything.

She said : " You might call it business, Johnny . . . nobody's business . . . ! "

He grinned at her. " So it's like that, is it ? When you have business that's nobody's business you have to come to Chennault Investigations. It sounds like a murky story. What have you been doing, Thelma ? "

"Believe it or not, Johnny, I haven't been doing anything. After Jim died——"

Vallon interrupted. "So he's dead? I'm sorry to hear that, Thelma."

She shrugged her shoulders. "I wasn't *too* sorry," she said. "It's only after one's married that one discovers it should have been somebody else."

Vallon said uneasily: "Meaning who?"

"Meaning *you*," she said. "But, as Mr. Kipling says, that's another story. However, this particular business doesn't concern me. It concerns a woman who is a close friend of mine—a very close friend."

"Yes?" He stubbed out his cigarette. He sat, his elbows resting on the desk, his long thin hands clasped, looking at her.

She went on: "This woman is a very nice person. Her name is Nicola Steyning."

Vallon said suddenly: "Would you like a drink?"

She shook her head. "No, thanks, Johnny. But you have one. I've never known you to be too far away from a whisky bottle."

He smiled at her. "You'd be surprised! I'm a reformed character." He opened the bottom right-hand drawer of his desk; took out the flask of Bourbon. He unscrewed the top; put the neck in his mouth; took a long swig.

She walked across the room; sat down in the chair in front of the desk. She said: "Still the same old Johnny."

He said: "Let's forget me. Let's talk about Nicola Steyning. Is it Mrs. or Miss?"

"It's Mrs. . . . She's forty-three and looks thirty."

"I know," said Vallon. "That type—beautiful and charming and nice! She's got to be beautiful; otherwise she wouldn't be in trouble. Because she's got to be in trouble; otherwise you wouldn't be here telling me about her. What is it—money or some man?"

" You're wrong for once, Johnny. It's her daughter
—Viola Steyning."

He said, with a grin : " I bet she's good looking too."

She nodded. " She has too much everything. Her
figure's too good, her legs are too good and she's got
too much money. You know how that adds up, don't
you ? "

He said : " Yes. Usually a bad sum of addition.
What's she been doing ? "

She snuggled back into her chair, resting her pink
gloved hands on the arms. She leaned her head against
the back of the chair ; looked at him through half-
closed lids.

She said nonchalantly : " She's a bad lot, Johnny.
Her mother, Nicola, thought it might be a good thing
for her if she did a little travelling. So she travelled.
Nicola hasn't heard from her for quite a time. Do you
know the Bahamas ? "

Vallon shook his head. " I've never been there, but
I've seen a picture of it. Which part are we talking
about ? "

" We're talking about the island called Dark
Bahama," she answered. " That's where she is now."

" And I suppose she's raising hell ? " Vallon queried.

She nodded. " Every kind of hell. I don't think I've
ever known a girl with such an aptitude for getting
herself into trouble."

" Well, we're narrowing it down," said Vallon.
" What is it ? Is she being blackmailed, or is Chennault
Investigations being asked to buy off some outraged
wife whose husband has strayed, or been deflected by
our little Viola, from the straight and narrow path ? "

" You're wrong again, Johnny. It's probably *all*
those things. But the main thing is her mother wants
her got away from the island. She wants her to come
home. She's been hearing all sorts of rumours—some
of them not very nice—about Viola."

" I see," said Vallon. " So I'm to send an operative out to this island—Dark Bahama—to bring the young woman home under his arm ? "

She shook her head. " No, Johnny, that won't do. *You* have to go."

He said : " I see. . . ." There was another—a longer—pause. Then he asked : " Why ? "

She shrugged her shoulders. " Well . . . this is one of those things. The girl isn't easy to handle. It's going to need somebody like you for this business. I told Nicola you were as clever as the devil himself ; that you were brainy, very tough ; that no matter how much you might be tempted by, shall we say, beauty, if you were doing a job you'd see it through."

Vallon grinned. " Thank you for nothing, Thelma. Are you suggesting that one of my operatives, if he were sent, might get himself seduced or fall by the way and never come home ? "

" I'm not suggesting anything, Johnny. But I told her this was a job for you, and I told her that you'd handle it for my sake."

Vallon said : " I don't think that was wise, do you, Thelma ? "

She looked at him seriously. " What do you mean by that ? "

Vallon said evenly : " I've never believed in trying to resuscitate old ashes, and I've a lot of business to look after here. Also "—he looked at her sideways— " I'm very happily married."

" I see. You're not turning this down, are you, Johnny—or should I have said you're not turning *me* down ? "

Vallon got up. He began to walk about the office. After a while he said : " Look, Thelma, why didn't Mrs. Steyning come to see me herself ? "

She looked at him over her shoulder. " Because she's not well. She's in a nursing home. Her nerves are shot

14

to pieces because she's worrying so much about this girl. And I'm her best friend. Isn't it natural that she should ask me to come and see you ? "

Vallon asked : " How ill is she, Thelma ? "

" Ill enough. I'm not suggesting that she's lying in a stupor, but she has to take things very easily."

He stopped walking. He sat on the edge of the desk. " Well, she could have written, couldn't she ? "

She said : " Look, Johnny . . . what is all this about ? You've got a bee in your bonnet about something."

" I haven't. And if I had, the only bee in my bonnet would be you."

" Meaning what ? " she asked. She was half-smiling. Vallon could see the gleam of her small teeth.

He said : " Listen, my sweet, I believe this Mrs. Steyning could have handled this business for herself if she'd wanted to. You're doing it because—well, I don't know why, but you've got some idea in your head."

She smiled. " So you still think I'm a dangerous woman ? "

He said : " I don't think . . . I *know* ! . . . Look at you. I've never seen you look so beautiful or be so attractive. Every year that goes by you become a damned sight more dangerous, more attractive than the one before."

" You're not telling me you're *scared*, Johnny ? "

He shook his head. " I'm not scared. I'm wise. Work it out for yourself. This daughter of Mrs. Steyning's seems to me like a pretty hot proposition. She's been out on this island, and she's caused plenty of trouble—the sort of trouble that needs "—he grinned at her—" a man like me—resourceful and tactful and who can't be bought. That means real trouble, doesn't it ? I wonder just *what* she's been doing."

She said : " That's for you to find out." There was

15

another pause. She went on : " There's a lot of money in this, you know, Johnny. Mrs. Steyning is a very rich woman."

He asked : " What sort of money ? "

She said : " There'll be a thousand pounds for a retainer ; another thousand for your expenses, and I should think that when you came back and brought the girl with you, having cleaned up any little difficulties she might have encountered in Dark Bahama, you could name your own price for the balance. D'you understand ? "

" I see what you mean." He lighted a fresh cigarette. He asked : " Where are you staying, Thelma ? "

She said : " I'm at the Hyde Park Hotel. I shan't be there for long. I shall be leaving to-morrow evening. I'm going to France."

Vallon said : " I'll think this over. I'll telephone you to-morrow morning. How will that do ? "

" It'll have to do, won't it, Johnny ? " She made a little moue. " Do you know, I think you're being just a tiny bit brusque with me, aren't you ? "

He shook his head. " If I'm being brusque with anybody, baby, I'm being brusque with myself." He looked at his strap-watch.

She got up. She said : " Well, I suppose you must go to the theatre and meet your wife ? I think she's very lucky. I've never met her, but I imagine you're much too good for her."

Vallon said nothing.

She adjusted her cloak. " Well, *au revoir*, Johnny. I hope it is *au revoir*. . . ."

He walked past her ; opened the door that led into the main corridor.

He said amiably : " So long, Thelma."

She stopped abreast of him. He said : " That's a very nice perfume. It's called Visa, isn't it ? "

She nodded. " Yes. You're an extraordinary man,

Johnny. Still the same old memory for perfumes. One sniff and it's never forgotten ! "

He stood smiling at her.

She asked : " Aren't you going to kiss me, Johnny ? "

He shook his head. " Why start something, my dear ? Run off home. I'll telephone you in the morning."

She moved out into the corridor. She flashed a quick smile. She said : " Good night, Johnny . . . and damn you ! "

He watched her walk down the passage-way.

II

Marvin, who was the staff manager of Chennault Investigations, went into the Blue Point Bar in Jermyn Street just after ten.

Marvin was of middle height, thin. His greying hair was brushed meticulously. His overcoat was of good cloth, well fitting. He wore tan cape gloves ; carried an umbrella. Marvin, who was in charge of the operatives, on both the day and night staffs, who worked for Chennault Investigations, was a man with a quiet, orderly mind. Vallon had once told him that his job was that of a very efficient sergeant-major—a business which required tact and quite a lot of brains. Anybody who has ever had the handling of twenty-five operatives in a detective agency will know exactly what I mean.

Marvin's one vice was the Blue Point Bar. It attracted him for reasons which even to him were vague. His small villa was at Walton, where he grew tulips, and lived a quiet and orderly life with a plump, quiet and orderly wife. But every time he went into the Blue Point Bar, which was on two or three occasions each week, and usually late in the evening, he had a vague feeling that one night he might find something

—something amusing. On this particular occasion he found it. He found Isles.

Isles was leaning up against the mahogany bar at the far end of the room. He was talking to a girl. Marvin thought she was a neat little trick. She was sitting on a high stool, leaning forward. She wore a coat and skirt and the skirt looked as if it had been pasted on to her. She was talking to Isles and smiling up at him. From where he was standing Marvin could see the peculiar, pale-blue eyes, which often seemed to change colour and which were Isles's most distinguishing feature, looking down at the girl almost benignly.

Isles was tall, slim. He had one of those figures that tailors love to hang clothes on. And his clothes were good—or had been. Marvin, with his eagle eye, thought he could detect the signs of a little too much brushing ; that the elbows of the well-cut grey sleeves were possibly a little shiny. He saw also that one of the well-polished semi-brogue shoes—the one nearest to him—merited a little attention from the shoemaker. He wondered why Isles would be like that.

Marvin walked farther into the room ; found a place at the bar ; ordered a White Lady. As the barman put the drink in front of him, he heard Isles's voice behind him.

It said : " Hallo, Papa Marvin. You're just the man I wanted to see."

Marvin turned ; smiled. " Hallo, Isles. I didn't think to see you here so soon."

Isles moved behind him. He looked down at Marvin with a good-natured smile. " Why not ? "

Marvin said : " We heard you'd got into a little trouble in South America. We heard you were in gaol ; that it would be a long time before you would be coming out. *That's* what we heard. I'd have spoken to you, but "—he looked towards the girl at the end of the bar—" I thought you were with a lady."

Isles said softly : " I very seldom have the opportunity to talk for long with ladies, and about that
South American thing, you were only half-right. It's
perfectly true they did sling me into gaol. Ever been
in a South American gaol, Papa ? Not very amusing,
I promise you." His face hardened. " However, I had
a good friend, so they decided to let me out."

Marvin said, with a smile : " I bet the good friend
was a woman."

Isles shrugged his shoulders. " That doesn't matter
now. The point is I'm here."

Marvin said : " And I'm glad to see you. By the
way, you said just now you wanted to see me. What
about ? "

Isles said casually : " I want to see you about a
double Bacardi, quickly."

" My God ! " said Marvin. " Is it as bad as that ? "

" It's worse than that, Papa."

Marvin ordered the drink. He asked : " Are you in
London ? "

" For a few days," said Isles. " I've a bed-sitting-
room—I think they call it—No. 14 Planters Road,
Streatham." His thin face broke into a whimsical
smile. " If you ever live in a bed-sitting-room, don't
take one at No. 14 Planters Road. But it's only for a
few days more," he went on. " Then I think I'm going
back to South America."

Marvin said in a quiet voice : " Things must be
pretty bad if you have to go back there. We thought
after that last thing that you wouldn't be awfully
popular."

" Needs must when the devil drives," said Isles. He
picked up the Bacardi ; sipped it ; looked at Marvin.
He said : " Here's to our next meeting." He took the
drink at one gulp. " Good night, Papa. I'll be seeing
you . . . one day . . . ! " He went out of the bar.

Marvin ordered another White Lady. When the

drink was brought he thoughtfully regarded it. Then he walked into the telephone box at the end of the bar. He called Chennault Investigations. He said to the girl on the switchboard :

" This is Mr. Marvin. Is Mr. Vallon there ? "

" Yes, sir. I'll put you through."

Vallon's voice came on the line. " What is it, Marvin ? "

Marvin said : " I'm in the Blue Point in Jermyn Street. Who do you think was here ? "

Vallon said : " You tell me. . . ."

" Isles. . . . He looks almost as well dressed as he used to be but only *almost* as well . . . understand ? He told me he was going back to South America, so things can't be very good. I wondered . . ."

Vallon interrupted. " You were quite right, Marvin. You wondered if I could use him for anything. You think it's a waste that a man like Isles should be going back to South America just because he can't find anything better to do. You didn't ask him his address of course ? "

Marvin said : " He's living in a bed-sitting-room at 14 Planters Road, Streatham. He's just gone home. I think he's broke."

Vallon said : " I see. Finish your drink and get a cab. Go to No. 14 Planters Road and bring him back here. I want to talk to him. Don't come back without him."

" Very well, Mr. Vallon."

Marvin came out of the box. Although it was his habit to drink only two White Ladys, on this occasion he stood himself a third. He liked Julian Isles. Then he went outside ; looked for a taxicab.

III

Vallon looked at his watch. It was nearly eleven o'clock. He thought that in a minute he would have to go to the theatre. Then he thought maybe he would not have time to get to the theatre. He called through to the switchboard.

He said : " I'm going to be busy for a little while. Send one of the night men round to the St. Martin's theatre. Tell him to meet Mrs. Vallon and see her home. Ask him to tell her that I'm busy. I'll be back in an hour. Understand, Mavis ? "

She said : " Very good, Mr. Vallon."

Vallon walked round the large office twice ; then he had another swig at the whisky flask. Then he picked up the telephone.

He said : " Mavis, get through to the Hyde Park Hotel and if Mrs. Thelma Lyon has arrived put me through to her."

" Very good," said the switchboard girl. " I'll ring you back, Mr. Vallon."

Vallon walked round the office twice more. He lighted a cigarette. He was thinking about Thelma Lyon.

The telephone bell rang. Her voice came, almost soothingly, over the wire.

" Hallo, Johnny. So you've decided."

Vallon said : " But not what you think. Listen, honey . . . don't go to bed. Stay up for a little while. I'm sending a man to see you. You can have the most complete trust in him. You'll find he'll handle the business you spoke of very well. His name's Julian Isles. He ought to be with you at a quarter to twelve."

" Well, I'm damned, Johnny." Her voice was cool. " How do you know that this man is going to be right? "

Vallon said : " I've never made a mistake about a

21

man yet, and I know this one *very* well. You'll find if anything he'll be better than I should be. If you've got any brains you'll use him. See what I mean ? "

" I understand, Johnny. All right . . . I'll see him. But, anyhow, I think you're a heel."

Vallon grinned. He said : " I know that. Treat him right, and you'll find he'll be very good."

She said : " Have you ever known me not treat anyone right ? "

" Like hell I have," said Vallon. " So long, honey ! " He hung up.

IV

The lift man, who had shown Isles to Suite 126 on the first floor at the Hyde Park Hotel, rang the bell once again ; waited ; shrugged his shoulders.

Then he said : " Well, it's very funny. The lady's in, sir, but she doesn't answer."

Isles said casually : " That's all right. Don't you bother."

The lift man went away.

Isles put his finger on the bell-push and kept it there. He could hear the bell ringing inside the apartment. Then, suddenly the door opened.

Isles said : " Good evening. I'm Julian Isles. Mrs. Lyon ? "

She stood in the hallway of the suite, holding the door wide open. She wore a garnet-coloured, silk velvet house-gown with gold mules. The sleeves of the house-gown were long, edged with chinchilla fur.

She said coldly : " You seem to be in a hurry, Mr. Isles."

He smiled. When he smiled his face became very attractive. She noted the good-humour lines at the corners of his eyes, his good teeth.

" I'm not if you're not," he said. " Mr. Vallon asked me to come round and see you. He said he thought it might be urgent."

She said : " I was changing. Will you come in ? "

He followed her across the hallway into the well-furnished sitting-room. A fire was burning. She walked over to the fireplace ; turned ; stood with her back to the fire looking at him.

She said : " Perhaps you'd like to leave your hat in the hallway. And would you like a drink ? "

" I'd like that very much, thank you." Isles went back into the hallway ; hung up his hat ; came back into the room.

She was busy at the sideboard. She said : " Tell me something about yourself."

Isles thought she had a charming voice.

" Is that going to get us anywhere ? " he asked evenly.

She looked at him over her shoulder. He was still smiling.

She thought he would be a rather difficult man to lose one's temper with. She brought the whisky and soda to him.

She said : " Isn't it rather natural, Mr. Isles, that when a woman entrusts a commission of some importance to a man she might like to know something about him ? "

Isles nodded.

She went to a table ; came back with a cigarette box ; offered it to Isles ; took one herself. He lighted the cigarettes.

" That's very reasonable," he said. " But supposing, for the sake of argument, my past history *wasn't* very good. I wouldn't be likely to tell you, would I ? On the other hand, as I have been sent to you by John Vallon, it might be in order for you to take that side of the question for granted."

She went over to the settee ; sat down. Isles sat in the armchair by the fire.

She said : " That depends on how well I know Mr. Vallon."

" Nonsense," said Isles cheerfully. " You know Vallon pretty well. No woman goes to a man and asks him to look after the safety of a—shall we say— ' reluctant ' daughter of a friend unless she knows something about him."

" I see. . . . Tell me, Mr. Isles, exactly what did Mr. Vallon say to you ? "

Isles said : " I imagine he told me what you told him. He gave me an outline of the job you wanted me to do. He said you'd be waiting to talk to me about it."

She got up. She began to walk slowly up and down the long room. He thought she was very effective when she walked, or sat down, or did anything else. He thought she was *good*.

She said : " I'm perfectly certain if John Vallon thinks you're all right for this business then you must be. I went to see him to-night because I'm concerned about the daughter of my friend Mrs. Steyning. She's really a very nice—very beautiful—girl. Actually, basically, she has a charming nature, but I think she's been worried and has become a little out of hand. You understand ? "

Isles said flatly : " No, I don't. I'd like to know exactly what you mean "—he was still smiling—" by a young lady who is basically charming but has become a little out of hand. *How* has she got out of hand ? Is it money, drink or love ? Has she got around with too many men ? Is she being blackmailed ? Is she drinking too many cocktails ? What sort of trouble has this young woman been creating ? "

She said quietly : " Mr. Isles, I'm beginning to wonder if I like your attitude towards this business."

Isles shrugged his shoulders. "Does it matter? My attitude doesn't come into it. You'll realise I'm thinking of Mrs. Steyning's interests. It isn't very much good my trying to do anything unless I know something about the girl, is it?"

There was a pause; then she said grudgingly: "I suppose you're right."

Isles grinned at her.

She went on: "What I meant was this. This girl was very nice—almost a quiet type—until a couple of years ago when she began to do a little travelling. I don't think she's ever been very good friends with her mother, if you understand what I mean. They like each other very much"—she smiled suddenly—"but perhaps they're both too good looking. . . ."

Isles said: "I think I know what you mean. I take it that Mrs. Steyning, who is rather nervous and in a nursing home at the moment, is a little bit jealous of her daughter—or vice versa. Is that why the girl decided to travel, or was that Mrs. Steyning's decision?"

"I don't know. I think they both liked the idea."

Isles asked: "Had she been making any trouble at home?"

She shook her head. "No, I'm quite definite about that. But suddenly they came to this decision that it would be good for her to travel and she went off."

Isles said: "When did she start going off the rails —in Europe, or did she wait until she arrived in Dark Bahama?"

She went back to the settee; sat down; crossed her legs. Isles saw that she had very good legs and ankles.

She said: "I can't answer that question, but I am inclined to believe that some sort of climax happened in Dark Bahama. Whatever it was or whatever had been going on came to a head there."

Isles said: "That means it's a man. Am I right?"

She answered : " There might even be more than one."

He asked : " Has she money ? "

She nodded. " She has money, and she'll have even more in a couple of years."

He drew on his cigarette. He said : " Maybe some tough egg has been making trouble for her. It's an old racket. Maybe somebody's been trying to compromise her and is asking her to pay up to keep him quiet. It *has* been known, you know."

" Yes, I believe it has. However, it's for you to answer these questions, Mr. Isles, when you get there."

He smiled at her. His smile was lazy. She thought to herself that she liked this man too much, but that in some vague way he irritated her. She thought that there was something devastating about Isles—something almost hypnotic. Yet, under his casual and charming exterior, there was, she thought, something caustic and cynical—almost as if, under his affable and well-groomed exterior, he was laughing at her.

He said : " So you've made up your mind I'm to go ? "

She nodded. " If you call here to-morrow morning and inquire at the manager's office there'll be an envelope for you with a thousand pounds in bank-notes inside. This will enable you to arrange your passage and make your own financial arrangements. I want you to get away as soon as possible."

" I understand," said Isles. " And after that ? "

" I want you to bring this girl back here as quickly as you can. How you do it is your affair. You may find she is a little tough."

Isles said : " Are you suggesting that I may have to use force ? " He smiled again. " Have I to abduct this young woman ? "

She shrugged her shoulders. " I imagine you'll find some other means. I should think that you've had very little difficulty in handling women, Mr. Isles. I expect that if you can't manage to deal with her one way you'll find another."

" I expect so," said Isles. " Maybe you've the idea in your head that if one man can blackmail her so can another."

" That depends on how expert you are at blackmail, Mr. Isles."

" I can always learn, Mrs. Lyon," said Isles. He went on : " I don't think you or Mrs. Steyning need worry about this. I'll bring her back."

She said shortly : " Good ! "

Isles got up ; stubbed out his cigarette in an ash-tray on a nearby table. He said : " I don't suppose I shall have any difficulty in finding her. I take it Dark Bahama isn't a very big place ? "

" You're quite right. It's a comparatively small island. However, you may be assisted in that. Some time ago Mrs. Steyning, in an attempt to persuade her daughter to return, sent out her maid—an elderly and very intelligent woman—to try and bring the girl back. She failed, but she's still on the island. I think when you get there she might telephone you. She'll probably tell you where Miss Steyning is."

He said : " That might be a help."

She got up ; came towards him ; took his empty glass.

She asked : " Would you like a drink ? "

Isles nodded. He thought to himself : What comes now ?

She mixed the drink ; brought it to him. " Yours must be an interesting profession, Mr. Isles. Have you always been a private detective . . . I suppose that's what you call yourself ? "

Isles drank a little whisky. " I suppose so. I've been all sorts of things. In the war I was in the S.A.S., and I was also what is usually described as an *agent*."

27

She said : " I see. . . . You must have had a very tough time."

He shook his head. " Not more than anyone else in my peculiar profession. And I found it amusing."

She helped herself to another cigarette. She said : " I suppose you knew John Vallon in those days ? I don't know if he told you, but I asked *him* to do this for Mrs. Steyning. He didn't like the idea." She smiled suddenly. " I should have thought it would have appealed to him."

Isles said : " It would have done. Johnny used to be a great man for getting around, but you know he's married now—very happily married. And Chennault Investigations has turned itself into a considerable business. I suppose he has too much on his hands— too much business, I mean—besides Mrs. Vallon. Do you know her ? "

She shook her head. " I never met her. Tell me— what is she like ? "

Isles said casually : " Well, she's what they call a very beautiful woman—a very attractive one." He smiled suddenly. " I might go so far as to say that she's almost as beautiful as you are, except maybe——" He shrugged his shoulders.

" Except maybe what ? " she asked quickly.

Isles said : " Women vary like everyone else. She's beautiful and attractive, but she hasn't quite so much of that thing the Americans call ' oomph ' . . . or allure . . . or whatever you like to call it, as you have."

She said almost demurely : " I'm glad you find me alluring."

" Not at all," said Isles politely.

She drew on the cigarette ; looked at him through the smoke. " I suppose you and John Vallon are great friends ? "

He hesitated. " I wouldn't go so far as to say that. Good business friends possibly. I've done work for him before—quite a lot of work. It doesn't mean to say that I have to be all that *fond* of him."

She raised her eyebrows. She said : " Really ! "

He went on : " Men are funny cattle, Mrs. Lyon. They can work together and not necessarily like each other."

She looked at him sideways. She said softly : " Don't tell me that you wanted to marry Mrs. Vallon ? Don't tell me that your lack of friendship is due to *cherchez la femme*—shall we say ? "

Isles said glibly : " You might be right."

There was a pause ; then she said : " Women would find you quite a person, Mr. Isles. I should think, with your romantic background they might find you a *very* attractive man."

Isles said : " Thank you very much. Tell me, Mrs. Lyon—how do *you* find me ? "

" You're certainly forthright." She smiled at him. " Shall we say that I find you amusing ? "

" I'm glad to hear it. I hope Miss Steyning will find me as amusing."

She said quickly : " Supposing you have some trouble with this girl, what are you going to do ? "

He shrugged his shoulders. " How do I know ? I've got to get there and absorb the atmosphere of this place ; find out if I can what's worrying Miss Steyning ; find out if it's a man or men, and if it is, discover something about them. If they're not good types one can usually get something on them. I also have to find out something about Miss Steyning from *my* point of view. Afterwards I shall formulate some plan of campaign."

She asked : " I suppose you'll report from time to time to Mr. Vallon ? "

He finished the whisky. " I don't know that that's necessary. Johnny's pushed this job on to me and I don't think he expects me to report to anybody. After all, there aren't any reports to be made—not unless Miss Steyning gets *very* desperate."

She looked at him quickly. " And supposing she does ? "

Isles said : " I shall have to use desperate measures, shan't I ? And even then I don't suppose I should have to talk about them to anybody. If I bring the girl back everyone's going to be satisfied, aren't they, Mrs. Lyon ? "

She said : " I suppose so. And that is the answer to the question."

Isles asked : " Is there anything else ? "

" No. . . . I think we understand each other very well." She went on : " I think it's rather funny that you and Johnny Vallon should not be such great friends. He has the ability to irritate one sometimes if you know what I mean."

He nodded. " I know."

She said : " Well, that's that. I wish you the best of luck. If you come here in the morning you'll find the envelope downstairs as I've said. I hope you succeed. I feel certain you will."

She led the way towards the door out into the hall. She put her hand on the latch of the front door. She said : " Good night. If you succeed, you'll find I shall not be ungrateful."

Isles said quizzically : " Does that mean that you'll find me a little more attractive than I am ? "

She smiled suddenly. " Why not ? And even at this moment you're not doing so badly, Mr. Isles." She put out her right hand ; took his chin in it ; kissed him on the mouth.

Isles said : " I think you're the most extraordinary woman."

She stood there smiling at him. " Quite a lot of people have discovered that, Mr. Isles. Incidentally, I think you're a rather extraordinary man."

He said : " That's fine. Let's be extraordinary again, shall we ? "

V

It was half-past one when Isles arrived at Vallon's apartment in Sloane Street. He rang the bell twice ; waited patiently. After a minute Vallon, in a dressing-gown, opened the door.

He said : " Come in, Julian. How did you get on ? " He led the way down the corridor ; opened a door on the right. Isles followed him into a comfortable library. He threw his hat on to a chair.

" I got on all right," he said.

Vallon asked : " Do you want a drink ? "

Isles shook his head. " I've had two." He helped himself to a cigarette from the box on the mantelpiece. " I wonder what the hell she's playing at, Johnny."

Vallon said : " So you think she's playing at something ? "

Isles nodded. " Look, this Mrs. Nicola Steyning—the girl's mother—who's so worried about her, is in a nursing home. Did Mrs. Lyon tell you where ? "

Vallon shook his head.

Isles went on : " She must know that no ordinary private detective or investigator is going to take on a job like this without receiving some definite instruction from the girl's mother. The only person who can really give them any authority to go after the girl is the mother, isn't she ? Maybe that's why she came to you. Maybe she thought that you being you wouldn't ask to see the mother."

Vallon said : " Why should you think that, Julian ? "

" I wouldn't know," said Isles. " But I expect she's been your mistress at some time or other, hasn't she, Johnny ? "

Vallon said : " That's an odd question, but I see what you mean."

Isles said : " She ought to have told you where the mother lived, anyway, so that you could have checked, or gone to see her. She didn't do that because she had an idea when she arrived at your office you wouldn't handle the job. She knew you'd put it on to someone else—someone you could trust. And she took it that that person, whoever he was, wouldn't check on anything because the job came from you, and the fact that the job came from you would be good enough for anyone, see ? "

Vallon said : " What's in your mind ? "

Isles began to walk up and down the room. He took long, easy strides. There was certainty in his walk.

He said : " I'll tell you what's in my mind, Johnny. Our Mrs. Thelma Lyon thinks she's got away with it. She's got away with the most difficult part of the job so far as she's concerned. She thinks that nobody is going to check on Mrs. Steyning ; that I won't check because I've been employed by you, and that you certainly are not going to check because you feel under some sort of obligation to her. She asked me what I thought of you. When she asked me a question like that I knew she didn't expect me to tell her that you were a first-class fellow, so I obliged her. I told her that I didn't like you very much ; that we worked very well together, but as man to man we didn't hit it off. She jumped to the wrong conclusion, but a very logical one for her to jump to. She concluded that there had been some sort of trouble between us over a woman."

Vallon said : " You were quite right, Julian. There aren't any flies on you."

" She told me," went on Isles, " that if I pulled this job off, when I came back I shouldn't find her ungrateful. We had quite a little love scene in the hall, and I'm not going to say I disliked it. See what I mean ? "

Vallon said : " Not quite. What are you getting at, Julian ? "

Isles said : " Look, *there isn't any Mrs. Steyning.* Don't you see ? Whatever tie-up there is between Thelma Lyon and this girl Steyning is something that concerns Mrs. Lyon. I'll bet you any money you like *she's* financing this job and that *she's* the person concerned."

Vallon said : " Well, I can check on that for you."

" Where will that get you ? " asked Isles. " Supposing we discover that there isn't a Mrs. Nicola Steyning, it doesn't help. It wouldn't stop the job, would it ? I'd still have to go to Dark Bahama ? "

Vallon nodded. " When are you going ? " he asked.

" As quickly as possible," said Isles. " I'll fly. I am to go to her hotel to-morrow morning and draw a thousand. I think I'll be off now."

Vallon said : " Well, have fun, Julian, won't you ? "

They stood grinning at each other. Isles picked up his hat.

" So long, Johnny. Remember me to Madeleine. Don't stick your neck out while I'm away."

Vallon laughed. " Don't you stick yours out whilst you're away, Julian. But I'm not worrying. Even if you did stick it out you'd pull it back in time. So long."

Isles went out of the room. Vallon heard the front door close behind him. He lighted a cigarette ; stood in front of the fire, smoking it slowly. He was thinking of the old days—and of Thelma Lyon.

CHAPTER THREE

I

THE TIME has arrived when it is necessary that you meet Mr. Ernest Guelvada, who began his rather peculiar and extremely arduous service with Mr. Quayle at the beginning of World War II. At this time he was what was called a Free Belgian but, as a result of war services—in addition to a superior decoration, which he promptly presented to a lady who had pleased him more than somewhat—he had acquired the status of an English national.

Guelvada was the result of his experiences which, since his early days, had been very interesting if not colourful. He had been born some years before World War I at a baconry near Ellezelles, in Belgium, and his mother—poor soul—had intended him for the priesthood. Events, however, interfered with his vocation.

Guelvada's mother had been stabbed by a German corporal who was annoyed because she put out one of his eyes whilst he was endeavouring to rape her. His father, who had arrived at this inopportune moment, had been shot by the Germans for strangling the corporal.

It is not surprising, therefore, that Ernest Guelvada developed an extreme, but very quiet, hatred of everything German and everything connected with that people. During World War II, as a member of Mr. Quayle's peculiar organisation, he had spent his time settling old scores with the enemy, being assisted in that process with a four-inch Swedish sailor's knife which he could throw up to twenty yards with complete accuracy.

It is not to be wondered at, therefore, that he found the post-war years a little tedious, even boring.

Guelvada was on the short side, and gave the impression of being slightly plump. He was hard and supple, nimble on his feet when he wanted to be and, physically, in superb condition. His main hobby was the quiet observation of the feminine sex and all the implications of that observation. His face was round, pleasant and inclined to good nature and, having regard to the half-smile that usually played about his mouth, it is surprising that most people felt a vague sense of discomfort when they were with him.

The only explanation for this peculiar attribute is, it seems to me, that most of the time Guelvada was thinking of his Swedish sailor's knife and wondering when he was going to use it again, and that somehow the hatred within him escaped, in spite of his smile, and permeated the atmosphere with discomfort and ruthlessness.

II

Not far from East Grinstead is a long and rather attractive road leading to the village of Balcombe. At the entrance to the village is an old-fashioned inn—small but with much atmosphere. At the back is a comfortable bar. And on this particular evening the only occupant of the bar was Mr. Ernest Guelvada, who sat on one side of the fire, smoking and thinking. His methods of thought, like some other things about him, were peculiar. He thought in several languages, five of which he spoke almost perfectly, and it amused him to switch from thinking in Portuguese to French, to Italian, with an occasional mental descent to his own language. He seldom thought in English, which he spoke extremely well except for a pedantic

35

use of words and occasionally, thrown in for good measure, some of the more outrageous American expressions.

The barmaid, who had been watching him for some moments—because there was something very attractive about Ernest Guelvada—said : " Do you want a drink, sir ? "

Guelvada got up. He walked to the bar. He leaned on it and stood smiling at the barmaid. He said : " I think so." He indicated the row of shelves behind the bar ; pointed to the top shelf.

He asked : " What is that bottle on the right of the shelf ? I feel I might be very interested in that bottle."

She looked behind her. " It's a very old liqueur, sir. It was left here by a gentleman during the war. I believe it's Turkish. It's called ' *Apple of Eden.*' "

Guelvada said : " I would like some of that, please."

She reached for the bottle ; poured a measure into a liqueur glass ; gave it to him. He put a pound note on the bar.

She said : " Do you like the liqueur, sir ? I expect you've drunk it before."

He shook his head. " I've never drunk it." He sipped at his glass. " And I don't like it. I think I will have a large whisky and soda."

She raised her eyebrows. She smiled. Then she said : " I wonder why you wanted to try it."

" I didn't want to," said Guelvada, with a little smile. " I wanted to see you reach for the bottle. You have a very good figure, Mademoiselle. The Greeks, I have no doubt, would have thought highly of it. For me, I believe women's figures are much better observed when they are reaching upwards for something."

She said nothing. She brought the whisky and soda.

He asked : " Do you take my meaning ? "

She said in a cool voice : " Yes, I think I see what you mean."

36

Ernest went on : " You will realise that I am what
is called an ascetic type of man. I love beauty. I think
I shall come here very often, Georgeous ! "

She put up her hand to push a tendril of hair into
place. She thought this customer had a nerve, but you
couldn't help liking him. She wondered why.

The telephone rang. She went round the back
of the circular bar ; answered it ; put down the
receiver.

She said over her shoulder : " You wouldn't be a
Mr. Guelvada, would you ? "

" Yes. . . . Mr. Ernest Guelvada . . . very much at
your service, I assure you, Mademoiselle."

She said : " Well, there's a call for you." She held
the flap of the bar open.

Guelvada picked up the receiver. He said : " Yes.
. . . Very well. . . . Thank you very much. . . ."

He replaced the receiver ; drank a little of the
whisky and soda ; went back to his chair ; picked up
his hat.

He said : " I wish you a very good afternoon. I
can't tell you what pleasure our meeting has given
me."

When he had reached the door she said : " You've
forgotten your change, Mr. Guelvada." Her voice was
almost arch.

He said : " No. . . . I assure you I never forget my
change. *Au revoir*, Mademoiselle."

He went out.

Outside, he got into the shiny Jaguar car ; turned
it ; drove out of Balcombe village. The long road,
leading into the heart of Surrey, stretched before him.
Here and there, set back from the road, were large,
comfortable houses, standing in their own grounds.
One of them had white entrance gates.

Guelvada got out of the car ; opened the gates ;
drove in. He left the car in the courtyard ; walked to

the entrance of the house ; pulled on the iron bell. He heard it jangling inside.

After a few moments the door opened. Standing in the entrance was a young woman. She was blonde, and lovely. She was wearing a heavy, ivory silk wrap ; high-heeled, black shoes.

Guelvada said : " M'selle Germaine . . . I am enchanted to see you again. My quick instinct tells me that you have either just got up from bed or propose to go back to it."

She laughed. Her teeth were white and even. She said : " I was working until five o'clock this morning, Ernest. Your second guess is right. I was just going to bed. But not now. Mr. Quayle's in his office. Will you go in ? "

He said : " Yes. I think it is a great pity that I have to indulge in affairs of business whilst you are around. However, I'll be seeing you, baby."

He threw his hat on to a chair ; walked down the passage-way which led to the back of the house. Over his shoulder he watched her going up the stairs. Just before she disappeared from his sight he blew her a kiss.

At the end of the long corridor was a velvet curtain and a door. Guelvada pushed aside the curtain ; opened the door ; went in. The room was a library, furnished in antique oak. A fire was burning in the grate. On the far side of the room was a large desk, on which there was no less than six telephones. And on the other side of the desk was Mr. Peter Everard Quayle.

Quayle was tall, burly, inclined to baldness. He might have been anything. He might have been a successful stockbroker or a financier. Usually, he managed to look like anything he wanted to look like. A strange, remote man, whose life since he was thirty had been spent, at great risk to himself and many other people, in sticking his nose into what might be called affairs of state; in trying to promote the peace by getting one jump ahead of sundry individuals of countries whose idea was to disturb that peace; working in his own way with unlimited funds from somewhere, controlling a network of agents throughout the world.

He said : " Come in, Ernest. You've had a long holiday, haven't you ? "

Guelvada shrugged his shoulders. " A busman's holiday I think you would call it. For me . . . I have been at peace with the world. I did a little travelling just to see if some places I had known and liked looked the same."

Quayle got up. He came round the desk. He asked : " Well, did they look the same ? "

Guelvada shrugged again. " Yes . . . and no. . . . Perhaps they were a little more . . . what you call it . . . tawdry ! Perhaps I am a little older and, shall we say, inclined to be a trifle cynical."

Quayle said : " But you had a nice, quiet holiday ? "

" Yes," said Guelvada. " Very nice—very quiet."

Quayle grinned. " I suppose you would call the incident which occurred in Andalusia ' quiet ' ? I understand there was a little trouble over a young Spanish lady, which culminated in somebody being stabbed. Was that the quietest part of your holiday ? "

Guelvada spread his hands. " Always, I assure you, I have been a misunderstood man." He went on, in spite of the widening grin on Quayle's face : " Figure to yourself, I arrive at this place and I encounter in an *estancia* a young, Spanish woman of great charm, culture and an extraordinary beauty. I look at her. I say to myself: ' Some baby ! This is for you, Ernest ! ' "

Quayle said : " Really ? And from what followed I imagine she didn't agree with you ? "

Guelvada looked unutterably shocked. " Mr. Quayle,

you astound me. How many years have I been working
for you—seven, eight, nine, ten—and you say that a
woman to whom I do the honour of falling in love is
not attracted by Ernest Guelvada ? "

" So she was attracted ? " asked Quayle.

" Definitely. But the situation was that there was
some other person with whom she thought she had
been in love until I appeared. This man became very
annoying. Something had to be done about it."

Quayle said : " It seems to me by the report I got
that something *was* done about it." He looked at
Guelvada intently.

Guelvada returned Quayle's stare with equanimity.
" Mr. Quayle, an instinct tells me that you believe that
I would sink to the depths of killing a man whom I
considered to be a rival. I assure you that is not so.
Two weeks after I met this young and delightful woman
the man, who was called Sebastian—which I think is
an indifferent name—became involved in a quarrel—
one of those appalling bar-room quarrels. He was
stabbed by a friend. They were quarrelling about
something—I don't even know what it was. I was a
long way away at the time. I had nothing to do with
it, I assure you."

Quayle said : " I bet you didn't ! I would also bet,
Ernest, that you were the cause of the quarrel between
the two gentlemen—the quarrel which led to the fight
in which Sebastian was stabbed."

" I am not denying that," said Guelvada. " But *I*
did not do it. No, sirree ! You know me too well to
think that I would become involved in some not-very-
good brawl, ending in death, unless it were necessary."

Quayle smiled. " Very well. How would you like
to go to work again, Ernest ? "

" I would like nothing better. You know, during the
war years I was happy. I was happy because I was
busy. I got into so much trouble through you that I

had no time to get into any trouble on my own account. But life was exciting. Very often I wonder why I am not dead."

Quayle said : " So do I. However, it will come to you one day. It comes to all of us, you know."

Guelvada shrugged his shoulders again. " Maybe. . . . Mr. Quayle, I think you are goddam right. But there does not seem much opportunity of meeting what you call a sticky end these days."

" I wouldn't bet on that," said Quayle. " Maybe we're all nearer to meeting a sticky end than we know."

" Ah ! . . ." Guelvada's exclamation was soft. He had put a world of meaning into it. " Now I am beginning to get an idea. . . ."

Quayle went back to the desk. He sat down ; opened a drawer ; produced a folder. He said : " Here are the facts. In the Bahamas is a small island called Dark Bahama. It is one of those places—a tourists' resort where you can buy liquor for almost nothing, where the sun shines all day and the sea is limpid and clear. You know the sort of place ? "

Guelvada nodded. " I know. . . ."

Quayle went on : " Nine or ten months ago I put an operative on Dark Bahama. He had important work to do. He was a very good operative until he arrived there—or so it seems."

Guelvada said : " It is possible that he became affected by the atmosphere of Dark Bahama. It is possible of course that he forgot to be a good operative."

Quayle said : " That's what I am uncertain about. Sandford was a very good man. He had definite work to do on that island. He had worked for me for years. He was one of my best men in the war. You never met him but he acted as a sort of liaison man between us and M.I.5, the Special Branch and some of the other cloak-and-dagger brigade boys. He never slipped up."

Guelvada asked : " What happened to him, Mr. Quayle ? "

Quayle said : " It seems that first of all he took to liquor. He was drunk most of the time. That may be true or not. Sandford was very good at playing drunk. He may have gone bad and become a drunkard, or he may have been fronting as a drunkard. He's used that pose before now. One night he decided to go shark fishing. He hooked a shark and it took him overboard."

" That has happened before," said Guelvada.

Quayle said : " Yes, but not in the same circumstances. Sandford was an experienced fisherman. He'd done a lot of shark fishing. However, there were two people on the boat with him. A negro—the owner of the boat—called Mervyn Jacques—and his man—a white man by the name of Mellin. Mellin's been doing a little drinking lately. Apparently, he had something on his mind. It seems that on the night that Sandford went fishing and went overboard Mellin had noticed before the boat went out that the straps on the fishing seat were badly frayed or cut. That didn't matter because Sandford wasn't even strapped in. Mellin said he was blind drunk at the time."

Guelvada said : " Have you considered the possibility of somebody having hocked his drink ? You know, a very tough man will take a Mickey Finn and not go right out. He's too strong for it. But he always *looks* very drunk."

Quayle said : " I haven't overlooked that possibility. It may be that Sandford had a meeting that night. It may be that he realised that somebody had doped his drink. Maybe somebody suggested to him that he should go fishing, or maybe he thought it would be a good thing to get off the island for a bit. But the fact remains he's dead."

Guelvada said : " What you think is that somebody killed Sandford. Somebody planned to do this."

Quayle nodded. " That's what I think. I want you to find out if somebody was laying for Sandford. If somebody laid this on it would in all probability be someone who knew what Sandford was doing on that island. So I'd like you to go to Dark Bahama. I would like you to find out all about Sandford if you can. I think that you might scare this Mellin into talking a little more. I understand that the owner of of the boat—Jacques—is a pretty tough sort of person. You might have trouble with him and you might not. But he also might be able to talk."

Guelvada looked at his finger nails. He said : " Mr. Quayle, they always talk to me. I have one or two little methods which have been very successful in the past."

Quayle said : " I am not asking about your methods. Go to Dark Bahama. Find out about Sandford's death. If you come to the conclusion that this was a deliberate plot to get him out of the way, find out who was behind it."

" And then ? " asked Guelvada.

Quayle said : " And then nothing. Then you come back and talk to me. Unless you have other orders in the meantime. You understand ? "

" I understand very well, Mr. Quayle. The Bahamas should be very nice at this time of the year."

Quayle grinned. He had a momentary vision of Ernest Guelvada improving the atmosphere of Dark Bahama. He said : " Call in at the office in Pall Mall to-morrow morning. Everything will be ready for you —your passport ; tickets, everything. I have arranged a drawing account for you at the Royal Bank of Canada. There's a branch on the island. There won't be any need for you to communicate with me until you come back. Don't come back until you can tell me what I want to know one way or another."

Guelvada said : " I'm very grateful. This should be

a very interesting holiday, Mr. Quayle. I hope it won't be too long a holiday."

Quayle said : " It better hadn't be. So long, Ernest."

Guelvada said : " Good-bye. I look forward to seeing you again, Mr. Quayle."

He went out of the room. In the hall, the girl Germaine was waiting.

Guelvada said : " Mademoiselle Germaine, for the last few minutes I have been thinking of you. Now I find you dressed for the road in a superb country coat and skirt. May I say that you look delightful ? "

She smiled at him. " Thank you, Ernest."

He asked : " Can I drop you anywhere ? I'm going to London."

She said : " You can drop me off at the grocery store in Balcombe. I have some ordering to do. But on one condition. . . ."

He put up his hand. He said : " Mademoiselle Germaine, I know what this condition is to be. It is that I am not to make love to you. Well, you know, for a man who is driving a car it is very difficult to make love, so I wish to tell you here and now that you are the only woman whom I have ever really loved in my life. Maybe there have been other incidents but they merely served to show how utterly deep my devotion is to you."

She said : " Like hell, Ernest ! Come on . . . and no nonsense in the car . . . ! "

CHAPTER FOUR

I

ISLES WAS very nearly asleep. He lay back in his comfortable seat in the rear of the plane, his eyes half-closed, his body relaxed. He was wearing a blue gaberdine coat and trousers, a silk shirt, a light-weight grey hat.

The hostess thought he was a type. She was a charming American girl from Miami, and she thought you could always tell an English gentleman. For most of the trip she had been wondering why. She still had not found any adequate reason, except that Englishmen either looked like gentlemen or they didn't. She thought this one did. So what !

Isles opened his eyes. A few thousand feet below, the sun shone on the still, blue waters. Away to the right he could see a small island with two or three large white houses dotted about.

He said to the hostess : " What is that place ? "

" That's Pigeon Island. It's shaped like a pigeon. If you look ahead and beyond it in a few minutes you'll be able to see Dark Bahama. It takes us just over half an hour from Miami."

Isles asked lazily : " What do you think of Dark Bahama ? Do you like it ? "

She shrugged her shoulders. " It's not so bad, but—for me—Miami ! " She smiled, showing pretty, white teeth. " I was born in Miami. I suppose that's why I like it, and although I've been on this run for a long time I still haven't got tired of this trip. Sort of pretty, you know."

Isles said : " Very. But you've been on Dark Bahama ? "

She nodded. " Yeah. . . . I stayed there once for three weeks. It was pretty good . . . swimming and fishing . . . and playing tennis. Everything you want. Lots of liquor and anything else you're lookin' for."

Isles said with a smile : " Meaning lots of babies."

She laughed. " Thousands of them."

Isles asked : " What are the men like ? "

" I reckon they're O.K.," said the hostess. " They got all sorts on Dark Bahama."

" Would you like to live there ? " he asked.

She shook her head. " Not for me. When it starts to rain I'd rather be in Miami. When it rains on that island it sure does rain . . . and blow . . . you can't imagine. They had a hurricane when I was there. Gee . . . it'd just blow you out to sea if it got you."

Isles said : " Nature always presents two faces. The more beautiful she is the more ruthless she is. Like women."

She said : " No, Mr. Isles. It's not as bad as all that. Don't tell me you're the type of guy who'd get a raw deal from a woman."

" You never know," said Isles. " It always depends on the woman."

" Well, maybe you're right," said the hostess. " Be seein' you. . . ." She went forward to the pilot's cabin.

Isles thought lazily that she had a very good figure. He lighted a cigarette ; leaned back. It was four o'clock in the afternoon. The whirr of the twin engines was almost like a lullaby. He closed his eyes and began to think about Mrs. Thelma Lyon.

Isles thought he was very intrigued with Mrs. Lyon. There was a woman, he said to himself, who had *something*. He wondered what had happened in the old days between Mrs. Lyon and Johnny Vallon. He thought he could guess the answer to that one. In the old days Johnny had been a harum scarum. A very good investigator but with an eye for women. And they went for him. Isles guessed that there had been something between Vallon and Thelma Lyon in the old days, which was the reason why Vallon was disinclined to handle this job for her.

But Isles's instinct, which was pretty good, also told him that there was something a little phoney about Mrs. Lyon ; that, possibly, the story she had told was not the truth, the whole truth and nothing but the truth. He thought it might be amusing to discover what was behind the façade of this search for somebody else's rather reluctant daughter. He thought it might be an amusing investigation, more especially if it brought him back somewhere in the neighbourhood of the beautiful Thelma. Isles, who had an eye for women, and in whose adventurous and interesting career they had played parts which the French might describe as *formidable*, found a strange attraction in Mrs. Lyon.

Not only was she beautiful and charming and graceful and with a definite character, but here was a woman with a peculiar and strange attraction, and a nerve. He remembered the scene in the hall. He wondered whether that scene was the result of a natural outburst of emotion from Mrs. Lyon ; whether she really found herself suddenly attracted to him, or whether it was part of an act. He shrugged his shoulders. If it were an act he didn't see what the idea could be. He didn't see how it could help her.

He sat there, dozing, relaxed, until the hostess tripped through the plane telling them to fasten their belts ; that they were going down.

II

Darkness falls suddenly on Dark Bahama. At one moment the sun is sparkling on the sea. A few moments later the shadows are falling and in half an hour it is almost night.

Isles, who had been asleep on his bed, got up; looked at his strap-watch. It was six o'clock. He rang room service; ordered a double dry Martini; went into the bathroom; took a cold shower and changed his clothes. When the drink came he went outside on to the balcony; sat in a wicker chair; sipped the drink; looked out towards the sea. It was going to be a lovely night, he thought. Away in front of the island he could see the light at the top of the old pirate watch-tower on Swan Cay.

He went downstairs; had another drink; began to walk about the grounds. He was at the far end of the palm-sprinkled lawn that ran for half a mile behind the hotel when the first drops of rain came. Ten minutes afterwards a strong wind was blowing, keeping the rain up, but there were clouds over Dark Bahama. Isles thought there was going to be a hell of a storm. He was right.

He had barely time to get back to the hotel before it broke. The rain came down in sheets. It hit the grass, the asphalt paths about the hotel, and the windows, almost as if it were imbued with hatred.

Isles went back to the bar. When he ordered his drink the negro bartender said:

" Mister Isles, ah got a message from the 'phone operator for you. She says that somebody called you here. They didn't say who they was. They just talked pretty quick and got offa the line."

Isles asked : " Was it a man or a woman ? "

" I don't know," said the barman. " I asked the

48

same question. She said it might have been either, Mister Isles. She said the message was that there is a telephone call comin' through to you at the call-box. The call-box is away down the road leadin' to the west of the island. It's about a quarter of a mile from here. The operator says that the message is comin' through for you at ten o'clock to-night."

Isles said : " All right. Thank you."

He finished his drink ; went into dinner. He thought that Mrs. Nicola Steyning—if it *was* Mrs. Nicola Steyning—wasn't wasting very much time.

III

At ten minutes to ten Isles got into the car he had hired from the hotel people ; drove slowly down the road. The rain was descending in torrents and with it there was a peculiar wind that made an odd sighing noise as it swished through the palms on the roadside.

After a few minutes he saw the call-box—an incongruous modern attribute standing in a clump of palm trees. He pulled the car on to the side of the road ; got out ; turned up the collar of the oilskin he had borrowed from the hotel porter. He went into the box ; left the door slightly ajar ; lighted a cigarette. He stood there, smoking, thinking about himself and life.

Life, thought Isles, drawing the tobacco smoke down into his lungs, was an odd proposition. Someone had once said that life was what you made it. He wondered if that was true or whether it was life that made you. Maybe, he thought with a grin, it was a bit of both. He thought it might have been so in his case.

He remembered the old days when he had been at a

public school and later at a university. He remembered the incessant urge he always found within himself in wanting to get away from the ordinary ways and boring routine of life. To get excitement—anything which broke the sequence of monotony. Well, he had got it all right. He remembered the old days when he had worked for John Vallon. He remembered the peculiar business that had sent him to South America ; that had landed him in a filthy gaol with a three-years' sentence.

Cherchez la femme! Isles grinned. Well, if it was a woman who had got him into the gaol, another one had got him out. He had cried quits on that job. But, he thought, he had been lucky to get out.

He wondered what life would have been like with the girl he had married if she had gone on living ; if the bomb that had killed her three weeks after their marriage had fallen somewhere else. That was bad luck, thought Isles. They had hardly had time enough to know each other. The devil with life was, he ruminated, that you were never certain as to whether any incident was lucky or unlucky. You never knew until you had gone the whole way.

The telephone bell jangled. Isles, the cigarette hanging from the corner of his mouth, picked up the receiver.

He said : " Yes ? "

He was answered by a peculiar voice—so peculiar that he was both amazed and intrigued. It might have been the voice of an old man or an old woman, and it might have been the voice of a young woman. Isles thought it might have been anybody's voice.

The voice said : " Mr. Isles, perhaps you were expecting a telephone call. Perhaps you'd heard something about the possibility of a telephone call ? "

Isles said : " Yes. I'm all ears ! "

The voice said : " Are you on foot or have you a car ? "

" I have a car on the other side of the road," said Isles.

" Very well. . . . If you drive back the way you came from the hotel and carry on straight past it, you'll come to a fork in the road. Your right-hand fork runs straight down the front of the island through the town. Your left-hand fork leads towards the middle of the island. You take the left-hand fork. If you watch the mileage register on your car and drive for two miles, you'll come to a small dirt road leading off at an angle. Not a very attractive road at first. It runs through a plantation, but if you drive down it for half a mile through a clearing you'll find a small road leading to wooden gates. Open the gates and drive down the carriage drive. It's a long carriage drive. You'll find the house at the end—a white, two-storeyed building with a veranda right around it. I'd say it would take you a quarter of an hour to get there. When you arrive ring the door bell which is at the side of the house. I'll be waiting for you. You understand ? "

" Perfectly," said Isles. " You wouldn't by any chance like to tell me your name ? "

The voice said : " Mr. Isles, at the moment I don't see that that would help, and I don't want to say more than I'm forced to—well, not on this telephone."

" Very well." Isles hung up ; went outside ; started the car ; turned it. He drove away.

In a quarter of an hour he found himself before the wide double gates of the house. Inside, he could make out the vague shape of a carriage drive curving into the blackness.

As he opened the gates the rain began to slacken off. He got back into the car ; drove along the carriage drive. On each side of him was thick planta-tion, palm trees, foliage, shrubbery. The air smelt fresh and clean, but Isles had an idea in his head that he didn't like the place. He didn't know why. He told himself that he didn't like the island very much. A lovely place—Dark Bahama—but there was something —some odd thing which he couldn't quite place. He grinned. He thought maybe he was getting a little fastidious ; getting to the time of life when one began to imagine things.

He stopped the car in the clearing in front of the house. The wide, paved paths that ran round it were neat and tidy. The small lawn which he could see on one side where the trees had been cleared was well kept. He switched off his lights ; got out of the car ; went round to the side of the house, up the six wooden steps —white painted—that bisected the veranda and led to the front door.

He put his finger on the bell-push and waited. He continued to wait. Five minutes went by. Nothing happened. Isles put his hand on the door knob ; twisted it and pushed. The door opened. He went inside ; stood in the hallway.

The hall was square, well carpeted, furnished after the Colonial style. There was a lamp on a small table in the far corner which illuminated the hall. In the left-hand corner, farthest away from him, was a wide staircase with an off-white carpet and wide, enamelled banister rails. On the right of the staircase was a wide passage leading towards the back of the house.

Farther towards him on the right-hand side of the hall were double doors. He tried the doors ; went into the room. There was an electric light switch by the door. He switched it on. The room was a dining-room. It was spacious, cool, distinguished. There was a long table down the centre of the room. The table-lamps on the table which had sprung to life when he had turned the main switch shone on the polished wood.

Isles sighed ; closed the doors ; went back into the hallway. He thought it was peculiar. He thought that if this situation had been written into some romantic novel it would have seemed mysterious. To him, for some reason which he could not understand, it seemed almost normal.

He moved along into the entrance of the passage leading towards the rear of the house; found a light switch; turned it on. He walked down the passage. There was a door facing him at the end; two doors on his right and one on the left which would lie approximately under the turn of the stairway above it. He walked down to the end of the passage; opened the door; switched on the light. The room was a wide drawing-room, furnished in off-white furniture and rugs, with a cherry-coloured frieze at the top of the cream-painted walls. There were two big chairs—one on each side of the old Colonial fireplace—and by the side of one of the chairs was a cigarette ash-tray supported on a bronze stand. Isles walked across the room; looked into the ash-tray. There were two half-smoked cigarettes in it. He picked them up. One of them, he thought, was a trifle warmer than the other, but that could be imagination.

He came out of the room; turned to his right; went through the smaller door—the one under the stairway. Strangely enough, this led into a small passage with a door at the end so that the passage ran under the stairway, but the room was beyond it. He went in; switched on the light. He stood with his back to the door, looking into the room. It might have been a library, a study or a small sitting-room. It had a large desk in one corner of the room, long book-shelves on the opposite wall. There was a settee set at an angle before french windows opposite him. The curtains were not drawn. A white fur rug lay across the settee.

Lying in front of the settee, with his head towards Isles, was the figure of a man. Isles thought the figure didn't look so good. Because the light-green carpet underneath the head was thickly stained with blood. Isles sighed once more ; thought to himself : Here it is again. Always you start some quite sweet, innocent-looking job and before you get well into it you encounter something like this. This was the sort of thing that happened to him.

He walked across the room ; stood looking downwards at the man. The lower part of the face was intact, but above the bridge of the nose from the line of the eyes the sight wasn't pretty. Isles thought that he had been shot at close range with a fairly heavy-calibred pistol or automatic. The bullet had smashed through the forehead ; taken off the back of the head. Isles thought it must have been at *very* close range.

The bottom of the face was youthful. Incongruously, one side of it was shaven, the other not. Isles thought that was a little odd, because the man had certainly not been interrupted whilst he was shaving—not unless he was shaving fully dressed. He was wearing an ivory silk shirt and a blue tie, with a cream alpacca jacket, slacks, white shoes, white silk socks. There was a lawn handkerchief of very good quality in his left-hand pocket. When he knelt down he realised that the handkerchief was scented with a man's scent—made in Paris—called " *Moustachio*."

He got up ; looked round the room. There was a telephone on the table in the corner. There was an ash-tray with three unsmoked cigarettes. Isles looked at these ; opened the silver cigarette box on one table ; found the brands were identical. In the corner of the room opposite the door was a drink wagon filled with bottles.

Isles went over to it. No glasses had been used. He took out his handkerchief ; picked up an open bottle of brandy ; poured a slug into a glass ; added some soda ; took the glass to an armchair ; sat down. He noticed there was no ice bucket on the drink wagon, which was strange in a place like Dark Bahama, where everybody used ice all the time.

Isles sat there, sipping his drink, thinking about Mrs. Thelma Lyon, the peculiar voice that had telephoned him at the call-box and the scene in front of him. One or two things were quite obvious. It was Mrs. Lyon who had informed him that he might receive a telephone call. Therefore, there must be a connection between her and the voice that had spoken to him. But Mrs. Lyon could easily deny she had ever said this would happen, and the voice could deny that it had made the telephone call. Isles thought it might easily be a frame-up. Why shouldn't it be ? "

Another thing that was obvious was that somebody had been waiting for him to arrive on the island. Because the message telephoned through to the hotel whilst he was out walking in the grounds had been telephoned a few hours after his arrival.

He finished the drink ; went over to the drink wagon ; poured himself another. He recorked the bottle ; cleaned it with his handkerchief and, when he had finished the drink, cleaned the glass. He went back to his chair. He wondered exactly what he was supposed to do. He wondered, supposing Mrs. Lyon were in the room, what she would advise him to do. He wondered what had happened to the voice ; whether the voice had really intended to meet him or not. Isles had an idea that this wasn't so. This, he thought, was a frame-up. Because he was going to do one of two things. He was either going to get in touch with the police or he was going to get out. But supposing he did get out—well, Dark Bahama was a small place. There weren't an awful lot of telephone calls. Any intelligent telephone operator would think it peculiar that a call should be put through to a call-box on a deserted road on the island. Any intelligent operator would have made a mental note of that call, and maybe heard what had been said, in which case if he got out he would probably be for it. Everybody knew who the new arrivals were and there were only seven people on his plane. Isles thought it might be amusing to try and have it both ways, not for any particular reason but that to do something incongruous invariably made things happen. Of course you didn't know *what* things would happen, but something would turn up.

He got up ; walked over to the telephone. When the operator answered he said : " I want to talk to the police—someone important."

She said : " Do you want the Chief Commissioner's office at the Police Barracks ? "

" Why not ? " asked Isles politely.

" Hold on a minute, please. I take it this is an urgent call ? "

Isles agreed. Two minutes afterwards he heard the click of the connection.

A voice said : " This is Bahamas Constabulary— Dark Bahama Police Barracks."

Isles asked : " Who is that speaking ? "

" This is the Inspector on duty."

Isles said : " There's been a murder. I'm sitting with the corpse now. I don't know what the name of the house is because I'm a stranger here, but I'll describe it to you, and tell you where it is. Would you like to make a note ? "

" Very good," said the Inspector.

Isles began to describe his route to the house.

The Inspector interrupted : " It's all right. . . . Ah know the house. So it's there ? "

Isles said : " Yes, it's here. I'm sitting in something that looks like a secondary sitting-room in the house. A man's been murdered. What do I do now ? "

The Inspector said : " Ah shouldn't do anything, sir, except stay where you are. Don't touch anything, please. In five minutes' time I'll send a wagon with a police officer. Just wait till he comes, will you ? "

Isles said : " Very well." He hung up. He had another look at the corpse. He thought it was rather a pity that a young man with such a long, slender, straight body should meet such a sticky end—literally sticky.

Then he went back to the drinks wagon ; poured himself another brandy and soda. He sat down in the armchair and waited.

He thought it was nice that the drinks were free.

IV

Isles heard a clock strike somewhere in the upper regions of the house. That, he thought, would be eleven-thirty. He sat down in the chair ; looked at the amber fluid in the glass in his hand. He wondered why it was that he had not even gone over the house. For all he knew there might be someone on the upper storey. His lips twisted into a smile. There might be some more bodies. You never knew.

There was a sound from the front of the house ; then footsteps. The door opened. An Inspector came into the room. He advanced a few steps ; looked almost casually at the body on the floor ; then looked at Isles.

He said : " Good evening, sir."

Isles was vaguely surprised. He thought he was going to meet a white Inspector of Police, but this one was not white. This one was a negro. He was short and thin. His khaki drill uniform was immaculate. He was a middle-coloured negro. Isles thought that the tint of his skin was rather attractive. His head was covered with short black and grey curls. His face was thin and the cheek bones were high. His lips were not the usual negroid type. They were inclined to be thin. His mouth was well shaped. Isles thought he looked very efficient.

He suddenly realised that he was in a place where most of the policemen and junior ranks were negroes.

The Inspector spoke again. He asked : " You are the gentleman who rang up, sir ? "

Isles said : " Yes."

" Ah'm sorry I took a little time getting round here. There was another call out."

Isles said coolly : " Don't tell me that somebody else has been murdered ? "

The Inspector shook his head. " No, we don't have a lot of murders on this island—just now and again. And even then we seem to get more than they have on the other islands."

Isles asked : " Why ? "

" Ah'm not suah, sir." The Inspector put his hand into one of the breast pockets of his tunic ; produced a notebook. " Ah wonder would you like to tell me all about it."

Isles said : " Certainly. I'll tell you all I know, and that's not a great deal. By the way, I don't know who this whisky belongs to but it's very good. I suppose you wouldn't like some ? "

The Inspector said : " No, sir. Ah've been taught not to drink when on duty. It's a bad thing. You don't think properly when you are drinking. Your brain's not quite clear."

Isles said : " I wish I were you. My brain's never been quite clear since I was born—or has it ? "

The Inspector looked vaguely shocked. He went over and sat down on the edge of the settee close to the white rug that was thrown casually across it. He did not even look at the corpse. Isles thought that the Inspector had been taught to concentrate on certain lines of duty ; that the teaching had become part of him. He watched him whilst he opened the notebook ; took out the pencil from its individual pocket by the side of the book.

The Inspector said : " Ah'd like to have your name, sir."

" My name is Julian Isles—I-s-l-e-s." He spelt it. " Julian Gervase Horatio Isles. There's a name for you. I think Horatio stinks, don't you ? I never did like Horatio."

The Inspector wrote down the name. " Now, if you'd tell me all about this, sir."

Isles said : " Certainly. Where do I start ? "

The police officer looked at him. His eyes, Isles thought, were very kindly. " Ah think it might be a good idea if you went on from the time you arrived on Dark Bahama. We have a list at headquarters of the passengers on each plane, and your name was among those who arrived off the Clipper late this afternoon."

Isles nodded. " I went straight to the Leonard Hotel," he said. " I arranged to hire a car while I am on the island. Then I went upstairs to my room. I was there some time. I had a drink up there. Then I went for a walk in the grounds. Then I went into the bar and was given a message that somebody was going to ring me up. Then I got into the hired car and drove off."

The Inspector asked : " Where did you go, Mr. Isles ? "

" I went to get the telephone message. I drove out because I was told the message was coming through at a call-box."

The Inspector said : " Ah know. That's the call-box on the main road leading west of the island—about a quarter of a mile from the Leonard Hotel."

Isles nodded. " I went into the call-box and I waited. The message came through. I was asked to come down to this house to meet somebody, and I was given the directions to get to the house. Well, I came here. This is what I found."

The Inspector asked : " Do you know what time that would be, sir ? "

" I can make a guess," said Isles. " I left the call-box at about ten o'clock. I imagine it would take a quarter of an hour to drive here. So I think I arrived at a quarter past ten. I stopped for a few minutes outside, because nobody answered the door bell. Then I put my hand on the door handle and found it wasn't locked. So I came in. I thought it was rather odd, you know, Inspector. There seemed to be no one in the house. I had a look round on the ground floor ; looked into one or two rooms. This was the last room I came into. I found what you can see."

" Yes, sir," said the Inspector. " What did you do then ? "

Isles said : " I didn't do anything for a few minutes. I was slightly shocked." He smiled at the Inspector. " I expect you understand that I'm not used to meeting corpses at this time of night."

The police officer permitted himself a small smile. " Well, sir, if you're not used to meeting up with corpses you seem to take it pretty good an' easy."

Isles said : " Exactly. When I was a little boy they taught me at my school not to get too excited about anything. It wouldn't have done any good, anyway. So," he went on, " I gave myself a drink. Then I got on the telephone to the police."

The Inspector made some notes ; then : " Ah'd like you to tell me, sir, who was the person who rang you up at the call-box ? "

Isles said : " I couldn't tell you. All I can tell you is that it was a rather peculiar voice—one of those voices. It might have been a man with a high voice or a woman with a low one."

The police officer asked : " Was it a white person's accent, Mr. Isles ? Or do you think it might have been some coloured person ? "

Isles said : " There again it might have been what you call a coloured person who spoke good English, but my bet would be that it was a white person—a European. Beyond that I can't tell you anything about the caller."

There was a little silence ; then the Inspector said : " Mr. Isles, so you expected that telephone call? Weren't you surprised when you were told at the hotel that somebody was going to ring you up at a call-box ; that they weren't going to do the normal thing and ring you at the hotel ? "

Isles said : " No. Nothing ever surprises me."

The Inspector said : " Maybe you knew someone was going to call you at the call-box ? You weren't surprised because you expected it ? "

" I was expecting a call," said Isles. " I wasn't expecting to be telephoned at a call-box, but after all, it's a free country. Maybe my caller didn't want the switchboard girl at the hotel to hear what was said."

" This voice you heard only told you to come here and meet them at this place ? There wasn't anything else said, was there ? "

Isles shook his head.

The Inspector said : " That seems a simple sort of message to me. You'd have thought they'd have put it through to the hotel, wouldn't you ? "

" No," said Isles ; " I wouldn't. Why should I ? The strangest things happen . . . like this. . . ." He pointed to the body.

The police officer made some more notes. He asked : " You wouldn't know this man ? "

" No. . . ." Isles got up. He walked slowly across the room, carrying his drink in his hand. He stood by the side of the body, looking down at it.

He said : " It's intriguing, isn't it ? "

The police officer got up. He came, carrying his notebook in his hand ; stood by Isles's side. " Yes . . .

sort of funny, isn't it, sir ? You see he's half-shaved. One side of his face is shaved. He's got quite a beard on the other. Now that's funny. Another thing, you see he's properly dressed, with his shirt and collar fastened. And his tie's all right. That don't look like he was interrupted while he was shaving. Ah think it's funny a feller should shave only half his face."

Isles said : " I think so too."

The Inspector went back to his seat on the couch. He asked : " Would you like to tell me what you've come on the island for, Mr. Isles ? "

Isles yawned. " I came on a holiday. I thought it was time I had a holiday. I heard this was a very interesting place." He grinned. " It looks as if my information was right. It *is* a very interesting place."

There was a noise outside. Some more men came into the room. They were all negroes ; all in police uniform. They carried the usual paraphernalia—cameras, fingerprint outfits.

The Inspector got up. He said : " All right, boys, you go ahead." He went on : " Mr. Isles, ah'm very sorry to inconvenience you, but it might be good for all concerned if you liked to drive down to Barracks and see the Police Commissioner—Major Falstead. Ah think Major Falstead would like to have a little talk to you about this. If you get in your car and follow close behind me you won't get lost."

" All right. I won't get lost." Isles finished his drink ; put the glass back on the drink wagon. He said : " I'll put this glass to one side so that you'll know the fingerprints on it are mine."

They went out together. The Inspector stopped on the top step of the veranda. The rain had ceased and the moon had come out.

He said : " It's a funny climate this. One minute it's raining like hell. The next minute the moon comes out. Dark Bahama's like that."

Isles said : " Yes ? " He went on : " Strangely enough, you don't seem very surprised about this killing."

The Inspector said : " When they was teachin' me to be a copper they taught me never to be surprised. Another thing, anything can happen here. Maybe this is just one of those things." He walked down the steps ; got into his car.

Isles went to his own. He started up the engine ; followed the rear lights of the police car as it drove slowly down the drive.

v

The Commissioner of Police was of middle height, tanned, with iron-grey hair. He was inclined to be a little cynical. Twenty years in the Indian Army had taught him that things are not always what they seem. In fact, he believed that they very seldom are. Another thing, he disliked Isles. He thought Isles was casual ; that no one had any right to be casual about a murder, especially when it took place in his—the Commissioner's —territory. And a murder to the Police Commissioner meant a lot of trouble.

He sat behind his desk in the square, meagrely-furnished office. He tapped on his blotter with the end of a pen. He regarded Isles, who was lounging in the one armchair on the other side of the room, with a serious expression.

He said : " I think I ought to tell you, Mr. Isles, that I don't find this matter very satisfactory as far as you are concerned. And I need not tell you that it is the duty of any citizen who has information which he should lay before the police to do so."

Isles nodded. " I know, Commissioner, but I'm in a very difficult position, aren't I ? "

63

The police officer shrugged his shoulders. " Possibly you are—from your point of view—but we cannot take cognisance of the fact that you are a private detective. We cannot make allowance for the fact that you regard the investigation or the business which brought you to this island as an essentially private affair between yourself and your client or clients. That is the position."

Isles said : " I understand that, and I'm sorry. But it doesn't make any difference as far as I am concerned, Commissioner."

The policeman nodded his head. " I understand. And you're not going to depart from that ? "

" I've told you what I'm prepared to do," said Isles evenly. " I'm prepared to make a statement to the effect that I came to Dark Bahama on the instructions of my principal Mr. John Vallon of Chennault Investigations in London. I'm not prepared to say anything else. Except that I received a rather mysterious telephone call, as a result of which I went to the house where I discovered the body."

" Exactly, Mr. Isles. But there must be in your mind some connection between this telephone call and the business that brought you here."

Isles shook his head. " Not so far as *I* am concerned. Why should there be a connection ? Quite obviously, if I'd been expecting a telephone call from somebody it would have come through to the hotel ; or if I'd known anything about that person I'd have telephoned them. I must say it looks to me rather like a plant."

The Commissioner said : " I don't understand what you mean by that."

" Maybe you don't," said Isles. " But there could be a few dozen reasons—maybe more than that—why a stupid call should be put through to me. Quite obviously, somebody on this island knew that I'd arrived at the Leonard Hotel. Quite obviously, that person didn't want to telephone me directly there.

Don't ask me why because I don't know. So this mysterious person goes to the trouble of sending a message through to the hotel asking me to receive a call in a call-box at ten o'clock. I've no reason to believe that any of this was connected with my business here. Supposing you received such a message, Commissioner? You'd probably go and take it, even if it was merely out of curiosity. You'd want to know who it was would take the trouble of telephoning in such extraordinary circumstances. Well, so did I. I don't know who it was. I don't know whether the voice was that of a man or a woman."

The police officer said : " Mr. Isles, you've never seen the murdered man before, I suppose? The fact that you saw him lying there dead brought nothing to your mind at all ? "

" Not a thing. I've never seen him in my life."

The Commissioner said : " Quite candidly, I don't see there's very much use in continuing this conversation, but I think I ought to tell you, Mr. Isles, that the happenings of this evening place you in an uncomfortable position, to say the least of it. The police doctor's report as far as it goes at the moment suggests that the murdered man was killed some time between a quarter to ten and ten o'clock, or thereabouts. You say that you arrived at the house at a quarter past ten, but there's no corroborative evidence to that effect. You merely say so."

" You mean I might have been there at ten o'clock or five to ten ? "

The Commissioner said : " A jury might easily think that, and there's another point which I think I ought to put to you. It is this : You say that you received this message at the Leonard Hotel—the message that asked you to go to the call-box and receive this call—and that you went and took it at ten o'clock. Someone might suggest, Mr. Isles, that you did not receive any message ; that there was no phone call to the call-box."

Isles said : " I don't care what anybody suggests. It is easily proved that the barman at the Leonard Hotel gave me that message."

" Exactly," said the Commissioner. " But no one knows exactly what you were doing before you went into the bar." He looked at Isles keenly. " I'm not saying this is true ; it is merely a suggestion, but it would have been quite easy for you to have slipped out of the hotel and from this very call-box to have phoned the hotel and left the message for yourself, disguising your voice. You then walk back into the bar and receive it from the barman."

Isles nodded. " That could be, but why should I want to do that ? "

The Commissioner shrugged his shoulders. " The reason's obvious. You received that message from the barman before dinner, and if you had put it through yourself—in other words if it were false—and if you did not go to the call-box at ten o'clock but instead went straight to the house, then you will agree you *could* have arrived there at, shall we say, five minutes to ten instead of a quarter past. Do you see what I mean ? "

Isles said : " I see what you mean, but it just isn't true."

The Commissioner said : " If I were you, Mr. Isles, I should be rather inclined to concern myself with what a jury might *think* might be true."

Isles grinned. The Commissioner, who was not very pleased with the result of his examination, thought it was an insolent grin.

He said : " I must say you seem to be taking a very casual attitude to this grim business, Mr. Isles."

Isles said airily : " Why not ? What am I supposed to do ? Am I supposed to do a couple of backfalls because some half-shaven young man gets half his head shot off? And as for your remarks about what a jury might or might not think, I think you're being rather stupid. If you think that sort of stuff intimidates me you'd better think again. If you accuse people of murder, Commissioner, you have to prove it. That's why I'm not concerning myself particularly about this business. What possible motive could I have for wanting this man dead? I don't even know him."

" So you say," said the police officer. " But, having regard to the fact that we don't know what your business is on this island, except that you are here on some mysterious errand, you mustn't be surprised if one disbelieved your statement that you didn't know this man."

Isles said nothing. He yawned.

Major Falstead got up. He said : " Well, frankly, I don't see very much use in prolonging this conversation. I think that some time to-morrow, possibly in the morning, when we have had a little more time to investigate this matter, I may want to talk to you again, Mr. Isles. Naturally, you will not leave the island."

Isles got up. " Very well. Good night, Commissioner."

The Commissioner said : " Good night."

Isles went out of the office.

Falstead walked over to the window ; stood there looking out on the palm trees outside. Then he went back to his desk ; picked up the telephone. He called a number. After a minute he said :

" Is that you, Stanley ? . . . Sorry to get you out of bed. We've a little trouble here. Young Gelert was murdered to-night by somebody up at Evansley—the house that was let to the Tinsley people. Remember ? . . . They're away anyway, so they don't come into it. But somebody does—a visitor by the name of Julian

Isles—an Englishman. Isles discovered the body and rang through to the police barracks. He might easily have been there at the time the murder was committed. It's a rather odd business. This Isles won't make any statement. His story is that he is a private detective employed by a firm in London, England, called Chennault Investigations, the owner of which is a John Vallon.

" Apparently, Isles came here working for this firm. He refuses to say what his mission is.; says it would be a breach of confidence between Chennault Investigations and the client. I think it would be a good idea if we tried to get a line on this Isles. Put a call through to Scotland Yard at once. Get a priority. You ought to be able to take the call up some time to-morrow morning. Ask the Yard to get everything they can on Isles and possibly they'll be able to go and see this Vallon at Chennault Investigations. Maybe he'll be more inclined to talk to them than Isles is to us. In the meantime I've told Isles not to leave the island. He's staying at the Leonard Hotel. Not that he can leave anyway, because there's no plane until the early morning plane to-morrow. So I suggest that some time to-morrow morning you might put a tail on him—just to see what he gets up to. Understand ? . . . All right. Good night, Stanley."

He hung up the receiver ; went home to bed.

Isles got into his car ; drove along the road to the right. He imagined the road would take him back to the sea-front and thence to the Leonard Hotel. But it was a long, winding road and Isles, sitting behind the wheel, thinking over the events of the evening, took no particular heed as to his direction. He turned to the left into a smaller side road, fringed with trees and occasional houses.

A hundred yards down this road he saw, sparkling not far ahead of him, an electric neon sign which, as he approached, showed the brilliant words " *The Golden Lily.*" The noise of a dance band came from within the building. There was a little crowd of coloured people round the entrance.

Isles pulled his car into the side of the road ; walked into the building. It was a club—a negroes' club. He went straight in. The dance floor was small, surrounded by tables. There was an eight-foot balcony that ran round the sides about three feet off the main floor. On it were more tables, and in the corner was a bar.

The place was crowded. The floor was filled with dancing couples. Isles, leaning over the edge of the balcony, watching the scene before him, thought that the dancing, if peculiar, was much better than in most places. The band was good.

He moved to the bar ; bought himself a drink.

He said to the bartender : " Are there any other clubs on the island ? "

" Not like this," said the bartender. " No, sir . . . this is the only coloured club on the island. There are other clubs, of course, but not for us. How d'you like the band ? "

" I like it a lot," said Isles. He drank half his drink. He asked : " What does one do on a night like this ? "

The negro raised his eyebrows. His eyes were large and round and surprised. He said : " That depends what you want to do, sir, don't it ? You stick around here. You stay as long as you like. You can drink all you like. Or you can go for a walk, 'cause ah think the rain's goin' to lay off. It'll be all right pretty soon. An' if you don't want to go for a walk you can go back to the hotel an' drink. An' if you don't wanta drink you can go to bed. Unless you wanta go bathin'. It won't be so cold. It's a nice night. Unless you wanta go fishin' for shark. That's certainly somethin', sir— fishin' for shark."

Isles said : " Is it ? "

" It's a great sport," said the bartender. " I never done it myself. I don' like the idea."

Isles asked : " How do they fish for shark ? "

The bartender said : " Well, you sit in a seat in the back of the boat, sir. Usually they go out about this time—or any time between eleven an' one o'clock. An' they take some blood with 'em in a bucket. An' you sit strapped into a seat at the back of the boat holdin' on to your line, watchin'. Then they sling the blood overboard. Most these boys here take the boats out, they know where to go to look for sharks. The shark likes the smell of blood an' comes up, see ? An' you hook him. . . ."

Isles said : " Very interesting. I suppose you know all the boys who take the boats out ? "

" You bet I do." The barman took Isles's empty glass ; refilled it. " I know 'em all. If you want to go after shark you go out with Jacques—Mervyn Jacques —a coloured gentleman—who knows more about the fish around this island than any guy. He's pretty good. Except one thing ; you wouldn't get him to-night."

Isles asked : " Why not ? "

" Jacques is takin' out Colonel MacPherson to-night," said the barman. " An' some other guy. He's goin' out with them at half-past twelve. Ah know ; he told me. But maybe if you went down along the front about a hundred yards this side the Leonard Hotel—there's a quay—a sort of pier, see—you'll find Jacques down there gettin' the boat ready. Maybe the Colonel wouldn't mind takin' you along with 'em."

Isles said : " Thanks." He put a dollar bill down on the bar. " Good night."

" Good night, sir," said the barman. " Whatever you do ah hope you sure have a good time."

Isles said, with a smile : " I'll try."

He went away.

The barman watched him walk round the balcony towards the entrance. He picked up Isles's glass ; swallowed the whisky. He said : " There is sure strange white man. He orders a drink an' don' drink it." He rolled his eyes. He said to himself : Maybe the guy's got somethin' on his mind. Who knows ?

Isles got into his car outside the Golden Lily ; drove back to the hotel. He left the car in the courtyard ; went into the bar ; drank a whisky and soda ; then went up to bed. He looked at his strap-watch. It was a quarter past eleven.

He lay down on the bed, smoked a cigarette and looked at the ceiling. He thought the situation was a little more than amusing. The idea was beginning to take definite shape in his mind that somebody was trying to frame him for murder.

He yawned. He understood the attitude of Falstead, the Commissioner of Police, perfectly. His story must have sounded very phoney. Not only that—the telephone message at the call-box asking him to go to the house must have sounded even more phoney. Isles thought it certainly looked like a frame-up.

He waited five minutes ; picked up the telephone ; rang room service ; ordered a pot of tea. He took off his coat, trousers and shoes ; put on his pyjamas over his underwear. A few minutes afterwards the waiter came up with the tea. Isles was in bed.

When the waiter had gone, he slipped out of bed ; put on his coat, shoes and trousers. His room was on a lower, first-floor corner of the hotel. He went to the side window that looked out on the plantation at the side of the hotel. Everything was quiet. Then he went to his document-case ; put his money and passport in the breast pocket of his coat, and slipped a small .32 Spanish automatic into his hip pocket.

He opened the french windows leading on to the

side balcony ; swung over it ; dropped on to the grass beneath. He walked through the plantation, out on to the dirt road that led towards the hotel ; circled the hotel ; came out on to the main road some three hundred yards below it. He crossed the road. Standing on the grass verge under a palm tree, he could see the wooden pier that the barman had told him about ; the white motor launch moored beside it. Keeping in the shadow of the palms that fringed the road, Isles walked towards the boat.

A negro was sitting in the stern. He was whistling. He got up ; touched his hat as Isles, bare-headed, his hands in his pockets, came down the quay.

Isles said : " Are you Mervyn Jacques ? "

Jacques grinned. " Yes, boss . . . that's me. But ah can't do nuthin' to-night. Ah'm booked up, see ? Ah'm goin' out with a party."

Isles said : " You're not. I've just walked down from Colonel MacPherson's place. He *was* going out with you to-night. He's changed his mind. I told him I'd drop up and tell you."

" O.K., sir," said Jacques. " Did he say when he wanted the boat ? "

Isles shook his head. " He'll get in touch with you to-morrow." He looked out to sea. " It's a nice night now," he said. " How'd you like a run round the bay for half an hour ? "

" Suah thing," said Jacques. " You don' want to do no fishin' ? Because my mate don' get around here till about twelve o'clock. If you wanta fish maybe we'd better wait for him."

Isles said : " I don't want to fish."

Jacques said : " Well you come aboard, sir. Ah'll take you a nice ride. Maybe we'll run towards Treasure Island, or Nassau or one of them places."

Isles got into the boat. He went forrard of the awning ; sat down on the deck, his legs dangling over the side. Jacques threw off the mooring ; started the engine. The boat moved out to sea.

Now it was a lovely night. The moon was out of the clouds, and the sea calm—almost limpid. Isles thought it would be a good night for bathing if you wanted to bathe. He grinned to himself.

Jacques called out : " Would you like a drink, sir ? I've some nice liquor aboard."

" It's an idea." Isles got up ; went aft ; jumped into the cockpit.

Jacques said : " You'll find the liquor and some ice water just inside the cabin, sir. Help yourself."

Isles went into the cabin. He found a bottle of Calvert, a glass jar of iced water. He gave himself three fingers of the whisky, drank it neat, then a little water. He sat in the cockpit looking over the quiet sea.

After a while he said : " This is a nice life. I suppose you don't have a lot to worry you here."

Jacques said : " Not me, sir. I never worry about nuthin'. Mos' the time I spend out in this boat fishin'. If ah'm not fishin', ah'm drinkin' or eatin' or sleepin'. Ah don' know what's the matter with that."

Isles said : " Neither do I."

Jacques began to croon softly to himself. Now the shore was almost out of sight.

Isles asked : " Where are we now ? "

" Well, ah'll tell you, sir. You know Nassau. We call it Nassau, but it's rightly Providence Island. It's away there over on your left. Right ahead is Burnt Island—a little sort of place—just two houses on it, both belonging to millionaires. Away past Burnt Island, over on the right, is Miami."

" How long does it take to get to Miami ? " asked Isles.

" Depends where you start from, but from here— well, in this boat—an' it's not a bad boat, she's fast enough—I reckon you'd be there some time in the early mornin'. Dark Bahama's really the nearest island to Miami, see ? Only takes just over half an hour in the plane."

Isles got up. " Look, would you like to earn yourself some money ? "

The skipper looked at him in the half-light under the canopy. Isles could see the whites of his eyes.

He said : " Suah t'ing, sir. Ah always like to make myself some dough. What do you want to do—take a fishin' trip to-morrow ? "

Isles shook his head. " I want to go to Miami. I suppose you could make it by about seven o'clock to-morrow morning ? "

" Maybe," said Jacques. " But ah don' want to go to Miami to-night, sir. I reckon maybe I got enough gas to get there, but I ain't enough to come back."

Isles said : " You could fill up there, couldn't you ? "

" Yeah. . . . I could fill up there. But ah don' want to. Ah got dates for fishin' to-morrow so ah don' want to go to Miami to-night. Ah don' want to go there any time."

Isles sighed. " You're going. And you're going now. . . ." He brought some notes out of his left-hand trouser pocket. " There's ten pounds English money. You get there the quickest way you can."

Jacques said : " Look, boss . . ." Then he stopped. He saw the automatic pistol in Isles's right hand. He said : " So it's like that ? What're you doin' ? "

Isles said : " You mind your own business. Just get cracking." He smiled. " I don't mean perhaps. Keep going till you get there ; otherwise there's going to be an accident. Understand ? "

Jacques shrugged his shoulders. " It's all the same to me, sir. But ten pounds ain't a lot of money for this job with the dollar the way it is. An' ah've got to fill up when ah get there."

74

Isles said : " Gas is cheap in Miami. But I'll make it fifteen."

Jacques shrugged his shoulders. " That's O.K. by me. You know what you're doin. But ah reckon Colonel MacPherson ain't goin' to feel so good when he ain't got any boat to-morrow for fishin'." An idea struck him. " Say, listen, boss. . . . I suppose you *are* a friend of Colonel MacPherson ? "

Isles shook his head. " I've never seen him. But when you get back to Dark Bahama give him my compliments. Tell him I'm very sorry if I've had to inconvenience him."

Jacques said : " O.K. If that's the way it is." He altered course.

Isles put the pistol back into his pocket. He went into the cabin ; helped himself to a little more whisky. Then he looked round the cabin. In a drawer underneath the chart case he found a .48 calibre automatic. He took it out of the drawer ; picked up the whisky ; went back into the cockpit.

He said : " Listen. Just to stop any trouble on either side, you get this gun back when I get to Miami. Understand ? "

Jacques grinned. " Suah, boss. You suah think of everythin'."

He turned back to the wheel. Isles sat in the stern, the automatic by his side, sipping the whisky, thinking about Mrs. Thelma Lyon.

CHAPTER FIVE

I

THE HOTEL YACHTSMAN occupies a block in a street running parallel with the Miami beach front and some five hundred yards behind it. Quite a lot of people believe that the Hotel Yachtsman is a very nice hotel. So it is. It is a quiet, not-too-fashionable place and, so long as guests behave themselves within certain limits and pay their bills, the management is not inclined to be too curious as to their business or their comings and goings.

Isles woke at three-thirty in the afternoon. He sat up in bed ; stretched. He was wearing an alarming pair of scarlet silk pyjamas dotted over with white stars which he had bought early that morning. He got out of bed ; looked at himself in the glass ; made a grimace ; walked over to the window and looked out. Far below him he could see people walking about in the sunlit streets.

He left the window ; sat on the bed. Then he telephoned room service ; ordered coffee and toast. When it came he sat there, relaxed, sipping his coffee, wondering about his next course of action.

Isles, who had found himself in many difficult situations in his life, was not particularly perturbed at the turn of events. He was a believer in the practice of following one's nose—a process which he thought always led somewhere in the long run. Now, in the light of the late, sunlit afternoon, and after a refreshing sleep, he knew exactly why he had got out of Dark Bahama so quickly, even if not so secretly, because it was a certainty that Jacques would talk when he got back to the island. Jacques would certainly talk when he found out that there had been a murder on the island in which an individual answering to Isles's description had been concerned, but at the moment that didn't matter. The main idea in his mind was that he *had* got out, and for the moment was not in a position where he could be subjected to any difficult cross-examination. He thought it quite possible that had he stayed on the island he *might* have been charged with suspicion of the murder and held. His story, he knew, sounded phoney enough for even that process.

He finished the coffee ; went into the bathroom ; took a hot and cold shower. He came back, wearing the legs of his pyjamas ; walked about the bedroom in bare feet. He was still wondering why somebody had found it necessary to make a date with him at a house in which a murder had been or was to be committed. He shrugged his shoulders. He thought that there was no chance at the moment of answering that one.

Isles turned as he heard the click of a key in the door. Then the door opened. Two men came into the bedroom. The first a tall, burly man, with a round face, little dark-brown eyes and thick lips. His ears were very large and his hands, which vaguely reminded Isles of bunches of bananas, hung down by his sides on long arms. The other man was short, square and grey. He was serious-faced and looked unhappy.

Isles said : " Yes ? Haven't you made a mistake ? "

The short man shook his head. " I haven't made any mistake, mister. I never do. I'm the hotel detective. This is Mr. Carno—Mr. Jack Carno. He wantsta talk to you."

Isles said : " Yes ? " He put on his pyjama jacket. " Since you're doing the talking, why couldn't Mr. Carno have telephoned ? "

The short man shrugged. " It looks to me as if Mr.

Carno wantsta talk to you sorta personal, an' he don't believe in wastin' no time."

Isles grinned amiably. "That's fine. I hope he doesn't propose to waste a lot of mine."

The hotel detective said : "Well, I reckon you'll find out about that." He opened the door ; said : "So long, Jake." He went away, closing the door quietly behind him.

Carno threw his hat on to the dressing-table. He pulled a chair forward ; twisted it round ; sat across it. He was big and burly. Isles though he looked unpleasant.

He said : "Well, so you're that bright little bastard, Mister Isles. I wanta say one or two things to you."

Isles yawned. "Well, that's a good start. What is it ?"

Carno said : "I'll tell you what it is, bright boy. I reckon you got yourself into a spot of trouble over on Dark Bahama, didn't you ? So you thought you was gonna take a run-out powder. So you got yourself over here on a fishin' cruiser. So what now ?"

Isles lay on the bed. He put his hands behind his head. He regarded Carno with a certain amusement. "What the hell's that got to do with you, pig-face ?"

Carno said : "Look, don't you talk to me like that because I don't like it. If you wanta stay all in one piece, Mister Isles, you behave yourself. See ?"

Isles said : "I think I'm behaving myself remarkably well. Who are you and what do you want ?"

Carno extracted a small, fat cigar from his pocket ; bit the end off ; spat it out. He put the cigar in his mouth ; scratched a match on his thumb-nail and lit the cigar. His pig's eyes remained steadily on Isles.

He said : "My name's Jake Carno, see ? I'm a private dick—what we call a shamus. Not only that, I'm pretty well known around here. I got a tie-up with the cops. Believe me, bright boy, they don't dislike me half as much as they're gonna dislike you if I open my trap about you."

Isles said : " Really ! I think you become more interesting every moment, Mr. Carno."

" You take it easy," said Carno. " Don't you get funny or sarcastic or start workin' yourself up, bright boy. The thing is what am I gonna do about you ? "

Isles said : " That would be very interesting to know." He yawned. " I don't know that I've broken any international laws. I have a British passport. I went to Dark Bahama via Miami. I don't know of any law that stops you leaving Dark Bahama on a fishing boat or any other boat and coming over to Miami. Perhaps I'm going to like the place. Perhaps I'm going on from here to somewhere else."

Carno said : " Maybe you are and maybe you're going where I tell you to. See ? "

Isles asked : " Why ? "

Carno removed the cigar from his mouth ; spat artistically into the fireplace. " I'll tell ya. Last night some guy gets himself croaked on Dark Bahama, after which you have a conversation with the Chief of Police there, and it's my bet that the Chief of Police asked you to stick around there until they'd cleared this murder up. You didn't do it. You took a powder, didn't you ? Because you murdered this guy. You're the guy who croaked him. So you come over here, plant yourself in this hotel, and think you're going to have a good time. How'd you like to go back to Dark Bahama, bright boy ? "

Isles said : " I hadn't considered the matter. It's quite on the cards I shall go back there some time. But tell me something, Carno. Aren't you rather exercising the prerogatives of the police here ? You're a private detective. So am I. The only difference is you're an American private detective and you've got a licence—

a process we don't have in our country. But you could lose your licence, you know, by doing something that's irregular. I think that's what you're doing now. How would you like it if I went to the police and laid a complaint against you for highly irregular conduct in bursting into my hotel room, threatening and trying a little blackmail ? "

He swung his legs off the bed ; sat there, regarding the American with equanimity.

Carno said : " Look, you try it. You go around an' see the cops. I'll tell you what they'll do with you. They'll sling you in the can. See, bright boy ? They'll smack you into the can for making an illegal entry into Miami. They won't argue about it either. Maybe they'll leave you there to cool off. Maybe they'll send you back to Dark Bahama and it's my guess you don't want to go."

Isles got up lazily. He walked across to the dressing-table ; took a cigarette from his case ; lighted it.

He said : " All right. You tell me what I'm going to do."

Carno said : " I'll tell you what you're gonna do. You're gonna get yourself up an' you're gonna dress. You're gonna get some clothes on an' you're comin' out with me. I'm takin' you down to the airport an' I'm gonna buy you a seat on a plane that's going to New York. An' when you get to New York you're gonna get yourself a passage on a boat an' you're going back to England an' you're gonna stay there. That's what you're gonna do, bright boy."

Isles went back to the bed and sat down. He said : " Really ! Why ? "

Carno got off the chair ponderously. " Look, Mister Isles, I'm gonna tell you why. An' you're gonna listen." He came over to Isles ; drew back his right fist ; smashed it into Isles's face.

Isles fell sideways off the bed. He hit the floor with

a bump. He lay there for a minute, tenderly feeling his nose, which was bleeding profusely. Then he sat up. He took the handkerchief from his pyjama pocket ; held it to his nose.

Carno said : " That's one of the reasons . . . see ? It's one of the reasons why you're going to do what I tell you, because if you think you're gonna make any trouble here in Miami ; if you think you're going around talking to people an' making yourself unpopular, you know what's gonna happen to you ? Somebody's gonna get to work on you, feller, an' when they're finished with you you won't even be interested in any goddam thing. Maybe they'll find you down in the dock, or there're lots of pools of water around here where they find bodies, an' who the hell is gonna take any notice of findin' yours—an unknown egg who got himself in off some fishin' boat ? D'you think anybody's going to bother ? "

Isles got up. He said : " Excuse me a minute." He went into the bathroom ; turned on the cold water tap. He soaked a hand towel in water ; came back ; held it to his nose. Carno had gone back to his chair.

He said : " Well, what do you think of it ? "

Isles bent down ; slipped his feet into his shoes. He found the process a little difficult using only his left hand. He straightened up.

He said : " As you would say, it looks to me as if you've got something." Before the words were out of his mouth he threw the hand towel in Carno's face. As Carno got up, Isles's left foot shot out ; caught him in the stomach. Carno went back against the wall with a groan. Isles went after him. Two minutes afterwards Carno was lying on the floor. His chest was heaving. There was a little froth about the corners of his mouth. Isles bent down ; put his hand underneath Carno's shirt collar ; pulled him up. He smacked him across the face ; knocked him sideways. He removed the automatic pistol from Carno's hip pocket. Then he sat on the bed.

He said : " You know, Carno, you only *think* you're tough."

Carno said nothing. He tried to get up. He got as far as his knees. Isles hit him again. This time Carno stayed down. Isles sighed. Then he knelt down beside the prostrate form of the detective ; began to go through his pockets. He found a wallet with a Miami private detective's licence, one or two odd letters, a thousand dollars in bills. There was nothing else except a fountain pen, some loose change and a small .22 vest automatic in a secret pocket of the skirt of Carno's coat. Isles put these things on the dressing-table. Then he went into the bathroom. He took the cords down off the plastic curtains over the large bathroom windows. He came back ; trussed up Carno.

He did it very satisfactorily, tying the wrists to the drawn-up ankles behind the man's back—a simple but very effective Japanese method. He stuffed a small hand towel into Carno's mouth ; tied it in place with a larger towel. Then he began to dress.

Three minutes afterwards Carno opened his eyes. Isles grinned at him. Carno's eyes followed him about the room as he tied his tie ; completed his toilet. When he put his hat on he walked over to Carno.

He said : " You be a good boy, Mr. Carno. Stay put and you won't get hurt any more, because if I set about you again you're going to feel it a lot more. Good afternoon to you."

He went over to the dressing-table. He put Carno's detective licence and the dollar bills in his pocket, together with his own pistol and his passport. He said : " So long ! " He smiled benevolently at the recumbent detective.

Then he went to the door. He took the " *Please don't disturb* " notice off the inside handle ; hung it on the outside of the door. He walked along the corridor; down the stairs for five floors. On the first floor he walked to the end of one of the long passage-ways. There was no one in the corridor. Isles opened the window at the end of the passage; stepped out on to the fire escape.

A minute later he was walking down a narrow street at the back of the hotel. He took Carno's licence from his pocket; found that his office address was 235 Greenacre Building, Palm Avenue. At the end of the street he found himself in a wider boulevard. He stopped a passing taxicab; told the driver to drive to the Greenacre Building.

II

Inside the cab Isles sat back in the corner. With the aid of the strip of mirror set in the corner of the cab he put in a little work on his bruised nose. He thought it could have looked worse. Then he lighted a cigarette and considered the position generally. He hoped that Carno would not be discovered for at least a few hours. Isles realised he was taking a chance but there was nothing else to do. Mentally he shrugged his shoulders. He was, as usual, following his nose, and wherever that process might lead at least something—some tangible fact—would emerge. The taxicab turned left into a wide boulevard edged with palms.

It stopped outside a large office block. Isles paid off the driver; went into the hallway; consulted the indicator board. He saw that the Carno Detective Agency was on the sixth floor. He went up in the elevator; walked along the long corridor till he found it. It was the end office and looked like a small one. Isles opened the door and went in.

The room was square and there was a door in the

corner leading off to another office. This door was open. Isles thought that that would be Carno's private office ; that the only other member of the staff was the girl who was sitting at the desk in front of him. She was a blonde, wearing the wrong shade of lipstick. She had four-inch heels and she knew that her ankles which showed under the desk were good. Isles thought that apart from the ankles she did not look too intelligent.

He said : " Good afternoon. I'm Julian Isles."

She stopped chewing gum. " Yeah ? What's that to me ? "

" Quite a lot. I've just been having a long and quite confidential talk with Jake Carno, your boss. Do you know anything about this matter ? "

" No, I'm just the typist around here. I never know anything about what goes on." She smiled. " Maybe that's good for me."

Isles breathed an inward sigh of relief. He said : " All right. Here's the thing. First of all, Mr. Carno asked me to tell you that he may not be back to-day, but he'll be here to-morrow at the latest." He put his hand in his pocket ; produced the thousand dollars. He put the bills on her desk. He went on : " Mr. Carno says if he's not back first thing in the morning you're to bank that. Understand ? "

" Yeah, I understand. If he's not back by the time the bank opens he wants it paid in. All right. Anything else ? "

" Yes," said Isles. He took a deep breath. " I want to talk to Mrs. Lyon. Get her on the phone for me, will you ? "

She looked at him. She put a piece of gum in her mouth and began to chew. She said : " Who's Mrs. Lyon ? Is that the one who was here this morning— the ritzy one—the one that looks like a picture offa *Vogue Magazine* cover ? "

Isles grinned at her. " That's right. You've got her phone number, haven't you ? "

She said : " I haven't. Maybe he has. Just wait a minute, will you ? " She got up ; went into the inner office. After a minute she came back. She had a pad in her hand. " There's an address and a phone number on this. Maybe that's the one you're looking for."

Isles took the pad from her. On it was written " *Orlando 22.264.*" The address underneath was " *Orchid House Apartments, Orlando Beach.*"

Isles said : " Do me a favour, will you ? " He put a dollar bill on the desk. " Take the elevator down and get me some cigarettes. There's a cigar kiosk on the ground floor. I'll get the number."

" O.K. . . ." She put the thousand-dollar bills in a drawer ; locked it ; picked up Isles's dollar note ; went out.

He sat down at her desk. He dialled the number. After a minute somebody answered.

Isles said : " I want to speak to Mrs. Lyon. Tell her it's Jake Carno's office."

" You hold on, sir. . . ." Isles thought the voice sounded like a negro maid. A minute passed ; then two. He wondered if he was going to have any luck. Then she came on the line.

Isles said : " Hallo. Mrs. Lyon ? "

" Yes. . . ." Her voice was charming and restful. Isles grinned happily into the transmitter.

He said : " How are you, Thelma ? This is Julian Isles."

There was a little pause ; then she said : " Well, now . . . isn't that strange ? How are you getting on, Mr. Isles ? "

" Actually, I'm not doing so badly," said Isles. " I had an interview this afternoon with a gentleman called Mr. Carno, who I take it is your favourite private dick. He wanted me to do all sorts of things."

There was a silence ; then she said : " I see. And of course you didn't do them ? "

" No. His arguments were, shall we say, very forcible, but mine were a little more successful."

She laughed softly. " Really ! How interesting. I told you that I thought you were rather an amusing person. How did you like Dark Bahama ? "

Isles said : " I think I liked it a lot. But at the moment I'm a little bit undecided about it."

She said : " Tell me just how you're undecided and why. You seemed to be like a man who'd make up his mind very quickly."

" Usually I do," said Isles. " But there are moments when I think that two heads are better than one." He went on : " You'll have to watch your step, won't you, Thelma ? In a minute you'll find yourself out on a limb."

She said slowly : " I don't know about that. Perhaps we ought to talk about it."

" I was going to suggest that," said Isles.

She asked : " Where are you now ? Are you really in Carno's office ? "

" Yes, I really am. I've just handed that thousand dollars you gave him this morning to his secretary to put into the bank to-morrow morning in case he's not here."

She said : " Dear . . . dear. . . . Did you hurt him very much, Julian ? "

" Not all that bad. Just bad enough to give him time to stop and think. What about this talk ? "

" Will you tell me the time, Julian ? " She sounded as if they were old friends.

" It's nearly half-past six."

She said : " I see. I expect you'd like a drink, wouldn't you ? "

" Yes, I would. Shall I come out ? "

She said : " Do that. if you hire a taxicab it'll get

you here in half an hour. It's straight along the coast from Miami Beach. Anyone will tell you where the Orchid House Apartments are."

Isles said : " I'll be with you about seven o'clock."

He hung up. The office door opened. The girl came in. Isles thought her figure and legs weren't bad, but that her face was quite alarming. Her hair was badly dyed too. He wondered vaguely why it was that women always wanted to look like something else.

She said : " I got Camels. Do you like Camels ? "

Isles grinned. He thought, looking at her, he preferred them. He got up. He said : " That was nice of you." He took the packet of cigarettes. " When you see Mr. Carno tell him I called in and left the money. Tell him I'm going out to see Mrs. Lyon. Tell him if he's as wise as I thing he is he'll just stay put until he gets a phone call."

She said : " O.K. Who's the phone call coming from ? "

" I'm not certain," said Isles. " But I think it'll be Mrs. Lyon. So long."

" Be seein' you. . . ." She sat down at the desk. Isles's last picture of her was her large, angular jaw working on the gum.

III

Isles stood on the palm-shaded sidewalk opposite the Orchid House. He thought he liked it ; that he liked Orlando Beach. He thought one of these days, when he was getting on a little bit, when his knees began to creak, he might consider the idea of settling in such a place—sunshine, blue seas, attractive women. He thought there might be a lot in the idea. The Orchid House was built after a Colonial Spanish fashion— a two-storey building, forming a square with a big wide arched entrance that showed a *patio* inside with a fountain. There was a long stretch of green lawn before the entrance and on the left and the right were terraces.

Isles crossed the road ; went through the entrance. Inside, set on the wall, was a glass-shielded indicator which showed that Mrs. Lyon was in Apartment 14 on the right of the *patio*. Isles walked through ; found the apartment. It formed a small, two-storey house standing in one corner of the *patio*.

He rang the bell ; listened with appreciation to the music and chimes that rang inside the house. After a moment the door was opened by a neatly-dressed negress.

She said : " You Mister Isles ? "

Isles nodded.

She said : " You come right in, boss."

He followed her through the cool hallway ; through the door at the end on the right.

She said : " This is Mister Isles, ma'am." She went away.

The room was long, cool and white. There was a black pile carpet on the floor and the furniture was covered with quilted glazed chintz—a floral pattern on a background of duck-egg blue. At the end of the room were long french windows looking out on to a secluded, white-fenced lawn. There were tropical flowers everywhere. On the left of the windows was a grand piano, and behind it Thelma Lyon was seated. She got up. She came into the centre of the room ; stood smiling at him. She was wearing an exquisitely-tailored frock in shell-pink sharkskin, the sheerest stockings and high-heeled nylon sandals. Two strings of pearls glowed against her camellia-coloured throat.

Isles said : " This is a very nice house to live in. And I think you have very good taste. But I thought you were going to France ? "

She shrugged her shoulders. "Did you? I thought I was too. But I wasn't quite certain. Instead I decided to come here."

Isles grinned at her. "And now you're feeling even more uncertain, aren't you?"

She said: "You're a little hard, aren't you, Julian? You don't mind my calling you Julian, do you? It's such a lovely name, so musical. By the way, what's been happening to your nose? I thought it was rather a nice nose."

"It'll be all right to-morrow or the next day. That was Mr. Carno."

She said: "I see. What did you do to him?"

"Not much," said Isles. "He makes a mistake common to many men. He thinks that being very big, fat and stupid means something." He smiled.

She said: "Sit down. Will you have a drink and a cigarette? I think we have quite a lot to talk about."

Isles sat down in the comfortable armchair. "You're telling me! And it *is* going to be a straight drink, isn't it? You're not going to cook me a Mickey Finn?"

She laughed. "No. . . ." She went to a sideboard; opened it; began to take out some bottles. She said: "To be quite frank I think I've given up experimentals with you, Julian. I think it's time that you and I talked sensibly."

"I think so too. If we don't I think somebody's going to get hurt and you never know, it might be you." He sat back and closed his eyes. He thought life was always amusing if you gave it the chance. He listened to the tinkle of the ice as she mixed the drink. She brought it over—a *Cuba libre* in a long, straight, hand-cut glass. The slice of orange poised delicately on top of the crushed ice.

She said: "I think you'll feel better after that. And I'd like to know what you think."

Isles said : " Just give me a minute, will you ? I have had a rather disturbing day up to the moment." He drank half the drink slowly and appreciatively. Then he said : " I'll tell you what I think. I think you are a very attractive and very beautiful woman. I think you've got plenty of everything. I'm very interested in you."

She said : " Thank you, sir. Do you mean generally or personally ? "

" I mean personally. . . ."

She moved over to the other big armchair. She sat down ; crossed her slim legs.

She said : " Go on, please. I like to hear you talk."

Isles took some more of his drink. Then he looked at her. Then he finished it.

She asked : " Would you like another ? "

He nodded. She came over ; took the glass from him ; went back to the sideboard.

He said : " You wanted to know something about me. I didn't tell you very much when we met at the Hyde Park Hotel, but I think you ought to know something now. I'm much tougher than I look, and nobody pulls my tail with impunity."

" Dear . . . dear. . . . Has someone tried to do that ? "

" I think *you* have," said Isles. " Consider for yourself. On the evening that Vallon got in touch with me I'd been back from South America only a few days. I was lucky to get out of that country." He smiled reminiscently. " I was a little foolish. I was doing some political work for one of the electoral parties out there. Unfortunately "—he grinned wryly—" it seems I picked the wrong party. I found myself in a not very pleasant gaol. However, I managed to get out. I had a good friend there. I came to England. I was very glad when Vallon gave me this job, but I'm beginning to wonder whether I haven't jumped out of the frying pan into the fire."

She came towards him. As she handed him the drink his nostrils caught a suggestion of her perfume.

He said : " You go and sit down in your chair and listen to me."

When she was seated Isles went on : " My experiences during the last two days have been a little odd. I arrived at Dark Bahama ; went to the Hotel Leonard. I got a mysterious message. Someone telephoned me at a call-box. You had warned me that I might receive a telephone call, so definitely that telephone message is linked in my mind with you. I was told to go to a house ; to meet the telephone caller at the house. I went there. When I arrived I found a young man—somewhere about twenty-five to thirty, I should think, lying on the floor. He was very dead."

Her expression did not change. " Oh, dear . . . how very annoying for you, Julian. I suppose you know what he died of ? "

He nodded. " He died because someone shot him at close range with a heavy-calibre automatic."

" Was anyone else there ? "

He shook his head.

" What did you do ? " she asked. " Get out while you had the chance ? "

Isles smiled. " Don't pretend you're so stupid, my dear. Someone was going to find out about me eventually. They were going to find out that I'd been there. Dark Bahama's a small place. It's easy to check on anyone. They'd have found I wasn't in my hotel at the time of the murder or afterwards. So I did the obvious thing. I phoned the police."

She said : " Yes. What then ? "

" I don't think the police liked me an awful lot," said Isles. " My explanation as to why I was in the house wasn't very convincing, was it ? More especially as I refused to tell them why I was on the island.

Chennault Investigations, as represented by Mr. Julian Isles, is always loyal to its clients. You see ? "

She nodded. " I see."

Isles went on : " But the Commissioner wanted to have another talk with me this morning. In the meantime I was supposed not to leave the island. He didn't think I *could* leave the island anyway ; there was no plane till this morning. But I didn't think I'd stay. I didn't think I'd stay because it looked as if I was in line for being framed for that killing. See what I mean, Thelma ? "

" I see what you mean."

" So," said Isles, " I decided to get out."

She asked : " Where did you think you were going ? And how did you get out ? "

" I got out by jumping somebody else's fishing boat. It was owned by a negro called Jacques. I showed him a gun, gave him fifteen pounds and made him drop me on Miami Beach to-day. I arrived there at eight o'clock this morning. That's how I got out. With regard to your other question, my reasons for getting out were : one, I wanted time to think and I had an idea that I was going to be pushed around if I stayed on Dark Bahama. The other reason was I wanted to get in touch with Vallon and get his instructions. I went to an hotel in Miami and I was going to put a call through to him. I knew that would take some hours and I hoped I would be undisturbed in the meantime."

She got up ; moved gracefully across the room. She helped herself to a cigarette from a carved ivory box ; lighted it. It was a fat, Turkish cigarette. Isles thought it smelt very good.

She walked over ; stood by the french window, looking out on to the lawn beyond. The sun was just beginning to die.

She said suddenly : " Tell me something. What did

you want to hear from Vallon ? What were you going to ask him ? "

Isles said : " That's easy enough. I was going to tell him exactly what had happened. I was going to say that unless I put some at least reasonable story up to the Royal Bahama Constabulary, I thought I had a good chance of being thrown in the can. I wanted to ask him if I could blow the whole works on you ; whether I could tell the Commissioner of Police the whole rather stupid story from the beginning—that lovely little fable about your wanting Mrs. Nicola Steyning's naughty daughter brought back home. I wanted to tell him that somebody—you—wanted this young man, whoever he was, killed ; that you'd elected me to be the murderer. I was going to tell him that I thought nobody would believe about this mysterious telephone call of mine ; that unless I substantiated what I had to say it might not be so good for me. In other words I was going to ask permission to blow the works on you."

She said : " In other words you believe that I'd arranged to have this murder synchronised with your arrival ; that I was responsible for the telephone call that got you to the house, and that you were going to be for it ? "

Isles said : " Yes. That was the idea, and everything that's happened since then rather supports it, doesn't it ? Quite obviously, Mr. Jake Carno knew that I'd arrived in Miami. Therefore, it's pretty obvious that he was only told by one person. That was you. And there's only one person could have told you about it."

She asked seriously : " Who was that ? "

" Jacques, the negro, who brought me over here. My guess is that that boy dropped me off that boat and then reported to you. He told me he was going along to the harbour to refuel his tanks. What he did was to come up here and tell you all about it. You must know this Jacques. Maybe he's a friend of yours. When he told you, you went down to Carno's office some time this morning and gave him a thousand dollars to persuade me to leave Miami very quickly. You did that probably for two reasons."

She said : " You know, I'm beginning to think you're very clever, Julian. What were the two reasons ? "

" First of all, if I'd done what Carno wanted and taken a run-out powder, as he would have put it, I'd have certainly been suspected of that murder. Here was I running away from the law ; getting out of Dark Bahama by force ; taking a plane to New York and disappearing. That was one of the reasons. The second reason was that if I'd stayed in Miami I might have discovered by some chance that you were here. I might have made inquiries. I might even have guessed that at some time or other you were going to Dark Bahama. Isn't that right ? "

She said : " You slip a little here and there, Julian, but perhaps you're not a bad guesser."

" One of these fine days I'm going to guess right," said Isles. " Don't you think it would be much better for all parties if you told a little truth." He went on : " There's another small point—just a tiny one but it *might* matter. When you went to Vallon's office you hoped *he* was going to handle this job, didn't you ? You hoped that for old time's sake—because it's my belief that there's been something between you and Vallon—he would come out here and handle this business. Maybe you'd already got it laid on that he might be framed for this murder. I wonder if it's a case of ' hell hath no fury like a woman scorned.' "

She sighed. She moved away from the window. She came slowly towards him ; stood in front of his chair, looking down at him. She said in a very soft, soothing voice : " What is it you want, Julian ? "

He smiled up at her. " I want another drink. I want some clothes. I've only got what I stand up in. I want a razor and all sorts of things like that."

She said : " That's perfectly simple. There are a lot of very good shops here, and they stay open quite late. Well, supposing you've got all these appurtenances, what do you want then ? "

Isles said : " I'm an adventurer. No matter how often I've tried to keep out of trouble, by some strange means I always get into it."

" Yes ? " Her voice was very low. " I rather like men like that. I certainly like the way you dealt with Jake Carno. I think you're quite a piece of a man, Julian."

He said : " Maybe. But when I've got the appurtenances I think you and I might eat a little dinner together. We might decide what is going to be done about Jake Carno, the Commissioner of Police on Dark Bahama, about Johnny Vallon, about you and last of all about me. Let me put it even more bluntly, What I have to decide, and I'm going to decide it in the next couple of hours, is whether I'm going to play around here with you, or whether I'm going on trying to work for Vallon."

She asked : " On what are you going to decide, Julian ? "

" On what you tell me. I want the truth, the whole truth and nothing but the truth. If I believe you I might even work for you. I might even double-cross Johnny Vallon if it's necessary."

She asked : " Why ? "

Isles looked at her sideways. There was a little smile on his mouth. She thought that he looked very attractive.

He said :

" You told me in England that in certain circumstances I might not find you ungrateful."

She smiled back at him. " I see. . . ." Then she laughed. " Where's Jake Carno ? "

He said : " I left him in my hotel bedroom, gagged with a towel and tied up with the bathroom curtain cords. I left a notice on the door : ' *Please don't disturb.* ' "

She looked at the clock. " I should think he'd be out of there by now."

Isles nodded. " So would I. By this time somebody will have found him. He's probably gone back to his office. He'll be very surprised that I left the thousand dollars for him there. When he's tried to work things out he's coming through here. He's going to ask you what he's to do next."

She said : " I don't think he'll have to. I think I'll tell him. I don't need his services any more. I'll do that now. Then we'll go out, Julian, and we'll look after your wardrobe and shaving kit. Then we'll have dinner and then we'll talk." She put her hands on the arms of his chair and leaned over him.

She said : " Honey, you may not know it, but you're going to work for me, and you're going to like it."

She kissed him on the mouth. She crossed the room to the telephone. She said : " I'm going to talk to Carno. Mix yourself that other drink you wanted, Julian."

Isles got up. Crossing to the sideboard, he thought women were strange animals. He felt a little resentful. He wondered why she should think that he would sell out Vallon so easily. Then he mentally shrugged his shoulders. You never knew with women. You certainly did not know with a woman like this one. He concluded that, possibly, the best and safest thing to do would be to drift along and see what happened. In any event, the idea of drifting along with Thelma Lyon was not too unattractive—not unless you woke up in bed one morning and found yourself with your throat cut.

Whatever you did you had to take a chance. So why not take an attractive chance?

She began to talk to Jake Carno on the telephone. He listened to her. The sound of her low-pitched voice was soothing. Apparently Jake found it so too. They seemed to part the best of friends.

She came back to him. She said : " There's a long corridor between this house and the next apartment. At the end of the corridor, on the right, is a bedroom and bathroom. I rent it for guests. So you can sleep there "—she smiled suddenly—" where I can keep my eye on you."

" You think of everything, Thelma." Isles's grin was mischievous.

" I try to," she said. " But I'm only a weak woman, and I slip up sometimes. Let's go shopping."

CHAPTER SIX

I

McMINNS parked his car in a lane on the Balcombe road ; began to walk towards the village, smoking a cigarette, admiring the weather and the signs of early spring. He was a tall, thin man, partially bald. He wore pince-nez, which gave him an owl-like expression. He walked slowly, with his hands in his trouser pockets, considering life and its implications.

McMinns was in fact beginning to wonder what life was all about. He was fifty-five years of age, and ever since the beginning of World War II had been employed as a liaison officer between M.I. 5 and Mr. Quayle's peculiar organisation. There is no doubt that McMinns found life unsatisfying because never, during that period of years, had he known anything about the real business with which he was concerned. He carried a message from here to there or from " A " to " B," and on many occasions had been sent to see Mr. Quayle, delivered his information and gone away, wondering, in the old days, what it was all about. Now he wondered less and less. He realised that he was merely a cog which worked between two important organisations, but that was all. And he concluded that it was better for him to concentrate on those things about which he did know something, like gardening and like matters, than to worry his head about questions to which he would never find an answer.

He went through the gates, up the drive that led towards Quayle's house. He thought it was a nice house. He stood for a moment admiring the architecture, wondering if he would ever see it again,

because McMinns found that Mr. Quayle's headquarters had a habit of changing quickly from one
place to another, even from one country to another.
McMinns, who had talked to Quayle on many
occasions, often wondered about him. There again he
drew a blank. Very few people knew anything about
Mr. Quayle.

He rang the bell; waited patiently. After a few
minutes the door was opened. The girl Germaine stood
in the hallway.

She said cheerfully: " Good afternoon, Mr. Mc-
Minns. It's quite a time since we've seen you."

McMinns said : " Yes . . . time does go by, doesn't
it ? "

She gave him a charming smile. " I expect one of
these days you'll think of retiring."

McMinns smiled at her. " I don't think I'd be
happy if I retired. I think there ought to be some
object in life."

" But of course. . . . What is your object ? " she
asked.

McMinns looked at her. " Now you come to
mention it, I don't really know. Can I see Mr.
Quayle ? "

She nodded. " You'll find him in his room. He's
rather good-tempered to-day."

He grinned. " That'll be a nice change."

He found Quayle seated at his desk, poring over
some papers. McMinns thought Quayle looked bene-
volent. He always did when he wore glasses.

Quayle said : " Hallo, McMinns. What can I do
for you ? "

" I don't know, I'm sure, Mr. Quayle," said
McMinns. " I have a little story for you."

" I like listening to stories," said Quayle. " Especially
if they're interesting. What's this one, and where did
it come from ? Sit down. Give yourself a cigarette."

McMinns sat down. He said : " It came from Scotland Yard. I'll give it to you as briefly as I can. It seems there's a private detective agency in London called Chennault Investigations. It is run by a certain John Vallon. I don't know if you've ever come across the organisation, sir, but it was originally owned by Joe Chennault—an American who worked in the war with the S.A.S. and S.O.E. He was also a liaison officer between the American Office of Strategic Services and our own organisation. When he retired he formed Chennault Investigations. He died about a year ago, and John Vallon, who was his office manager, took the business over."

Quayle said : " I see. Go on. I've met Joe Chennault."

McMinns went on : " It seems that John Vallon was approached recently by a lady called Mrs. Thelma Lyon. She had known Vallon for some years. Mrs. Lyon was very worried about the daughter of a friend of hers. Apparently the girl had been making a damned fool of herself at a place called Dark Bahama—one of the islands in the Bahamas. She had been drinking a little too much, she had too much money and, apparently, she was a little too beautiful."

Quayle said : " A nice combination."

" Possibly . . ." said McMinns. " However, Mrs. Lyon wanted Vallon to go out to Dark Bahama and bring the girl back before she got into any further trouble. But Vallon couldn't go. He sent a man called Julian Isles. I should point out, sir, that Vallon is a very good man. He's done quite a little work in connection with one or two Government departments. But we don't know an awful lot about Isles except that he worked on several cases with Vallon some years ago. He seems to be a fairly good type ; a public schoolboy and a University man. Just before Vallon gave him this job Isles had returned from South America."

Quayle asked : "What was he doing in South America ? "

McMinns shook his head. "Vallon wasn't quite certain about that, sir, but Isles was put into gaol on a fairly long sentence. He'd got himself mixed up with some political party out there, and apparently chose the wrong one. Anyhow, he was released after serving only nine months of his sentence."

Quayle nodded. "So he went to Dark Bahama to find this woman, and bring her back, instead of John Vallon ? "

"Yes," said McMinns. "And it seems, sir, that on the evening he arrived on the island—and this information comes from the Commissioner of Police on Dark Bahama—he says that he received a mysterious telephone call at a call-box. He doesn't know who made the call and the voice was so disguised that he didn't even know if it was a man or a woman. But this mysterious caller asked him to keep an appointment a quarter of an hour later at a house on the island, called Evansley. This house belonged to some quite well-known people who were away holidaying on one of the other islands. When Isles arrived he found the door open and the place empty. Everything was apparently in order except when he went into a room which they call the breakfast-room where he found a man of twenty-eight lying on the floor with half his head blown off by a .45 automatic bullet."

Quayle said : "I see. Go on."

"Isles rang through to the Police Barracks. He told them the story ; was told to wait at the house. He waited. The police arrived and the corpse was identified as one Hubert Gelert—a popular young man on the island, who lived there on an income and seemed to have a very good time. This Gelert was a great favourite with most of the young women. The Commissioner on Dark Bahama had a talk with Isles and naturally found his explanation very unsatisfactory, more especially as Isles would not say what he was doing on the island. His excuse was that a private detective couldn't talk about his client's personal affairs. The Commissioner said he'd talk to him on another occasion and told him not to leave the island. Then Isles went off.

" The Commissioner got through to Scotland Yard and asked them to check Isles's story as quickly as possible. So they sent a man round to Chennault Investigations to see Vallon, and Vallon confirmed what Isles had said."

Quayle said : " That's all right. But what's all this to do with me ? "

McMinns said, with a smile : " I don't know, Mr. Quayle. But then I never *do* know anything very much. When the Yard had seen Vallon they checked as far as they were able on the parties concerned. They knew nothing about Mrs. Thelma Lyon, or for that matter, about Isles. So as a matter of routine the report was put through to M.I. 5 just in case *they* knew any of the parties. M.I. 5 didn't know anything very much either, but my chief thought that one of the names might mean something to you ; that possibly at some time or other you'd come across one of these people. In any event, he thought purely as a matter of routine that you might like to know something about it."

Quayle said : " It's very kind of him. Give him my compliments and say I'm much obliged to him, but nothing rings a bell with me."

McMinns got up. " That's all, sir. I'll give your message to my chief."

Quayle said : " Good afternoon, McMinns. I expect I'll be seeing you some time."

" I hope so, sir. Good afternoon, Mr. Quayle." McMinns went out of the room.

When he had gone Quayle lighted a cigarette; began to walk about the room. He thought life was a most peculiar thing, especially in his particular business. You threw a stone into a pond and the stone created ripples which became wider and wider until, although almost invisible, they embraced the whole surface of the pond. He thought for a moment that he was annoyed; then came to the conclusion that it wasn't worth while being annoyed about anything.

He went back to his desk; picked up the house telephone.

He said: " Germaine, put a call through to Mrs. Wellington. Tell her that I'd like to look in and see her for half an hour at six o'clock this evening."

The girl Germaine said: " Very good, Mr. Quayle."

Quayle hung up. He sat back in his chair, drawing slowly on his cigarette. He thought that Mr. Julian Isles was a damned nuisance.

II

Mrs. Wellington was an attractive, well-tailored lady of fifty-five. The story was that her husband—a wealthy Birmingham manufacturer—had left her an immense fortune when he died a year before the Second World War; that she spent most of her time globe-trotting; that she was an indefatigable tourist who was never so happy as when she was walking through ruins in out-of-the-way places, reading uninteresting plaques, or sitting on a hotel veranda absorbing dry Martinis and the local guide book.

Mrs. Wellington was in fact an extremely intelligent woman who had for years acted as runner for Mr. Quayle. Like McMinns, she was always going somewhere and very seldom knowing why. She was good-figured, round-faced and pleasant. Also she loved experimenting with hair styles which, after all is said and done, is a harmless hobby.

Quayle arrived at five minutes past six. Mrs. Wellington, smiling and relaxed in her well-furnished Kensington drawing-room, greeted him with a pleasant smile and a cocktail.

She said : " I've made it very carefully, but strong— I hope it's all right. I think you'll find it just as you like it."

Quayle said : " Thank you, Mary. Sit down, I want to talk to you."

She sat down. Quayle sat in an armchair ; sipped his cocktail ; put the glass on the table at his elbow.

He said : " How long is it since you've been to the Bahamas ? "

She answered promptly : " I was there two years ago."

Quayle said : " I don't think I want you to go quite so far as that. I think you want to stop at Miami."

She said : " That's about half an hour's flying distance from the nearest island, which is Dark Bahama."

" Right." Quayle drank some more cocktail. He went on : " Some days ago I sent an operative— Ernest Guelvada—out to Dark Bahama to do some work. What you have to do is to park yourself in a good hotel in Miami. Give yourself a proper background. You'd better be doing a little globe-trotting and finish up at George Washington's birthplace, or something like that, so that you only need stay in Miami for a day or so. Understand ? "

She nodded.

Quayle said : " When you've got there, send Guelvada a telegram. You'd better send it to the post office and ask for delivery. They'll know where he is. Everybody knows where everybody is on Dark Bahama. When you send the telegram, say that you have some information about the apartment he wanted to get in Miami ; that perhaps he'd like to drop in and see you. Let him know where you're staying."

She said : " Very well, Mr. Quayle. And then ? "

" That'll bring him over to you," said Quayle, " pretty quickly I should think. When he comes tell him this : Say that an individual by the name of Julian Isles, who went out to Dark Bahama to do some work for a detective agency in London called Chennault Investigations, has got himself mixed up in a murder which occurred on Dark Bahama two or three days ago. Tell Guelvada that the murder was that of a young man by the name of Hubert Gelert, and possibly Isles might be suspected. Tell Guelvada to get Isles out of it somehow." He smiled. " He'll find a way. And tell him to meet this man Isles if it's possible and see if he knows anything or has picked up any information. Tell him to handle the whole thing with kid gloves. Tell him that I don't know Isles and therefore don't trust him particularly. Tell Guelvada that the client of Chennault Investigations who was responsible for Isles's employment was a woman called Thelma Lyon. Tell Guelvada that I have an idea at the back of my head that there may be some connection between this killing and the business on which I sent him to Dark Bahama. Tell him not to waste any time. You understand ? "

" Perfectly, Mr. Quayle."

Quayle said : " All right. Now get yourself a sheet of foolscap and a pencil. I want you to take a note."

She went to a desk in a corner of the room ; opened a blotter. She said : " I'm ready."

" Take this down," said Quayle.

" *Dear Thelma,*

" *What goes on ? I imagine that either nothing does and you're trying to make something happen, or something's gone radically wrong. When you get this message you might answer these questions direct to the lady who'll give it to you:*

" *Exactly who is Julian Isles? Why was it necessary that he should go to Dark Bahama for the purpose of bringing some unknown young woman back from there? I suppose she isn't by any chance working for one of my people, is she? If she isn't who is she and why should she be removed from the island?*

" 2) *I had the idea that by this time you would be on the island yourself. I take it you're still in America. Perhaps I could know about this some time.*

" 3) *If you are in any sort of jam it might have been advisable for you to let me know exactly what is going on. I know that you are fully aware of the fact that once a job is started I don't want to know anything about it till it is finished, but there is an exception to every rule.*

" 4) *Ernest Guelvada is operating on Dark Bahama. You may make contact with him through the lady who is giving you these questions. I think, as you seem to be in some sort of difficulty, that this might be a good thing in any event.*

" 5) *If you do find it necessary to contact Guelvada he had better take the job over. You are to do what he wants. You know Ernest. His methods may be forcible but they're usually very successful. In any event Ernest will get his own way, I promise you.*

I am sending this to the Orchid House because some time ago a little bird told me you were there.

" *Let me have back, through the lady concerned, a complete picture of the operation up to date.*

" *Good luck to you.*

" *Quayle.*"

When she had finished writing Quayle said : " Learn that off by heart, Mary. Then burn it. Recite it to Mrs. Lyon. You'll find her at the Orchid House Apartments in Miami. Write down her reply. Learn it by heart, destroy it and get back here as quickly as you can."

She said : " Very well. Tell me something. Who do I see first—Mr. Guelvada or Mrs. Lyon ? "

Quayle said : " You see Guelvada first. Then you'll know where to get at him if you want him again. But before you see him check that Mrs. Lyon is still at the Orchid House Apartments. And tell Guelvada she's there. You understand ? "

She said : " Perfectly."

Quayle finished his drink. He said : " Now tell me exactly what you're going to tell Guelvada when you see him."

She told him.

He said : " You're a good girl, Mary. You've a marvellous memory." He got up.

She asked : " When do I leave ? "

" Get away as soon as you can to-night. I'll be seeing you one day, Mary." He went to the door.

She said : " It is quite some time since I went to the tropics for you. Do I get some new kit this time ? " She stood smiling at him.

Quayle said : " What a woman ! All right. But not over a hundred and fifty pounds. So long, Mary." He went out ; closed the door quietly behind him.

Mrs. Wellington sighed. She smiled. After all, she thought, it *was* the season in Miami. And at a pinch she might make it three days instead of two.

III

Guelvada turned over on his back and floated on the quiet, blue waters of Fisherman's Bay—a small bay, carved into the western end of Dark Bahama. He lay, his arms outstretched, congratulating himself on the

107

fact that one could lie on the sea without moving. Above him the afternoon sun sparkled. Guelvada thought that life was restful, but perhaps not sufficiently interesting. He thought that the time had come when he must do something about this. He had spent some days absorbing the atmosphere of the island, considering its inhabitants. He had wandered through the streets, visited the Golden Lily Club. Ernest, who had the ability to shrink within himself when he wanted to, presented a picture of the usual quiet tourist who is satisfied to swim, do a little fishing, a little drinking in the evening and to laze through the halcyon days.

He turned over—he was a good swimmer ; swam farther out towards the sea. It was only when he saw the fin of a shark two hundred yards away that he turned ; swam slowly back towards the shore. He walked up the beach ; draped his towel round his shoulders ; sat in the chair the negro servant had put up under a large, coloured umbrella. He lighted a cigarette ; put his hands behind his head ; began to work out a plan of campaign in his mind.

Like everyone else on Dark Bahama, Guelvada was concerned with the latest news—the Gelert killing. Although this affair had, apparently, nothing to do with his own mission, he considered that it was interesting—interesting because an individual called Julian Isles, who had been questioned by the police, had suddenly disappeared. The story of how Isles had managed to get off the island was by now public property. He had got off on a fishing launch owned by Mervyn Jacques. This was the connecting point that interested Guelvada.

He finished his cigarette, got up and, draped in his towel, walked from the beach, across the main road and into the apartment he had rented in one of the side streets not far from the Leonard Hotel.

Arrived there, he bathed, shaved and dressed himself

in a cream tussore suit ; sat on the veranda, drinking rum cocktails. It was only when the shadows had begun to fall that he went round to the garage at the back of the apartment and drove away in the car he had hired on arrival. On the main road, he turned left. He sat relaxed behind the steering wheel, driving at a level thirty, admiring the scenery and the shadows that were falling across the sea.

He kept on, through the town, past the Club, straight on until the asphalt of the road turned into a dirt track. The track was narrow and rutted. Between him and the sea were thick trees and foliage. The road was almost dark. Here and there, through the branches of overhanging trees, the dying daylight speckled the uneven road.

After ten minutes he came out into a clearing. On his right was a broken-down pier leading out to sea—a deserted memory of the time when this place had been used as a yachting club. Now the pier and the buildings about it were derelict. On the left of the road was a small lane leading into the thickness of a wood.

Guelvada stopped the car. He parked it in the shadow of a hedge ; walked down the road ; turned into the lane. He walked, whistling softly to himself, for twenty minutes. The path disappeared into a clearing. On the other side of it was a broken-down shack which somebody had endeavoured to repair. There was a small veranda in front, rotten with age and exposure to seasonal hurricanes. There was a figure sitting on the veranda steps. It sat there, arms on knees, shoulders hunched forward, a native straw hat tipped over its eyes.

Guelvada thought it was not a happy figure. He whistled a little louder. The face under the wide straw hat was raised. Guelvada found himself looking at Mellin.

He said : " Mr. Mellin, I believe ? I should like to introduce myself to you. My name is Ernest Guelvada

—a name which, possibly distinguished, is unknown to you. You look very unhappy. I think you ought to have a drink."

Guelvada put his hand to his hip pocket ; produced a pint silver flask. He held it out.

Mellin said : " Thank you very much, sir. I haven't had a drink for days." He looked at Guelvada suspiciously. " Maybe you wanted to inquire about a boat ? "

Guelvada shook his head. " Give yourself a drink, my friend. I promise I will be very frank with you. I do not wish to inquire about a boat. On the contrary " —he smiled benignly—" I want to talk to you about a murder, which I think is a goddam sight more interesting. And what do you think about that, hey, baby ? " There was a peculiar, metallic tone in his voice.

Mellin looked scared. He took a long swig at the flask ; handed it back to Guelvada.

Guelvada took his handkerchief from his breast pocket ; spread it delicately on the wooden step beside Mellin. He sat down. He put the flask in his mouth ; took a long swig at the rum inside.

He said : " My friend, you will listen to me and when I say listen I mean *listen.* Do not miss any of the pearls that fall from my lips. And I don't mean maybe. Be very careful to absorb everything I say, because a very great deal might depend on it—for you, I mean."

Mellin said : " What the hell do you mean—for me ? " Now he felt a little braver. He looked at Guelvada sideways, suspiciously.

Guelvada said : " Believe it or not, you will find that the law, as it applies to England, also applies to islands in the Bahamas. Do you understand that ? "

Mellin nodded.

Guelvada said : " It might easily be said that you were an accessory before and after the fact of the murder of one Sandford. You will not deny, Mr.

Mellin, will you, that you have heard of Mr. Sandford? If you did, I should describe you as a goddam bonehead. Let us consider the facts. This Sandford hires the boat of Mervyn Jacques to go shark fishing on a delightful night not very long ago. You were on that boat. Before the boat went out you noticed that the straps on one of the fishing seats were worn, or perhaps they had been deliberately frayed or cut. Sandford arrived. He sat in this seat. Because the straps were not secured, which is possibly because he was thought to be drunk, when Sandford hooked a shark he was taken overboard, and I have no doubt was properly consumed by this denizen of the sea, hey? There is no question about the fishing seat strap being frayed because, Mr. Mellin, you yourself in an alcoholic moment informed a friend of yours of this fact.

" After the accident you returned to the island, where the mishap was reported to the police by Mervyn Jacques. No further action was taken. The death was considered to be accidental. After all, such things have happened before. But if it was *not* accidental, my bright Mr. Mellin, it was murder, and you had a part in it."

Mellin said hoarsely : " It's a damned lie. I was the mate on the boat—not the skipper. I told Jacques about the straps. Well, it wasn't his fault if Sandford was drunk. A man out shark fishing ought to be able to look after himself."

" Precisely," said Guelvada. " I agree with you—like hell I do ! What you mean is Sandford ought not to have been drunk ? "

" That's what I mean." From the torn pocket in the breast of his soiled shirt, Mellin produced a pack of cigarette tobacco and some papers. He began to roll himself a cigarette. Guelvada noticed that his fingers were trembling.

He asked : " Had you been fishing with Sandford before ? "

Mellin nodded.

" Was he drunk on those previous occasions ? "

Mellin said : " Well, yes, he was always slightly cut. He used to do a lot of drinking around the island. But I've never seen him so bad as on the last night."

Guelvada said : " Exactly what you mean, my friend, is that on the night of his death he was peculiarly drunk. Is that right ? That he seemed to be more drunk than usual ; that this man, who was able to carry his liquor so very well that he could drink all day, was on this occasion so very drunk that he did not know what he was doing. Would that be right ? "

Mellin said : " Yeah . . . something like that. So what ? "

Guelvada said airily : " I suppose it never occurred to you that Sandford might not have been drunk ? "

Mellin asked : " What the hell do you mean by that one ? "

" I'll tell you," said Guelvada. " Have you ever overlooked the possibility that he might have been drugged ? Have you overlooked the possibility that someone had given him a hocked drink ? "

Mellin drew on the cigarette. " For chrissake ! . . . You might be right."

Guelvada said : " What makes you think that so suddenly ? Where do you get a sudden bright idea from, baby, hey ? "

Mellin said : " Whenever he went fishing before he always had whisky. He used to drink it most of the time. But that never stopped him strapping himself in. He knew how to look after himself. But the last night that he went out he had some coffee."

Guelvada smiled. " You see . . . already your brain is beginning to work." He produced the flask. " Give yourself a drink. Then listen."

Mellin took the flask : drank. He handed it back to Guelvada, who put it in his hip pocket.

Guelvada said : " On this night, before Sandford came down to the quay, you told Jacques that the seat was unsafe ; that someone had been at the straps, or that they were frayed. In spite of this Jacques put Sandford into that seat, and in spite of the coffee Sandford had still not enough sense to strap himself in. Where were you when he went overboard ? "

Mellin said : " I was forrard. . . ."

" And you didn't actually see him go overboard. If you were forrard how could you ? The canopy of the boat would be between you and the stern. You might have seen him in the water but I'm going to suggest to you, my friend, that you did not see him *leave* the boat."

Mellin said : " Well, I saw him in the water astern of the boat."

" Precisely," said Guelvada. " Then you are not in a position to swear that he was not actually assisted out of the boat by Jacques. Consider the picture, my friend. The shark takes the hook. Sandford is pulled forward, but he had the rise of the stern between him and the sea. It might be that he was assisted over the stern—a sudden push ! You understand ? "

Guelvada smiled. He said amiably : " You will think it over. You will find that you remember eventually."

Mellin said : " What the hell are you gettin' at ? I might have talked a little one night when I was drunk, but that's not evidence. When I talked I wasn't in a court of law."

Guelvada shrugged. " It won't help you. The only question that is in my mind is what I am actually going to say to the police. You understand ? That is if I should decide to go to the police."

Mellin asked : " What has this got to do with you, anyway ? "

Guelvada spread his hands. " Not very much . . .

except that I am a person who takes an interest in previously unconsidered trifles ; that I have an aptitude for sticking my nose into other people's goddam business." He looked at Mellin. Mellin saw that his eyes were as hard as steel ; that they belied the smile about Guelvada's mouth.

"What I am considering," said Guelvada, " is whether I am going to implicate you in this murder. See what I mean, big boy? Whether one of you or two of you are going to be hanged."

Mellin said : " My God . . . ! " His voice was hoarse.

Guelvada put his hand into the pocket of his coat. He brought out a collapsible, Swedish sailor's knife. The handle of the knife lay delicately across his palm. Mellin looked at it. Then Guelvada touched the spring with his left hand, and the blade shot out— a four-inch, pointed, razor-edge blade. Guelvada casually adjusted the knife on the palm of his hand. Then, with a sudden movement, he threw it. The knife flew across the clearing in front of the veranda. It struck, quivering, into a tree fifteen yards away.

Guelvada said casually : " A hobby of mine. I never miss." He went on : " My good friend Mellin, let us go inside your so delightful shack. Let me rehearse you in the story of what actually happened that night, and you will learn it very well and you will repeat it if and when I ask you to do so. And you will not talk to anybody ; otherwise, so help me God, you are going to swing off the gallows ! Do you understand that ? "

Mellin said : " Yeah." His hands were trembling.

" Or, alternatively," went on Guelvada, " you might slip one day and fall off a headland into the sea. You might be run over and killed by a car driven by a rather stupid driver like myself. All sorts of things might happen to you, my good Mellin, unless you do as you are told."

Mellin said nothing. Guelvada lighted a cigarette. He smoked in silence for a few minutes.

Then he said : " Tell me. Tell me about our friend Jacques, the skipper of this boat. Do you remember how he was dressed on that night ? "

Mellin said : " That's easy. He's always dressed the same way. Some days he wears a floral silk shirt. Some days it is white. He is a snappy dresser. He always wears rope-soled shoes, no socks, a pair of dark gaberdine slacks and a leather belt."

Guelvada asked : " What does he wear on his head ? "

" A sun cap," said Mellin. " A sort of skull cap with a long peak. He always wears coloured ones. He has half a dozen of them. He's always losing them. He puts a cap down some place and leaves it there. It's a thing with him. He has a lot of caps."

Guelvada said : " That's excellent. Now, my good Mellin, let us go inside. Let us discuss this thing as between friends, and we are friends, aren't we ? "

" Yeah. . . . I suppose we are. I suppose I gotta be."

Guelvada said : " Why not ? The police would be very interested if they knew the truth of the death of Sandford. Maybe it will not be necessary. Maybe it will. For your sake, if it is necessary, I hope you'll do as you are told. By the way, how are things with you, Mellin ? Are you doing well in your profession ? " He looked behind him at the broken-down shack.

Mellin said : " Things aren't so good."

Guelvada said : " Perhaps by some chance you're not doing so much work as you usually do for Jacques. It may be you are a little afraid of Jacques. I understand he's a very tough baby. It may be he has got to hear about what you said when you were drunk. It may be he does not like you a lot. Tell me, good Mellin, are you afraid of Jacques ? "

Mellin said : " He's not a good guy to be at outs with. He can be tough."

Guelvada looked at him and smiled. It was a terrifying smile. " But, my good Mellin, you are much more afraid of me, are you not ? It will be much better for you to be at ' outs ' as you call it, with Jacques and be at ' ins ' with Mr. Guelvada, don't you think ? " His voice rasped.

Mellin said : " Yeah. . . . I guess so ! "

Guelvada put his hand in the breast pocket of his tussore jacket. He brought out a roll of bills. He said : " There is a Spanish proverb which says that a good dog is worth a bone." He held out the roll of bills. " Here is the bone."

Mellin took the roll. He put it in his trouser pocket.

Guelvada said : " You will forget that you have spoken to me. Even when you get drunk you will not mention my name. Mellin, go and get me the knife."

Mellin got up a little unsteadily. He walked across the clearing ; pulled the knife out of the tree. It took quite an effort. He came back with it ; gave it to Guelvada. Guelvada threw it again. It struck the same tree in the same spot. He got up ; strolled casually across the clearing ; retrieved the knife. He came back.

He said : " Come on, baby. Let us have our little talk."

They went into the shack.

·   ·   ·   ·   ·

It was dark when Guelvada left the shack. He walked quickly back to his car ; turned it. He drove for a mile without lights. When he had reached the asphalt road he switched them on. He drove through the town ; turned ; took a side road ; came up at the rear of the Leonard Hotel. He parked his car ; went into the hotel bar. He drank two rum cocktails. Then he walked out into the hotel grounds, smoking a cigarette.

The grounds were deserted. Guelvada went out quietly through the side gate on to the main road. Keeping in the shadow of the palms that fringed the grass verge between the road and the sea, he moved quickly down towards the quay. The place was deserted. Most of the boats were back and tied up after the evening's run. Few of them would go out again, except those that went out after midnight for shark.

Guelvada moved along the rear end of the quay. Tied up nearest the shore he recognised Jacques's boat from the description Mellin had given him. Guelvada moved as swiftly and silently as a shadow. In a minute he was in the cockpit of the boat. He opened the door on the left of the cockpit that led into the cabin. Then he began to search expertly and with incredible speed. He went through everything in the cabin. At the bottom of a locker used for odd papers and magazines he found what he wanted. There were three sun caps —old, going at the seams, screwed up in a ball, under a roll of Miami newspapers. He smiled amiably.

He put one of them into his pocket. He came out of the cabin ; looked around. He left the boat. Walking alongside the wooden pier in the shadows he reached the main road. He sighed. He lighted another cigarette. He walked back towards the Leonard Hotel, singing an old Spanish love song.

CHAPTER SEVEN

I

Isles lay back in his bath ; drew placidly on his cigarette ; he thought it was a good thing to give a woman her head, especially a woman like Thelma Lyon.

The tropical Miami sun came through the cracks of the screen window ; formed amusing arabesques on the walls and on the ceiling. Isles flicked the cigarette ash over the edge of the bath on to the floor and wondered how long this quiescent period would continue. But life was amusing. Isles remembered that not so very long ago he had been in England and broke. Now he was in Miami, well housed, well fed, with money in his pocket. He was doing the best he could for Johnny Vallon, even if it wasn't very much of a best. But that wasn't his fault. He had no doubt that in time Thelma would talk.

He wondered just what she would have to say and just how true it would be. He shrugged his shoulders. Always Isles had had an open mind about women's confidences. Sometimes they were true. Sometimes they were told for a purpose. But it did not matter to him. Why should it ?

He got out of the bath ; took a cold shower ; dressed himself. When he had finished he regarded himself in the cheval glass. He thought he did not look too bad. Freshly shaven, in a white linen suit, a silk shirt and a quiet tie in contrast to the gorgeous neckwear which Americans were sporting, he thought he might pass easily as almost anything—he grinned to

118

himself—even something remotely approaching a gentleman.

He shut and locked the bedroom door behind him ; walked down the long passage-way that led to the Lyon apartment. Arrived, he tapped on the door. The negro maid opened it.

She said : " Good mornin', Mistah Isles. The missus is in the dining-room. Will you go right in ? "

Isles said : " Yes, Mary Ann." He grinned at her cheerfully. He walked across the hallway into the dining-room.

She was seated at the breakfast table. She wore a pale green, chiffon house-gown. The room was cool and quiet.

She said : " Good morning, Julian. I hope you enjoyed your night in the town last night. Did you have fun ? "

He sat down at the table. He said : " Good morning to you. I did not have a lot of fun and I didn't have a lot of no fun, if you know what I mean. I kept to the outskirts. I thought it might be a wise thing for the moment."

She nodded. " Possibly . . . although I don't imagine that there is a police alarm out for you." She poured coffee for him.

Isles took the cup. " I wonder why you think that ? "

She said : " I'll tell you in a moment." She got up from the table ; walked to the window ; pulled the transparent curtain to one side. She stood looking out on to the flower garden. She said : " I suppose you've wondered why I haven't talked to you yet."

" Not particularly." Isles smiled at her. " I'm a patient man, you know, and after all, it's only a couple of days since I made my first appearance here. I thought perhaps you wanted to think things out."

She turned to him. She stood, her back to the window, looking at him. " You are right. I have been thinking things out. Most of the time I've been wondering if you're going to believe me."

Isles asked : " Has that been worrying you a lot ? " He began to butter toast.

She smiled. " You're pretty cute, aren't you, Julian ? May I ask why you should think that whether I told you the truth or not hadn't been worrying me ? "

" Yes." Isles's voice was cheerful. " You see, I've been told an awful lot of things by an awful lot of women in my life . . . some of them true, some of them not true. . . . But in the long run it doesn't matter, you know, because nobody could go on telling lies success-fully—permanently—if you see what I mean."

" I see what you mean. Well "—she smiled again—" supposing I don't talk ? Supposing I give you permission to ask questions ? That might make it easier."

Isles refilled his coffee cup. He said : " I take it that the original story you told me about Mrs. Nicola Steyning and her naughty daughter isn't quite true. It might be half-true or a quarter true, but it wasn't the real reason why you wanted someone to go to Dark Bahama, was it ? That's the first thing. The next thing is," he went on, " you really wanted John Vallon to come out here for you. You really didn't want *me* to come, did you ? But someone had to come, so when you couldn't get him you had to settle for me. What about those two things for a start ? "

She walked slowly over to the mantelpiece ; helped herself to a cigarette ; lighted it.

She said : " Believe it or not, there was quite a lot of truth in what I told you. There is a Viola Steyning on the island and her mother is Mrs. Nicola Steyning. Did you think she didn't exist ? "

Isles shrugged his shoulders. " I thought there might not be a Mrs. Nicola Steyning. I thought the girl might be some relative of yours in a jam, and that you didn't want to divulge the fact."

She shook her head. " She isn't a relative of mine and, as I told you, she's a pretty tough proposition. She does much too much drinking and, I believe, occasionally takes a little dope. She's in a bad way, that girl."

Isles nodded. " I gathered that. And you wanted her got away from Dark Bahama. *You* wanted her removed from there either by guile or force. Is the suggestion that if she were somewhere other than Dark Bahama she wouldn't get drunk or do the other things, or is it that she might cause *you* more trouble if she stays there ? "

" Your guess is fairly correct," she said. " And the answer is also the answer to your second question as to whether I really wanted John Vallon to go there. Yes, I did. I'll tell you why. When I was on the island— before I returned to England and met you—I was quite happy—almost contented, one might say. Un- fortunately, a man arrived. I'd known him a long time ago, Julian. He wasn't a very nice man."

He said : " I understand. Was he making things tough for you or her ? "

She said : " He might have made things very tough for both of us. First of all—and I've got to admit this, Julian—he knew one or two things about me that weren't very good. He had some rather stupid letters that I'd written to him years ago—the sort of letters that I wouldn't like to have made public. When I was out on the island Mrs. Steyning—Viola's mother—met a friend of mine in London who told her that I was there. You must understand that at this time I didn't even know Viola Steyning. But her mother had heard one or two not very good rumours about her, so she wrote to me. She told me that she thought the girl was making a fool of herself. She asked me if I could see her ; if I could do anything about it. I wrote back and said I'd try.

" I went to see Viola. I liked her, but quite candidly, I think she's a hard case. She's still beautiful, young, wealthy and headstrong, and she's got to the state where she's half-tight most of the day and quite tight after about six o'clock in the evening. Not a very nice situation."

Isles nodded. " Not very good for her. But what did it matter to you ? She wasn't *your* daughter."

She said : " It mattered to me this much ; that the man I was telling you about began to pay Viola attentions. Unfortunately, she seemed to fall for him too. He's an attractive devil. Perhaps she regarded him as somebody to lean on. It was quite obvious to me what he was after. What he wanted was her money. This man is a despicable cad—a hopeless type. Now are you beginning to understand ? "

Isles, his mouth full of buttered toast, nodded. " It sounds to me like the old story. Perhaps I could make a few suggestions as to the finish. You go to your new friend Viola and you tell her this man's a bad lot. But she thinks she's in love with him. So she tells you to go to hell because she believes you're jealous. I suppose he's pretty good looking. He *must* be good looking."

She asked quickly : " Why ? "

" Well, he must have had something for you to fall for him in the old days." He smiled cheerfully at her.

She said : " You're very logical, aren't you, Julian. Yes, that's true. She thought I was jealous."

" And," continued Isles, " I suppose you next considered going to see him. Perhaps you did go to see him. And then I imagine you got a rather nasty surprise. I should think, if this story is going to run true to form, he told you to mind your own business, and he also told you that unless you stopped interfering and got out of the way he was going to have a few words with Viola, and tell her about you. Maybe he even threatened to show her your letters."

She nodded her head. She said cynically : " You're quite right, Julian. As you say, it's an old story—a thing that's always happening to women—even intelligent women like myself. It shows that we seldom learn very much about men."

Isles said nothing. He drank some more coffee.

She went on : " I thought it was time I had a rest from Dark Bahama, so I went back to England. I went back first of all because I wanted to meet Viola's mother—Mrs. Steyning. It was quite true when I said she was in a nursing home. She was in such a state of nerves about her daughter that I hadn't the heart to tell her the whole truth. So I told her that Viola was getting on fairly well ; that she had sent all sorts of messages to her mother ; that I was going back to Dark Bahama and returning to England in a few months, and that I could more or less promise her that when I came back I'd bring Viola with me."

Isles said : " I see. Now I'm beginning to understand."

" I thought you would, Julian. I knew I hadn't a chance of bringing the girl back with me. I knew that by the time I got back to Dark Bahama this man might have poisoned Viola's mind against me. I thought the safest thing for me to do was to go to Johnny Vallon ; to ask him to go out and somehow get the girl away. You know Johnny's pretty cute ; very clever, and he can be very tough. I thought he'd manage to do it even if no one else could. I thought he'd do it for me."

Isles grinned. " That's what I'd have thought. Tell me, Thelma, was Johnny another *affaire* of yours ? Is that why you thought he'd do it ? "

She smiled a little sadly. " You're only half-right, Julian. One time—quite a long time ago—before

123

Johnny took over the Chennault business—I thought there was a chance of him and I being married. I met him during the war. But when I came back I found he was very much married to a Miss Madeleine Thorne."

Isles nodded sympathetically. " That's the way it goes, my dear. Well, that's that."

She asked : " Julian, do you believe what I've told you ? "

He got up ; lighted a cigarette ; began to walk about the room. He said : " Yes, I believe you. This is one of the things that happen to women like you. The trouble is you're too beautiful."

" It hasn't got me anywhere, Julian."

He grinned. " It seldom does. Beauty is like a two-edged sword. I forget who said that, but somebody did some time—even if it was only me. So what does ' X ' do now ? Am I still employed by Johnny Vallon or am I to return and mark the case closed, or what am I to do ? " He sat down in the armchair ; stretched out his long legs.

He went on : " There's another little point ; we mustn't forget that I'm a murder suspect. Or am I ? And maybe it wouldn't be easy for me to go back to Dark Bahama, supposing——"

" Supposing what, Julian ? "

" Supposing you asked me to," he said.

" I wouldn't worry too much about that if I were you—about being a murder suspect I mean. Because I think I'm going to ask you to go back."

He sat up. " Now this begins to be very interesting. So I am to go back. What do you think I shall be able to do on that charming and mysterious island ? I should imagine that directly I show my nose I shall be thrown in the can, and I'm rather tired of that process. It wasn't so long ago that I succeeded in getting out of another one by the skin of my teeth. I'd hate to go back unnecessarily." He smiled. "Of course if you want it I'll go back for *you*. Chennault Investigations never lets its clients down—well, not much."

She said seriously : " Listen to me, Julian. One thing we know. There's no particular hue and cry out for you ; otherwise it would have been in the papers here. Remember that a murder on one of the Bahama Islands is news—big news. There's been practically nothing in the papers. If the Miami police had been looking for you they'd have found you. It's my belief that they're not even looking for you ; that no one has asked them to."

Isles said : " That's very interesting. Why do you think that ? "

" Work it out for yourself. You saw the Commissioner of Police on the night when you discovered this murdered man. You told him a story that must have sounded extraordinary, but you don't think he'd be so stupid as not to check on that story, do you ? "

He sat up again. He said : " I'm beginning to see what you mean."

She smiled. " Precisely. You can take it from me that when you left the Commissioner that night he made arrangements to get in touch with Scotland Yard in London. The first thing he'd do would be to check your story. Well, what would happen ? Scotland Yard would go and see Johnny Vallon. Johnny would be forced to talk. Probably he wouldn't mention my name but he would confirm your story. He would say that a client had sent you out to Dark Bahama to make an investigation, even although he knew nothing about the mysterious phone call. Johnny, who has a very quick brain, would have guessed that I had suggested to you that somebody would get in touch with you. He'd confirm everything. Do you understand ? "

Isles said : " I see what you mean. That once my extraordinary story was confirmed by the Yard, the fact that it was so extraordinary would be in my favour ? "

She nodded. " It's my belief that they're not even looking for you ; that the police on Dark Bahama are on another scent."

Isles said : " That could easily be." He got up ; yawned. " I wonder what this murder was all about."

She moved a little. She stood, one hand on the mantelpiece, looking at him. She said. " Something's occurred to me, Julian. It's only a guess, but it might easily be the truth. You remember I told you at our first meeting in the Hyde Park Hotel that you might have a telephone call from a maid on the island. I suggested to you that this maid was an old employee of Mrs. Steyning's. That wasn't true. The truth of that is this : When I left the island I asked Viola Steyning's maid—a dear old negro woman—to watch the list of arrivals—it's easy enough in a place like Dark Bahama—and when Vallon, as I hoped, arrived at the hotel to get into touch with him ; to talk to him and let him know how things had gone in my absence. I sent word to her that *you* would be coming, not Johnny."

" I see," said Isles. " And this negro maid just dramatised the situation a little bit and thought she'd ring me up at a call-box ? "

She said : " That would be sensible of her, if she wanted to meet you secretly, as apparently she did. She wouldn't want the call to come through the hotel switchboard."

Isles said : " That's true enough. So you think——"

She said : " I think this : That it is quite possible that since my absence Viola has got wise to the man I told you of. Maybe she's learned something about him. Maybe he's frightened her. Maybe he's trying to blackmail her. If her maid knew this, as she probably would do—all the servants listen on Dark Bahama—

it is quite on the cards that she would have told her mistress that somebody who might be a friend was coming out from England. Maybe it was Viola who wanted to meet you at that house."

" All right," said Isles. " If she wanted to meet me there, why wasn't she there ? Why does somebody—some young man—have to be murdered ? "

She said : " That young man's name was Gelert. He wasn't a bad type of young man and he was very keen on Viola. It is a great pity that she wasn't as fond of him. Don't you see what might have happened ? "

" I've got it," said Isles. " What you mean is this : Viola gets her maid to ring me at the call-box to ask me to meet her at this deserted house—a house belonging to someone else who was probably away—to which she had the key. But she doesn't like the idea of going there by herself so she rings up this young man who was considered to be a friend and asks him to meet her there. Possibly she wants him to hear what she has to say to me. Maybe she was good and scared—leaning on anybody. That's possible."

She said : " It's more than possible, Julian. And it's just on the cards that someone else knew that this meeting was going to take place—this other man. Maybe he knew somehow. Maybe he followed her there, and when he arrived there he found Gelert."

" It could be," said Isles. " Your ex-boy friend has a gun in his pocket. There is a row between the two men. Gelert tells him where he gets off and your ex-boy friend kills him. That's easy enough if two men are in bad tempers and have had a little too much to drink —not an unusual process on Dark Bahama, I imagine. It all adds up. Maybe that's what happened."

" I believe it to be possible, Julian—or something very like that. Now imagine her position. Probably she was present when this murder took place—in a bad state—not really herself. She'd be scared stiff. She probably ran back home and maybe hasn't put her nose outside the door since. She was like that. Like most people who drink too much, she scares easily."

There was a pause. Isles stubbed out his cigarette on the ash-tray. He said : " And so you want me to go back and pick up the pieces."

" I want you to go back, Julian, and get that girl off the island. If I'm right in this ; if this ex-boy friend of mine, as you call him, is responsible for this murder—and I think he is—my going back isn't going to help very much. It's not going to help *me* very much, is it ? "

" Not if he's got something on you," said Isles.

She said : " Precisely. Now you understand, don't you ? "

Isles nodded. He smiled at her. " Well, my dear, when do I start ? "

She said : " We'll wait another day or two. That can't do any harm. Then I suggest you go back. I think it would be clever of you if you went to see the Commissioner of Police ; if you told him that you'd been thoroughly scared because you thought he didn't believe your story ; that you got over to Miami and after a few days here you realised that you were doing a rather stupid thing, so you'd gone back." She smiled. " That, after all, is the action of an innocent man."

Isles said : " I think that's the thing to do. I believe your reasoning's right. If the police on Dark Bahama still suspected me they'd have been after me. As it is, perhaps they're on some other line. All right, when you want it, Thelma, I'll go."

She said : " Thank you, Julian. I knew I could rely on you. You're not letting anybody down—either me, yourself or Johnny Vallon."

He grinned at her. " What a strange position for Mr. Isles to be in ! Everybody's pleased."

She asked demurely : " Except Mr. Isles ? "

" Oh, no," said Isles. " Believe it or not I'm very

happy. I like gathering roses while I may even if I'm only *metaphorically* gathering roses."

She laughed at him. " Don't be impatient, Julian. All things come to him who waits."

He laughed back at her. He said : " I know . . . all the things nobody else wants."

II

It was eight o'clock in the evening and very dark. Guelvada came out of his apartment ; strolled down to the main road ; turned left ; began to walk towards the interior of the island. He was hatless, neatly dressed in a suit of dark blue gaberdine, wearing brown rubber-soled shoes. As usual, he was crooning softly to himself.

Ernest was interested and happy. He was happy because he considered that events on the island were beginning to take shape. He considered that Mellin was sufficiently scared to do as he was told. Ernest felt secure on that point. These things being so, he was beginning to see daylight.

Now the road had narrowed. Few people were about. Away somewhere to his left Guelvada could see the sparkling neon sign of the Golden Lily Club. He began to walk more quickly, keeping in the shadows of the trees which lined the road.

After another twenty-five minutes he found himself outside the wide gates of the house Evansley. He opened the gates ; walked thirty or forty yards up the path ; stood silently in the shadows observing the house. It was dark ; appeared to be deserted. Guelvada considered that it was unnecessary for the police to have left anyone inside the house. He continued up the curving carriage drive ; tried the side door of the house. It was locked. Guelvada moved silently round to the back of the house ; opened a window ; got through. He closed the window quietly behind him ; moved across the room until he found the door. He passed through it ; closed it ; then switched on a dim electric torch. Moving as silently as a cat he went through the rooms on the ground floor of the house, finishing in the breakfast room, in which the body had been found. Now the moon came out from behind a cloud. It was light enough for him to see.

Guelvada moved across the room ; sat down on the couch beside which Isles had discovered the corpse. Guelvada put himself in the place of the murderer. Having shot somebody, this gentleman, he thought, would have had to get out by the quickest possible way. That was by the french windows. Guelvada tried them. They were unlocked. He unlatched the window ; stepped through to the lawn outside. He stood, close against the wall, looking about him. The lawn extended some fifteen yards down to a gravel pathway. On the other side of the pathway were trees, and a thick shrubbery. Guelvada crossed the lawn, his flat-soled rubber shoes making no impression, across the pathway into the shrubbery. He smiled to himself. Policemen, he thought, were sometimes clever and any object produced could easily be checked for its recent background. He thought it would be a great pity to make a mistake in the case of the sun-cap of Mr. Jacques.

A few yards inside the shrubbery was a water culvert. A thin stream trickled away from this, soon to be lost in the surrounding earth. Guelvada stood beside the culvert. He thought it might be a good idea to stuff the cap into the culvert, so that the water would throw it out. This would carry the cap a few feet. It would end up in the slimy puddle where the water finished. He bent down ; took from his pocket Jacques's red and blue cap ; rolled it into a ball ; pushed it lightly into the culvert. Within half a minute it appeared ; floated on the water down into the slimy patch. He let it stay there.

Guelvada walked quickly away from the house to his left. Twenty minutes walking brought him to his second destination—a small but well-designed white house that stood in a little clearing off the road. Guelvada could see a light on the second storey. He went to the front door ; rang the bell. He waited patiently, leaning up against the door-post. Two or three minutes went by ; then the door was opened. A voice said :

" What do you want, sir ? There ain't nobody wants to see you here, boss."

Guelvada looked into the placid face of the negress who held the door half-open.

He said : " On the contrary, I assure you somebody does want to see me. Miss Viola Steyning wants to see me. And don't tell me she's not in."

The maid said : " Ah'm tellin' you, boss, Miss Steyning don' want to see nobody. Ah reckons she's not so well."

Guelvada smiled disarmingly. " I assure you she's going to see me. Tell me, where is she ? " The dollar bills made a crackling sound—they were new bills. As Guelvada took them from his pocket and folded them, her eyes went towards the sound. Guelvada held out the notes. He repeated : " Where is she ? "

The maid said : " She's in the room at the back of the house, boss . . . end of this corridor. But ah reckon she ain't gonna to be no good to anybody to talk to."

He smiled at her. " Never mind. You go back to your own room. I'll see myself out."

She said : " All right, boss. But ah tell you she ain't no good to anybody." She held the door for Guelvada as he entered the house ; then she closed it. She disappeared up the stairs.

Guelvada walked slowly down the corridor that bisected the house ; opened the door at the end. It was a large room, well furnished. A gramophone had been playing in the corner ; had come to the end of the record ; had not been switched off. It was making the odd whirring sound of a needle running round a record, playing nothing. Near the gramophone, on the couch, was a young woman. She was half-sitting, half-lying back against the head of the couch. Beside her was a table with a dozen bottles and a few glasses.

She looked at Guelvada with dull eyes. She said in a peculiar, almost broken voice : " What do you want ? " She mouthed the words at him.

Guelvada picked up a chair. He carried it across the room ; put it down by the couch. He sat on it. He said : " Miss Steyning, permit me to introduce myself to you. My name is Ernest Guelvada and, whatever you may think to the contrary, I assure you I am a most delightful person—well, sometimes—and this is one of the moments when I am utterly delightful."

She looked at him dully ; then she almost smiled. She asked : " What is it you want ? "

Guelvada shrugged his shoulders. " I'd hoped you'd ask me to have a drink. I wanted to talk to you about something very important."

She moved a little. Guelvada saw that, in spite of the fact that she was drunk, she was attractive. Her skin was youthful and clear.

She said : " If you want a drink you give yourself one. You'll find anything you want there. Help yourself."

Guelvada looked at the bottles. He selected one ; took a glass ; poured himself a drink. He drank a little of the rum.

He said : " Miss Steyning, believe me, I sympathise very much with you. I know you don't want to talk to anybody, but yet the matter is so important that I think I would like to talk to you."

She said : " Nothing's important. I don't want to talk to anybody."

Guelvada sipped some rum. " Nevertheless, I think you will talk to me."

" Yes ? Why should I talk to you ? "

Guelva said : " Because Hubert Gelert was very much in love with you. Surely a woman wants to talk about any man who was in love with her."

She asked slowly : " How do you know ? Have you been snooping around too ? "

He shook his head. " I never snoop, Miss Steyning. Everybody on this island knows that Gelert was very much in love with you. Everybody knows that he is dead. I suppose you wouldn't know why he died, would you ? "

She said : " Who the hell are you ? Are you a policeman ? I'm sick to death of policemen."

Guelvada nodded. " I bet you are. For me . . . I don't like policemen either, and I am not one. Supposing I were to tell you "—he lied glibly—" that I was a friend of Hubert's ; that I knew him a long time ago before he came to the island ; that I would like very much to discover who killed him. I suppose *you* wouldn't know ? "

She said : " No, I don't know. Why should I know ? "

Guelvada asked : " You wouldn't know why he went to Evansley on the night he died, Miss Steyning ? "

She shook her head.

Guelvada leaned forward. His voice was soft, almost sympathetic. He seemed to have a peculiar effect on the girl. Her eyes, a little brighter, stared into his.

He said : " But you saw him on that night, didn't you—or you spoke to him ? "

133

She said dully : " I don't remember. . . . I don't remember. . . ."

" You knew him well ? He was very fond of you. He wanted to marry you, didn't he ? Can you by any chance think of any reason why he should have gone to the house Evansley on the night that he died ? He couldn't by any chance have had an apointment that you knew about ? He couldn't by some chance have had an appointment with you ? " Now his voice was harder.

She said : " What business is it of yours ? He's dead and nothing's going to bring him back again. There's nothing to talk about."

Guelvada finished his drink. He thought that he agreed with her. He said : " I won't bother you any more, but if at some time or other, Miss Steyning, you should think you need a friend, get in touch with me. I'm staying at the Cleveland Apartments, close to the Leonard Hotel. Don't forget. If ever you want to talk, come and talk to me. Good night."

He went quietly out of the room. When he had gone she sat up for a moment trying to think. Then she shrugged her shoulders ; reached out for the drink beside her.

Guelvada walked slowly back in the direction of his apartment. He was satisfied with his talk with Viola Steyning. He thought it was hard luck on a girl as good looking as she was to be in the state she was in. But the maid had been right. She wasn't any good for anyone to talk to.

He wondered how he was going to play it from now on. He thought that unless something else happened he must bring things to a head. He smiled to himself. At least he would create a situation from which something might happen.

It was ten o'clock when he went into his apartment. He went into the main room overlooking the veranda ;

switched on the light. He went to the sideboard ; poured himself a drink. When he turned and walked towards the table he saw the telegram. He opened it. It said :

" Reference your inquiry about an apartment to rent on Miami Beach I have some information for you which might help, if you are prepared to pay the usual commission."

It was signed : *" Mary Wellington."*

Guelvada smiled. He finished the drink. Then he undressed ; put on his swimming trunks and a robe ; lighted a cigarette ; strolled out of the apartment towards the beach. He felt almost happy.

He began to croon his favourite Spanish love song.

CHAPTER EIGHT

I

THELMA LYON had just finished breakfast when the telephone rang. She got up from her chair ; put down her napkin ; looked at the telephone ; then began to walk slowly towards it. Telephone calls might mean a lot or very little.

She picked up the instrument. A quiet and motherly voice spoke. It said : " Is that Mrs. Lyon ? My name is Wellington—Mrs. Wellington. Perhaps you've heard of me. Perhaps you haven't. I'd better identify myself. I think I wrote you a long time ago. Do you remember? I was getting up a subscription in London for a special sort of aviary. You remember I was interested in birds belonging to the quail family. I told you I had an amusing collection."

Thelma said : " I see. . . . Perhaps you'd like to come along some time and talk about it. I think I might be interested."

" I'd like to come as soon as I can," said Mrs. Wellington.

Thelma asked : " When can you get here, Mrs. Wellington ? It's half-past ten."

" I could get there almost at once," Mrs. Wellington answered. " I'm talking from a pay-box just round the corner. And I'd like you to be by yourself."

" Very well," said Thelma. " If you'll come right round I'll be waiting for you."

She hung up ; rang for the maid. She said : " Go along and give a message to Mr. Isles. I have some important business to do this morning, and I want to be alone. Say I'd be very glad to see him about lunch time, but not before. You understand ? "

The maid nodded ; went away.

Thelma walked across to the mantelpiece ; opened the compact that she found there ; powdered her nose. She experienced a vague sense of annoyance. She realised that never before in the course of some of the very peculiar work which she had done for Mr. Quayle had he intervened or sent a message—the idea always being that an operative started a job and finished it without interference. She shrugged her shoulders. She thought that you never knew with Quayle, which was perhaps a very good thing.

She lighted a cigarette. By and large, she thought, the Quayle system was good. You knew just as much as you were meant to know—unless you were very good ; then sometimes you even knew what you were doing. She came into this class. She knew that too. She wondered why Quayle was becoming impatient— if he *was* impatient.

Three minutes later Mrs. Wellington arrived. She was dressed in a floral print frock. She looked very tidy, rather Victorian. Thelma thought she liked her.

She said : " Won't you sit down and have a cigarette or some coffee or something ? "

Mrs. Wellington said : " No, my dear, I won't. I'll just do what I have to do and then I'll go away. You see, I'm only here for two days—at the most three— and I want to get in as much sight-seeing as I can before I have to be bumped about in an airplane."

Thelma said : " So you're going back to England immediately ? "

" Unfortunately, yes. It's so nice here and I'd have liked to have stayed, but needs must when "—she shrugged her shoulders—" our employer, shall we call him, drives."

Thelma smiled. " I think that's an apt quotation."

Mrs. Wellington sat down. She said : " I think I *will* have a cigarette. Then I'll tell you exactly what I have to." She repeated Quayle's message.

Thelma said : " It rather looks as if he's getting a little impatient. Tell him I'll reply in due course. D'you think he thinks I've been dawdling ? "

" I wouldn't know about that," said Mrs. Wellington. " But I saw a Mr. Guelvada very early this morning. He arrived at such an impossible time—half-past five in the morning. Goodness only knows how he got over from Dark Bahama. I expect he chartered a plane."

Thelma, standing with her back to the mantelpiece, regarded the glowing end of her cigarette. She asked : " What did you think of Ernest Guelvada ? I've heard of him. I've never had the pleasure of meeting him."

Mrs. Wellington said : " I think he's rather interesting, my dear. He's a little on the short side and a trifle plump, but he's quite fascinating. He makes you feel important for a few minutes, and then suddenly *very* unimportant. I was vaguely uncomfortable most of the time he was with me. He has a very quick mind. He seems to know exactly what you're going to say and what he's going to do. I should think he'd be quite easy to work with."

Thelma said : " Would you ? And so I have to work with him ? "

" Yes. He has to be the boss. But I should think it would be easy provided you did what *he* wanted you to ; provided nobody argued with *him*. He's coming to see you this evening. He said he was coming round here to take a look at the place. He was only with me for half an hour ; then, I imagine, he came round here. He came back and saw me again. He said he'd be here after dinner, about nine ; that he'd come through the french windows of the drawing-room. He said he didn't like meeting *too* many people."

Thelma said : " I see. . . ." She thought she was not going to like Mr. Guelvada.

Mrs. Wellington got up. " Well, my dear, I'll be going. I wish you the best of luck." She sighed. " I often wish I knew exactly what was going on, but I never do, and for a woman that's very unsatisfying, isn't it ? "

" For a woman all sorts of things are unsatisfying, Mrs. Wellington." Thelma held out her hand. " I'm glad to have met you."

Mrs. Wellington said : " So am I. I like new faces. Well, good-bye, my dear. Don't bother to see me out. I'm so awfully used to going in and out of places and wondering if I shall ever go to that place again, if you know what I mean. My errands are so very spasmodic. Oh, there's just one thing, my dear. About this gentleman, Mr. Isles. . . . Mr. Guelvada said the thing to do with him was to get him back on Dark Bahama as quickly as possible. Mr. Guelvada said he'd pick him up there and look after him."

Thelma said : " I wonder what he meant by that."

Mrs. Wellington shrugged her shoulders. "I couldn't tell you. To me, it seems a very ordinary remark to make."

" You think so ? It all depends on what Ernest Guelvada means by looking after him, doesn't it ? "

Mrs. Wellington did not answer the question. She smiled pleasantly. She went away.

II

Isles came in just after lunch time. He walked across the dining-room, through the french windows on to the lawn. Thelma was sitting in a deck-chair reading a book.

Isles said cheerfully : " Well, how do you feel to-day ? It's lovely weather, isn't it ? "

She nodded. " Yes . . . but I'm not particularly interested in weather."

He drew up a deck-chair ; sat down at her side. He said : " Something's worrying you, isn't it, Thelma ? "

She nodded. " That's perfectly true. Let's face the fact. I'm worrying about this girl Steyning. Every day that she stops on that appalling island with no one to look after her scares me more and more."

" I see. . . . That means to say that you want me to do something about it ? "

" I think you ought to, Julian. I'd like you to take the afternoon plane to-day. Do as we suggested. Go back to the Leonard Hotel. Tell them some story about your absence. They've probably got their own ideas in any event. Then go and see the Commissioner of Police. Tell him the story we arranged. Put yourself right with him."

He said : " That's easy enough. If, as you suggested, they're on some other scent they probably won't bother too much about me. And then what do I do ? "

She said : " Something will turn up."

Isles smiled at her. " You know, things don't turn up unless you make them. Don't you think it would be a good idea if I went to see this girl ? Don't you think it might be a good idea if I talked her into going back to England ? "

She said slowly : " It might be. But I can't say at the moment and I don't want you to do anything like that. Perhaps I'll be able to get some sort of message to you. In any event, I'd like you not to see her until you've heard something more from me."

" Very well." He grinned. " I don't know why I'm being so awfully good about you ; why I'm carrying out your instructions so implicitly. I wonder what

Vallon would think I ought to do—if he were here, I mean."

She smiled at him. " I'm perfectly certain, Julian, that if he were here he would tell you to do as I ask. After all, I'm the client, you know. Chennault Investigations is supposed to be working for me."

He nodded. He was still smiling. " I like the process. But you're a strange person, aren't you, Thelma ? During these last two or three days I've been with you quite a lot, but when I try to add up what I know about you it seems all very unsatisfactory."

She laughed. " So you consider I'm the mysterious woman who is always supposed to figure so much in the life of a private detective ? "

He said : " I think you're damned mysterious—and *very* attractive."

" Thank you, sir. So I take it that you'll be on the afternoon plane ? "

He nodded. " That means to say I should be on Dark Bahama by four-thirty. Maybe when you come to some decision about this girl you'll come over ? You don't have to be afraid about coming over, because I shall be there."

She said : " I'm not afraid, Julian. If it's right for me to come over I'll come."

He got up. " Well, I'll be on my way. I think it's an interesting case—this case of the unruly Miss Steyning. I rather wish I knew what the end was going to be."

" I shouldn't worry if I were you," she said. " All we have to do is to remember that the means are always worthy of the end—or are they ? "

They laughed. She got up.

She asked : " Do you want a drink before you go ? "

He shook his head. " I think I'll get out of here as quickly as possible, or I might begin to make love to you. So I'll go at once."

She said : " I think that's a very good idea, Julian. I don't think I feel like being made love to at the moment. Good-bye. Good luck. I expect I'll see you soon."

He walked back through the french windows. As he went into the dining-room he turned and looked at her. He had a vague idea in his head that it might be the last look he would have. Then he walked into the cool interior of the room, out through the other door.

III

Guelvada stood at the far end of the lawn, listening to the music, admiring the moonlight glinting on the flowers and foliage. He thought that the scene was perfect ; the music most appropriate. He shrugged his shoulders. He strolled slowly across the lawn ; tried the outside handle of the french windows ; found they were unlocked. He pushed them open ; stepped into the room. He stood there, spick and span in his white tuxedo, looking across the room towards the grand piano.

It was a few seconds before she saw him ; then she stopped playing ; got up ; came into the middle of the room. Guelvada's eyes moved appreciatively from her hair to her shoes. He thought she looked exquisite. She wore a chiffon dinner frock of pale primrose yellow. The bodice was tight fitting. The folds of the wide skirt billowed about her. Round her white shoulders was a draped scarf of the same colour as the frock. She wore one large diamond clip, and her high-heeled sandals of primrose yellow were covered with tiny rhinestones. With her colouring, and superbly-dressed hair, she made an entrancing picture.

He said : " I assure you, Mrs. Lyon, that when I look at you I realise what an extremely clever person

our esteemed boss is. Boy . . . what a picker ! . . .
Never in my life have I seen a woman so utterly lovely
as you, and I don't mean maybe, hey ? "

She smiled. " Mr. Guelvada, I presume ? "

He came into the room. " Very much at your
service. Everything that Ernest Guelvada has is at
your disposal, Madame."

" That's very nice," There was a hint of sarcasm in
her voice. " What is it that Mr. Guelvada has ? "

He shrugged his shoulders. " God forbid that I
should talk about myself, but I am not without certain
attributes. I have an unerring eye, a superb instinct
and, I think I may say, one of the quickest brains on
record. Apart from these things I have other qualities
which I have no doubt you will discover in due course."

She laughed. " Including modesty, Mr. Guelvada? "
she asked.

" But of course. It is quite impossible for a man to
present such a heroic picture to the world as I do
without being at the same time modest." He went on :
" I feel I have known you for a considerable period. I
should like to call you Thelma. My name is Ernest.
Very often people call me Ernie because they like me
so much."

She laughed again. " Very well, Ernie. In the
meantime would you like a drink ? Then are you going
to talk or shall I ? What do you know ? Do you know
anything about the work I am engaged in ? "

" No. . . ." Guelvada walked back to the french
windows ; closed them carefully. " I take it you have
been living for some time in this place and you know
that there are no microphones in the walls, or eaves-
dropping servants ? "

She said : " You may be quite content about that.
What would you like to drink ? "

" I consider this to be a most important question,
Thelma, because my first drink with you must be to

toast your beauty, your intelligence, everything about you. I think you are unutterably charming. Therefore, it must be a long drink—a long, cold, rum drink. That would be delightful."

" Very well." She went to the sideboard ; mixed a long *Cuba libre.*

Guelvada stood watching, admiring the deftness of her movements. He thought the glitter of the rings on her fingers in the half-shadows on that side of the room was delightful.

After a while she brought him the drink. He held it up.

He said : " Your health, and to your success, Thelma. Now, shall we sit down."

She sat down in the large chair facing him. Guelvada seated himself ; took some more of his drink. His eyes, almost gentle and benign, regarded her over the rim of the glass.

He said : " First of all I talk, and then you talk. Do you like that ? "

" Yes," said Thelma. " But there is one thing I should like to say. I don't know whether you have talked to Mr. Quayle about me and my mission, but if he's dissatisfied——"

He interrupted. He put up his left hand. He made a clicking noise. " That is not so. It would be quite impossible for anybody to be dissatisfied with you, Thelma. Let me tell you I know nothing about your mission. Of course I had heard of you. You work for Quayle. For a long time you have been very successful. But maybe in a woman's life in our peculiar work the time comes when a little male influence is, shall we say, beneficial. Do you understand, my sweet ? "

" Yes. I understand very well."

Guelvada finished his drink ; got up. He said : " If you will permit me to make another of those delightful drinks I will begin to talk."

She said : " Of course."

Guelvada went to the sideboard ; began to mix his new drink. He said : " Quayle sent me to Dark Bahama because some little time ago an agent by the name of Sandford who was working on the island died a little mysteriously. This Sandford was supposed to be a drunk. He'd been on the island for some time as a holiday-maker. Well, lots of agents put up a front of being drunken and dissolute. Often it is a very good part to play. People will often talk in front of a drunkard when they would be careful if he was sober. I don't think Sandford was sober when he died."

She nodded. " I understand."

" He went over the back of a fishing launch," Guelvada went on. " A shark pulled him over. And, remember, this Sandford was an experienced fisherman. There is a possibility that he was half-drugged at the time ; that he was on the boat because he thought it would be a good thing to get off the island for a little while. Maybe—who knows "—he shrugged his shoulders—" someone was gunning for him. He wanted a few hours to think. I went to Dark Bahama to try and find out about this. I arrived there ; got the atmosphere of the place ; made one or two contacts. I contacted the mate on the fishing boat on which Sandford met his death—an individual by the name of Mellin—who has confirmed that the death was not accidental. Therefore, my suspicions were aroused. I was about to take some further steps when I was interrupted by a message from one of Quayle's runners —Mrs. Wellington—who has already been to see you. Is that not so ? "

" That's perfectly right," said Thelma. " I found her a very charming person."

" She is," said Guelvada. " I think she's a sweet. We used to call her the globe-trotter because she is never in the same place for more than a week. Quayle keeps her busy, I can tell you. I went to see her and she told me the story which had got back to Quayle via Chennault Investigations, Scotland Yard and M.I. 5, who had passed it to him purely as a matter of routine. This is the story of your visit to Chennault Investigations, of your employing the man Isles to go out to Dark Bahama and by some means to remove from the island this charming "—he smiled—" if somewhat indiscreet—young woman, Miss Steyning. You know, my Thelma, I think it would have been very difficult for Isles to have removed her. I saw her not very long ago and she was very drunk.

" She has arrived at that stage," he went on, waving one hand in the air, " when nothing seems particularly to matter—not even the process of talking to Ernest Guelvada.

" The next thing that is brought to my notice is that the man Isles, having arrived on the island, was somehow implicated in the murder of a young man called Hubert Gelert. My instructions are to remove Isles from the implications of this murder. Now it occurs to me that you were using Chennault Investigations and the man Isles for your own ends ; that you told them some sort of fairy story—one of those little fables we so often use in our peculiar profession in order to bring about some situation that we desire. Now, Thelma, talk to me."

Guelvada adjusted the crease in his black evening trousers ; leaned back in his chair ; put his glass down on the occasional table beside it ; took a thin red and white gold cigarette case from his pocket ; lighted a cigarette ; relaxed.

He said : " Tell me, Thelma. I have an idea in my head that a great deal depends on this."

She asked : " Why do you think that ? "

He spread his hands. " Consider to yourself, my sweet, I know quite a lot about you. You are considered to be a superb operative. Your record in the last war, I know, was very good. I don't think that on any previous occasion you have ever worked with a man. Therefore, when Quayle instructs me to see you and to take over the conduct of this affair, I take it that it is first of all very important and, secondly, that you are placed in some position of difficulty. Is my guess right ? "

She nodded. " It's perfectly right, Ernest. Here, in a nutshell, is the story. The principal in the business in which I was concerned was *not* Viola Steyning, but her brother. Her brother John Steyning was a young scientist. He was working secretly under allied directions on one of the new nuclear fission processes. *You* know ? "

" I know," he said. " Atom bombs, ' H ' bombs, ' A ' bombs—all those things which we have threatening our existence—and how terrible they are ! " An expression of humorous dismay passed over his face. " Consider to yourself, even Guelvada cannot argue with an atom bomb ! But continue."

She said : " John Steyning either made some discovery which he considered to be important or was in possession of papers which he considered important. Someone on the other side got wise to this. They began to work on him. You know their methods are sometimes very odd."

Guelvada nodded grimly. " I know some of the methods."

She went on : " Very well. Steyning was unshaken in his fidelity to the people he was working for and to his work. There was no doubt that he thought himself in some sort of danger. He disappeared and certain papers disappeared with him. That was when Quayle first came into this matter. One of Quayle's operatives who was working in conjunction with Sandford picked up Steyning's trail. He came out to one of the islands in the Bahamas. When Quayle's operative arrived Steyning was dead."

Guelvada said : " Most interesting. Tell me, Thelma, how did he die ? "

She shrugged her shoulders. " Officially, suicide ! He shot himself, but in rather peculiar circumstances."

Guelvada said : " You mean he may have been murdered ? "

She nodded. " That was what was thought. Either his nerves were in such a state that he decided to kill himself or someone had done it for him. The point was that the documents which he was supposed to have in his possession were gone."

Guelvada said : " I see. So they had those ? They got them from him ? "

" I don't think so," she said. " The only available information there was, was that on the day that he died he wrote a letter to his sister Viola. It was more than a letter. It was a package. It was thought that, knowing the end—whatever it was—was close at hand, he sent those things to his sister."

Guelvada said : " Ah ! Now I am beginning to understand. You were put on to the sister ? "

" Precisely, I was put on to Viola Steyning."

Guelvada said : " Things are beginning to make sense. You are sent to Dark Bahama. Sandford was also operating in Dark Bahama. Now I understand. Quayle had sent Sandford there possibly to keep an eye on you—his usual habit. They discover this and get Sandford first. Tell me, my dear, how did you get on with Viola ? "

She said : " I didn't. Viola had been having a very good time on the island, but she had been behaving herself more or less until she heard the news of her brother's death. You understand ? "

" I understand. And after she had also received the letter he sent her ? "

" Precisely," said Thelma. " Either because she was unnerved at hearing of her brother's death, or because of the importance of the letter which he had sent to her, she went to pieces. She began to drink heavily. She did all sorts of things. I thought the only thing that I could do would be to get her away from the island. I thought if I could get her back to England and look after her for a little while we might get some sense out of her."

" I see. . . . I see . . . ! " Guelvada stubbed out his cigarette. He picked up his glass. " Already in my mind there begins to form a very clear picture. I think it is very interesting. I am glad to be part of it."

" I'm very pleased to hear that, Ernest. I hope you'll like the picture."

He shrugged his shoulders. " Life is made up, my sweet one, of things which are good and bad. If we appreciate the things which are good we must also not be too dissatisfied with those that are bad. But go on with your story. I find it entrancing."

She said : " I came back here to Miami. I have used this place as my headquarters for a long time. I knew it was impossible for me to try and get Viola Steyning back to England by force. It would also be a very bad thing for me to do to become too closely connected with her."

Guelvada. " You were right. Who knows, you also might have been devoured by a shark." He smiled pleasantly at her. " The idea almost makes me wish that I myself were a shark. But I think you were right. So you made a plan ? "

She said : " I made a plan. I went back to England. I met Mrs. Steyning. I told her that I thought it would be a good thing for Viola to go back to England to her mother. I said I'd do my best to persuade her to do that. In other words, I was providing myself with a

ready-made excuse. Then I went to Chennault
Investigations. I had known John Vallon for some
time. He's a good type. I evolved a story about Viola
Steyning's behaviour. Vallon believed it, and I thought
at first that Isles did. Now I think Isles doesn't believe
it."

" I see," said Guelvada. " Most unfortunate. So
what did you do about Isles ? "

She smiled. " I gave him another story, Ernest—
much more interesting. After he became involved in
the Gelert murder he came back here to Miami. He's
clever, this Isles. First of all I tried to get him out of
the place. I realised he could no longer be of much
use to me. I employed a private detective here—a
strong-arm man named Jake Carno who had heard
that Isles had landed here—to get him out of Miami
and back to England."

Guelvada nodded.

She went on : " It was no good. Isles was too good
for Carno. He's quite an intelligent type. He came
here, so I gave him my story No. 2. I suggested he
went back to Dark Bahama. I said that obviously the
police did not suspect him because they'd made no
attempt to get in touch with the American authorities
here about him. I said that a man who had been my
lover in the past had several letters of mine ; that this
man was making a play for Viola Steyning because he
thought she had money ; that I could do nothing
because if I attempted to interfere he was in a position
to blackmail me. Isles believed this story. He went
back on the afternoon plane to Dark Bahama."

Guelvada said : " I see. And what does he propose
to do when he gets there ? "

" I hope nothing. I told him not to do anything
until he hears from me."

" And you think he'll do as you want ? " asked
Guelvada.

150

" I'm fairly certain of it. I believe he thinks he's in love with me."

Guelvada said : " Very convenient. And why not ? You said he was intelligent. Any man with any sort of brain would fall in love with you, my Thelma. I will tell you a secret. Believe it or not, I—Ernest Guelvada—find myself strangely attracted to you. And I don't mean maybe ! "

She said, with a little smile : " How nice of you."

" Not at all," said Guelvada airily. " It is natural. Charming and beautiful women appeal to me." He went on : " So if Julian Isles does nothing and is on Dark Bahama, and if he is intelligent—if he doesn't scare easily—if he was good enough for Jake Carno, your private detective here—it may easily be that I may use him if I want a stooge."

She said : " Possibly. I have heard, Ernest, that sometimes your methods are what is usually called tough."

" But why not ? " he said. " Sometimes life is tough, and if it is, one must be tough also. Are you afraid for Julian Isles ? "

She said : " I should not like anything too unpleasant to happen to him unless it is necessary."

Guelvada said : " I assure you, Thelma, I never do anything unpleasant unless it is very necessary." He went on : " I would like another drink and perhaps you will join me. We will drink to the success of our joint mission. Then I will go back. I have a small and very fast plane which I flew here. But it is not a very safe plane. The engine sounds as if there were a tin can in it. However, it is a short journey and always Ernest Guelvada trusts to the goodness of God."

She asked : " Is it easy to make a landing on Dark Bahama at night ? "

" No. But on a night such as this when the moonlight makes everything look like day, and when you are using such a stupid little plane as mine you either come down in the right place the right way up or you don't. Besides "—his voice became confidential—" I did not tell you I am considered to be a superb aviator."

She got up. She walked slowly to the sideboard.

Guelvada said : " This time I will have a little drink—a very dry, very good Martini—if I may."

She laughed. " What a head you must have, Ernest, drinking Martini on top of rum ! "

Guelvada shrugged. " I have never been troubled with mixing my drinks. To me it is all right. The head of Ernest Guelvada is very strong."

She mixed the drinks.

Guelvada rose ; came towards her ; took the glass from her hand. He said : " Madame, here's to our joint enterprise. It could, of course, have but one ending—a good one." His voice became serious. " You will stay here. You will amuse yourself in Miami. You will swim, sail, go to cocktail parties. But you will always be in this apartment at ten o'clock at night, because from ten to eleven I might telephone you. You understand ? And when I say that you will be here at ten o'clock you will please be here punctually. After eleven do what you like, but from ten to eleven you stay in this apartment with the telephone."

She said : " I see. You're *very* decided, aren't you ? "

Guelvada smiled. " My dear Thelma, are you not glad of that ? Would you like to work with a man who was not certain of himself ? Be a good girl. Do as you are told. Which you *will* do because you *are* a very good girl."

She said : " I suppose I've got to. Very well. I'll wait to hear from you. Good luck to you, Ernest."

Guelvada took her hand ; bent low over it. He kissed the back of her hand softly. He said : " One day I may be permitted to kiss your arm—if I am very lucky I may finish in the region of your lips. *Au revoir*, Thelma. My felicitations."

He put down his glass ; went through the french windows like a white-coated shadow.

She stood motionless for quite a minute after he had gone. She had begun to realise, as many people had realised, the devastating quality that went with Mr. Ernest Guelvada. She shrugged her shoulders ; went back to the piano.

Guelvada, on the other side of the lawn, stopped ; listened appreciatively to a few bars of the music. Then, humming to himself, he moved across into the *patio* and, keeping in the shadows, went out of the back entrance of the Orchid House. Just along the narrow boulevard, on the grass verge, he stopped to light a cigarette.

A quiet voice from out of the shadows behind him said : " Mr. Ernest Guelvada ? "

Guelvada did not move. He flicked off his lighter ; stood, smoking. He said : " Yes ? "

The voice went on : " Just step back a little. I'd like to talk. My name's Willie Frim. I'm an agent of the Federal Bureau of Investigation."

" O.K. . . ." Guelvada walked a few steps as if in thought ; returned ; moved into the shadows.

A man was standing with his back to a tree. He was about thirty, slim. Guelvada liked his face.

Frim said : " Your boss Quayle has been in touch with Hoover, and an instruction came through to the Field Office in Miami. Mr. Quayle has the idea that you might be needing a little help from us sometime. I've been appointed to act with you."

Guelvada smiled. " My esteemed boss thinks of everything. The joke is, he is usually right. I'm delighted to meet you, Mr. Frim. I expect you have heard of me. Most people in your business have heard of me."

Frim grinned. " I guess we've heard of you, buddy. I heard you thought plenty of yourself, but that usually you were right. Well, here I am." He put his hand into his pocket ; produced the usual leather case with the identity disc of a Federal Agent set inside it.

Guelvada looked at it. " That's good enough for me."

Frim said : " If you want to talk I've an automobile down the road. We can sit in it. I've been waiting for you to come over. We've been watching the Dark Bahama planes. When you got in at the airport this morning they let me know. I've had a tail on you all day. I thought this might be a good chance to talk to you."

Guelvada said : " Extremely intelligent and, believe it or not, my good friend, you have arrived at an opportune moment. Let us go into your car and smoke cigarettes. There are lots of things I have to discuss with you."

Frim said : " That suits me. This way, buddy."

He led the way into the shadows.

CHAPTER NINE

I

IT WAS eleven o'clock and a hot morning. Guelvada got out of bed ; bathed ; shaved ; put on a dressing-gown ; went out on to the veranda. He sat there, drinking coffee, humming softly to himself, thinking over the implications of the very interesting situation in which he found himself.

Eventually he went into his sitting-room ; telephoned the Leonard Hotel. He asked to be put on to Mr. Julian Isles. He waited, smiling pleasantly to himself.

When Isles came on the telephone, Guelvada asked : " Mr. Isles ? . . . Permit me to introduce myself. My name is Ernest Guelvada. I'm a traveller—a travelling salesman—and I sell the most interesting products. Your name was given to me by a very beautiful lady whom I met in Miami. And I think it might be a very good thing if you and I talked a little together, hey ? "

There was a pause ; then Isles said : " By all means. Did this lady give you some instructions for me ? "

" But of course," said Guelvada airily. " Some very important ones. How would you like to come and drink some whisky with me this evening about six o'clock ? "

Isles said : " I'd like that very much."

" Excellent," said Guelvada. " I am at the Cleveland Apartments—very near to your hotel. I shall expect you at six."

Isles said : " I shall be there."

Guelvada hung up.

He dressed leisurely ; got into his car. He drove

slowly through the town, out the other side. It was half an hour later when he turned down the side road ; stopped his car in front of Mellin's shack.

Mellin was sitting on the steps outside the broken veranda. He looked up as Guelvada appeared.

Guelvada sat down beside him. He said : " My friend, I am sorry that this time I have no liquor with me, which is perhaps as well because I want you to listen very carefully. I have some instructions to give you."

Mellin said morosely : " I wish to God I'd never seen you."

Guelvada shrugged. " There are many people in this world who wish they had not met Mr. Guelvada. However, their eventual fates should not interest you —providing *you* do what you are told. Now, listen to me. There is on this island a gentleman by the name of Mr. Julian Isles. Mr. Isles is, I think, a very intelligent man. He is staying at the Leonard Hotel. At some time to-night he will contact you. Probably, I should think, about eight or nine o'clock. He will give you some instructions and you will do exactly as he tells you. Do you understand ? "

" Yeah," said Mellin. " I understand. What am I running into now ? "

Guelvada replied : " If you do as I tell you, you will not run into anything—at least, nothing that will hurt you *very* much. I have already explained to you that you will be much safer in doing what I tell you than not. If you want this little matter about being an accomplice in Sandford's death forgotten, my advice to you is to behave yourself."

Mellin said : " All right . . . all right. . . . I am behaving myself, ain't I ? "

" Excellent," said Guelvada. " Now, this morning you will make arrangements to hire—or secure by some means—a fast motor boat. Have this boat filled

with oil and gasolene. Moor her somewhere not far
from the quay where she will not be noticeable. When
you have done that, come back here and stay here
until you hear from Mr. Isles. You understand that ? "

Mellin said : " O.K. I can get the boat but it costs
dough."

" Naturally. . . ." Guelvada took a roll of bills from
his pocket ; gave it to Mellin. He said : " Now tell
me what you have to do."

Mellin told him.

Guelvada got up. " See it's a good boat. Be back
here by the afternoon. Wait till Mr. Isles comes to see
you. And no liquor. See that you are sober ; otherwise
I will deal with you. Good day to you."

Guelvada went off.

II

It was just after six o'clock when Guelvada, looking
through the long windows of his apartment, saw Isles
crossing the street. Guelvada looked admiringly at the
tall figure approaching. He liked the look of Isles—
the indolent, casual walk, the well-fitting clothes. He
sighed. He murmured to himself : " *Le style c'est
l'homme!* "

He went into the hallway. As Isles arrived at the
head of the veranda steps Guelvada opened the door.
He stood in the cool hallway, smiling. He was wearing
black crêpe-de-chine pyjamas, with a scarlet and black
dressing-gown, with a delicately perfumed handkerchief
emerging from the breast pocket.

He said : " Mr. Julian Isles ? May I present myself
to you ? I am Ernest Guelvada . . . very much at your
service. . . . And what do you know ? "

Isles grinned. He put out his hand. " Not very
much. In fact, I am a little bemused."

Guelvada shrugged his shoulders. " Follow me. . . ." He led the way into the drawing-room. " Sit down, Julian—I propose to call you Julian because I feel towards you almost as a brother. And you will call me Ernest. Many of my friends call me Ernie because that is the way "—he flashed a smile at the Englishman— " that friends who are engaged on such important business should behave towards each other. In the meantime I will mix you a long, very cool drink."

Isles sat down. He helped himself to a cigarette from a box on the table. He said : " So it's going to be important business, is it ? I'm glad about that. At least something is going to emerge."

Guelvada, who was busy with the bottles on the sideboard, looked over his shoulder. " And how ! My friend, you will be amused at the implications, repercussions and what-have-you that will emerge at any moment. Or can a repercussion emerge ? " He waved his hand airily. " I promise you life is about to become very interesting for you. It is always interesting if you are associated with Ernest Guelvada."

He brought the glasses of rum and iced lemon to the table. He began to walk about the room.

" Drink, my Julian, and listen. But listen carefully."

Isles said smilingly : " I always listen carefully. I have to. I've been told so many stories at different times that I have to check carefully to keep my facts straight."

Guelvada spun round. " There is no necessity for you to worry about keeping your facts straight." Now his face was serious and his voice a little grim. " You may always rely on Guelvada to keep facts straight. All you have to do is to do as you are told—exactly as you are told."

Isles smiled amiably. He picked up his glass ; drank. He said : " That's a very good drink. I like it very much. Thank you." He was still smiling. He asked casually : " Supposing I don't like doing what I'm told ? "

Guelvada raised his hands in astonishment. " That is a complication which never occurred to me. And believe me, I know what I am talking about. All right. Supposing you don't like doing what you are told ? " Now the tone of his voice had changed. The peculiar, metallic note had come into it. Even Isles, with his phlegmatic nature, was affected by the strange atmosphere which seemed to emanate from Ernest Guelvada.

" Supposing you don't like it," went on the voice. " Well, then I should have to reconsider matters, my Julian. For instance, there is the little matter of this murder of the man Gelert. You have returned to the island here and I have no doubt you have seen the Commissioner of Police. You have told Major Falstead an adequate story. You have explained your sudden disappearance. But the fact remains, my friend, they have not yet found any other murderer. And they are not likely to find him, unless, like a conjurer who produces a rabbit from a hat, he is produced . . . by whom ? Who else but Guelvada ? "

Isles said : " So you know the murderer ? "

Guelvada nodded. " I know who the murderer is. . . . I *think* ! At least I know who I think I can make appear to be the murderer to such an extent that eventually I shall prove him to be the murderer. If I do that it would be very nice for you, wouldn't it, Julian ? But supposing I don't do that ; supposing by a wave of a magic wand I managed to dig up a little further evidence against Mr. Julian Isles ? What do you think would happen to him ? "

Isles moved a little uneasily. He thought Guelvada was a very difficult person to deal with. He thought that beneath the sometimes placid and smiling exterior of this man was a tornado—an utterly ruthless personality, capable of anything.

He said quietly : " What the hell are you playing at . . . Ernie . . . since we're such friends ! "

Guelvada picked up a cane chair which stood by the wall. He carried it across and set it down a few feet from where Isles sat. He straddled across it ; reached out for his drink from the table ; took a long gulp.

He said : " I'll tell you just as much as I wish to tell you about what I am playing at. But first let us talk of other subjects. I am beginning to understand quite a lot about you. Always," he continued, " I have what they call a very good sense of applied psychology. Goddam it, there are times when I am almost a witch. I have been talking in Miami to a mutual friend of us both—the most beautiful and adorable Mrs. Lyon, who was, I believe, your client."

Isles shook his head. " Why *was* ? " he asked. " Why not *is* ? "

Guelvada smiled benignly. " *I* am your client. . . . But I will continue. I think that you have a regard for Mrs. Lyon, isn't that so ? You have a regard for her in spite of the fact that she has told you at least one little fairy story."

Isles drank some more liquor. " I don't know that she's told even one fairy story. She gave me an outline of the case I was supposed to be working on when I met her in England. Well, that wasn't quite true, but it was almost true. When I saw her in Miami she explained to me why she hadn't told me the complete truth in the first place. She gave me the true story— the true set-up. She asked me to come back here and to await her instructions."

He shrugged his shoulders ; smiled pleasantly at Guelvada, who was watching him like a cat.

He went on : " I expected to receive some in- structions—a little information to go to work on." He laughed. " I didn't expect to meet a tornado like you ! "

Guelvada leaned forward; pointed with a plump forefinger at Isles. He said: "This is one of the pleasant surprises in life for you. But let us keep to our muttons. I am telling you now, and this is Guelvada who is speaking, that Mrs. Lyon has *never* told you the truth. She has never told you the truth because she has never told you the whole truth, and if you wish to know why the beautiful Thelma has not spoken the truth to you I will tell you. It is because she is a honey, because she is a great person and because she always does what she is told. Also," he continued, "she is going to be in a very tough spot, my friend, if you don't do what Ernest Guelvada tells you to."

There was silence for a moment; then Isles said: "Is she? I wonder why."

Guelvada got up. He began to roam about the room. Now a late breeze from the sea began to move the flimsy curtains at the window.

Guelvada said: "All my life, ever since I could think, I have been dividing people into groups. It is a great plaything for me to try to divide people into groups; to try to decide for myself what they will do or not do in any given group of circumstances. Primarily, when coming to conclusions about my fellow human companions I ask myself one question: Can I trust this person? And the answer is inevitably no. Because, my Julian, I find it is a very good thing not to trust anybody, or if you do, trust them not so much that you cannot put the affair right at any given moment. Understand also that I wish to trust you."

Isles said: "I see. . . . May I fill my glass?"

Guelvada nodded. Isles got up; wandered over to the sideboard; refilled his glass. He stood, leaning against the piece of furniture, regarding Guelvada quizzically.

He said: "So you have decided to trust me, Ernie? But only so far as you can put the matter right if I let you down. I wonder how you'd do that." He took a pack of cigarettes from his pocket ; extracted one ; threw the packet to Guelvada, who caught it. Isles came across the room with his lighter. Guelvada drew the cigarette smoke into his lungs.

He said glibly : " With you, my friend, it is important that you should not betray my trust. If you did, I should kill you without the slightest scruple. And what is more important "—his face was smiling but his eyes were blue and cold—" I should get away with it. I should not even dislike you when I killed you, but I should know that your death was necessary because you knew a little too much and had not behaved too well. Now sit down. I am going to talk to you."

Isles went back to his chair. He sat back, relaxed, watching Guelvada.

Guelvada began to speak. His voice was soft, almost caressing. He said : " As you know, my friend, there is a great deal of trouble in the world. Everywhere there are the forces of good, but unfortunately they do not make so much noise as the forces of evil. Never has our poor world been in such a devastated state ; everywhere, all over the place, people are trying to invent things to eradicate the other half of the world —a process which, to my mind, is entirely unnecessary."

He shrugged his shoulders. " This would not matter so much," he went on, waving his cigarette airily, " except for the fact that, in the process, all sorts of innocent people become involved. For the protection of these people there are in every country forces which work silently and quietly for, shall we say, the preservation of mankind." He smiled at Isles. " I, Guelvada, am one of those forces."

Isles said : " Some force ! " He laughed. " I think I'd like to be on *your* side."

Guelvada nodded. " Believe it or not, my friend,

you are on my side, because you've got to be. Now I will talk of Mrs. Lyon. Mrs. Lyon has told you of the young woman—this naughty young woman Viola Steyning. Miss Steyning, who is always drunk, who is stupid with drink, whose nerves are wrecked and who is very unhappy." He spread his hands. " Another victim of the forces of evil. Well, it was Mrs. Lyon's business to try to look after this girl ; to keep an eye on her, not because of some stupid love affair as she told you, but because of something very much more important—vitally important. I will tell you briefly this : The brother of this Miss Steyning was a young scientist who was working on a most important invention—an invention which might possibly have put an end to threats of atom bombs, of hydrogen bombs and all those other peculiar deviltries we hear so much about. You understand ? "

Isles nodded.

" So, naturally," Guelvada continued, " he had enemies. He became affected too. You, I am sure, would not like to live day after day wondering about the evil eyes that were watching you from morning to night, wondering what the owners of those eyes were going to do next ; when they would strike. Would you like that thing, my friend ? So you will realise that he didn't like it either. So he did what most people "— he smiled—" except perhaps Guelvada—would do. He did what anybody would do—anyone who was becoming scared. He ran away. He took his secret with him because, you will understand, he was not a traitor to the people who employed him—these people who were working for what they thought was good.

" Then it became apparent to him that forces were closing in on him. So he wrote to his sister, and he sent her a package which contained the notes of his discovery. Poor boy. . . ." Guelvada shrugged his shoulders. " It was all he could do. One would have thought he could have found a better recipient for his secret, but that's what he did. The person who has that secret, or knows where it is, is Viola Steyning. Now you understand why Mrs. Lyon was employed to look after Miss Steyning."

Isles nodded. "Strangely enough, I believe every word you say."

Guelvada asked : "Why not ? Why should I tell a lie ? Only cowards lie. I am an extremely brave man. Goddam it, I am ferociously brave ! "

Isles said quietly : " I don't wonder Thelma Lyon wanted help."

" Of course," said Guelvada. " Imagine her position —because she is a woman of beauty, of charm, of great personality, it is hoped that she will be able to handle this girl." He shrugged his shoulders again. " Who could handle Miss Steyning . . . except with a coke hammer ? And what good would that do ? I talked to her the other night. If I could have got that secret from her by hitting her with a coke hammer I would have done so. The process would have been quite redundant. Besides, I do not like coke hammers, and it would have got me nowhere.

" When Thelma Lyon was here there was another operative on the island. His business was to keep an eye on both of them. Unknown to either of them he was in the vicinity. He died. You understand ? In one of those strange ways in which people like our-selves often die and no one is very concerned with the death. There is an inquiry and it is forgotten. The world goes on. One brave man or woman goes ; there is always another to take the place."

He stopped suddenly. He said : " She's a lovely person, isn't she, this Thelma ? "

Isles said : " I think so."

Guelvada leaned forward. He dug his plump fore-finger into Isles's chest. " You *think* so. You lie. More

than that, my friend, you love her. That I know.
When you speak of her I see the look in your eye. I
have discovered your secret. I will tell you something
else. I also love her. I, Guelvada, who loves every
woman in the world, love her at least as much as the
other few million. Therefore, what I ask you to do,
you will do for Mrs. Lyon. And I will tell you exactly
why you will do it."

" I'm listening." Isles lighted a fresh cigarette.

Guelvada said : " When I go into action, my friend,
I like a lot of room and a lot of space. Like great
armies I must have room to develop. Like great fleets
I must have space to manœuvre. You understand ?
It is for this reason that I do not wish this island to be
cluttered up with non-essential women, and at the
moment our beautiful and adorable Thelma is non-
essential. Therefore, she will stay in Miami. But do
you think she is safe in Miami ? " He shook his head
dramatically. " Look, it is all the tea in China to a
very small and insignificant bad egg," continued
Guelvada, " that the forces who removed the other
agent on Dark Bahama know all about Mrs. Lyon,
and even if they do not they will not take a chance of
her not knowing anything. They associate her with
Miss Steyning. They will remove anybody who is
close to Miss Steyning or appears to be interested in
Miss Steyning."

Isles nodded. " And eventually they will remove
Miss Steyning ? " he queried.

" Precisely," said Guelvada. " Precisely. But not
until they know where the package is that her brother
sent to her. When they know where it is ; when they
have it, they will remove her. But they are going to
find the matter a little difficult because even these
people—desperate and ruthless as they are—are re-
stricted by events. This is a small island. It is not
easy to leave quietly. It is so small that everyone

knows who arrives or leaves by plane. After to-morrow
it will be even more difficult for them."

Isles asked : " Why ? "

Guelvada got up. He puffed out his chest like a
pigeon. " I propose to throw a spanner in the works.
I am going to create a little sensation by producing
some news of the murder of the first agent, which was
supposed to be an accident. Then, for a little time,
they must be careful. Then may come a possibility of
you, my Julian, being able to do the job for which I
have ear-marked you. Are you interested ? "

Isles asked : " What do you think ? "

Guelvada said : " I take it that you will comply
with my conditions. You will do as you are told.
You will continue to be an operative employed by
Chennault Investigations, but in fact you will be an
operative employed by Mr. Guelvada. When the time
comes I propose by fair means or foul to have the
package which young Steyning sent to his sister.
Where I am going to get it, I don't know ; how I'm
going to get it, I don't know, but I am going to get it,
and when I have it I have to get it away from here. I
have to get it away from here to Thelma Lyon at
Miami, and you are the man who is going to take it
to her. Because "—he grinned wryly—" I am going to
be very busy."

Isles got up. " You're an interesting person, Ernie.
Strangely enough, I believe everything you say. I will
play ball with you. I'm doing as I'm told."

" That being so," said Guelvada, " it would be very
nice if you would mix me another drink." ·

Isles went to the sideboard. Guelvada came over ;
stood behind him ; watched him mix the drinks. He
said : " Are you all right for money ? "

Isles nodded.

Guelvada went on : " Get yourself a hired car if you
haven't one—a small car that is not noticeable. To-

night at eight o'clock drive through the town. Drive
openly through the main street. Don't skulk in the
alleyways. When you are out of the town and on
the dirt road keep on until you come to the narrow
path by the old pier that leads into the interior. Turn
down it. Keep to it. Some way down you will find a
clearing and a shack. In the shack you will find a
man called Mellin. He is a white man. He has been
a mate on one of the fishing launches. He knows the
coast and the boats well. By this time he will have
a launch moored somewhere near the quay, ready
for sea.

" Now, consider. . . . It may be that sometime to-
night a fast fishing launch may leave the island. Well,
where will it go to ? " He turned ; walked to the
window on the left of the door ; pointed to the sea.
" Standing here," he said, " on our left, miles away, is
the island of Nassau. On our right is the long coast of
America, with Miami almost opposite to this island.
Farther ahead, slightly to the right, between us and
Miami, are a little group of cays. One or two of them
have natives living on them. Some are deserted, or
thought to be deserted. It is my belief that a person
wishing to reach the mainland ; wishing to avoid
Miami as he would naturally do, and sail down the
coast when he reaches America, must have a store of
gasolene in order to refuel his boat. It will be your
business, with Mellin, to lie off those cays to-night. It
will probably be a fine night. You must be careful,
but there are a dozen places where you can conceal a
boat."

Isles said : " I understand. You say it is a fast boat.
Supposing he doesn't call at one of the cays. What do
we do ? "

Guelvada said : " He must call. All the launches
here—even the largest ones—carry only enough
gasolene to reach Miami. That would be of no use

to him. He dare not land there. He must stop at a cay."

" And even supposing he does ? " asked Isles.

Guelvada said : " It is simple. He must not leave the cay. Somehow or other, you sink the boat. Do you understand, my friend ? " He took the glass from Isles's hand.

Isles said : " I understand all right. Remember I am putting my shirt on you, Ernie."

Guelvada said : " Why not ? It looks to me like a very nice shirt."

III

It was eleven o'clock. A full moon rose from behind a patch of dark cloud, illuminating the waters of the bay. Guelvada, seated on the grass, his back to a palm tree, smoked a cigarette and regarded the beauty of the picture before him. Guelvada was not dissatisfied. Always he had regarded life as a game of chess and he liked the game providing the pieces on the board moved as he wished them to move. If they did not he did something about it. Guelvada was fearless, unscrupulous and tough, because he believed implicitly in his mission and in himself.

Now he began to think about Jacques. He tried to get inside the mind of this clever, quiet negro, who had the ability to plan adequately so far and after that not to be very good. Guelvada concluded that Jacques, like many other people, was not aware of his limitations, unless of course, also like many other people, he was scared.

Guelvada shrugged his shoulders in the shadows of the palm tree, thought it was easy for some people to become scared. People were brave enough to consider a job because they saw something to their advantage in it ; because they thought they could get away with it. Usually they missed one or two little points. They slipped up. They became a little too involved, and then the process of being scared set in. This was the time when Guelvada liked to make his entrance on the scene. He thought that time had come with Jacques.

He got up ; brushed an imaginary blade of grass from his dark-blue, gaberdine slacks. He began to walk slowly towards the quay. On the way he sang softly to himself.

He began to think about Isles. Guelvada, who was a considerable judge of mankind, thought that, beneath his airy exterior, Isles was a man of loyalty and principle. That was one thing. Secondly, thought Guelvada, Isles was crazy about Thelma Lyon. He smiled to himself. That was another thing, he thought, possibly the most important thing. For those two reasons Isles would do as he was told.

He slowed his walk. He was approaching the moorings of the launch. He could hear the quiet, low voice crooning somewhere in the cockpit.

" *Nut-brown baby, you got rovin' eyes.*
You don' say nothin' but yo' sure is wise
You don' say nothin' with dem honey lips
But yo' sure say plenty when you swing dem hips.
Ah feel de knife in ma breeches when yo' swing dem hips
At dem high-yaller bastards off de sailin' ships."

Guelvada walked down the wooden pier. He stopped at the spot where the boat was moored. He called out : " Jacques. . . ."

Jacques came astern, out of the shadows of the cockpit. He said : " Good evenin', Mister Guelvada. Ah got everythin' ready like you telephoned. Yes, sir !

Everythin's all right. We're gonna take a big fish to-night."

" Excellent." Guelvada stepped on to the stern of the boat down into the cockpit. He said : " It is a lovely night. My friend Jacques, I have come to the conclusion that it is much too beautiful a night to pursue a fish—even such a monster of the deep as a shark. To-night I am poetic. I love the moonlight on the waters, the dark shadows of the cays. Start your engine, my friend. Let us go and wander about the moonlit waters of the bay. Let us go where we want to go. Also, if it is possible, we will drink a little whisky."

Jacques grinned. " Yo're the boss, Mister Guelvada. Ah got the best whisky in the island on this boat. Ah got coffee. Ah got everythin'. You'll find the bottle in the cockpit . . . an' glasses an' ice water." He started the motor.

Guelvada went into the cabin forrard ; came out with the bottle, the glasses, the jug of iced water that he had drawn from the cooler. He sat down on the seat that ran round the cockpit, looking at Jacques.

Jacques stood by the wheel, slim, wiry, relaxed. His right hand was on the spokes of the wheel, his left hand down by his side. Guelvada noted the strength in the slim fingers, the lean stomach, the thin, wiry legs, the tough shoulders. Jacques's fishing cap, red and blue, was pushed over one dark ear. He was half-smiling and the glint of his white teeth showed in the half-light. Guelvada though he was quite a type.

He poured out the drinks ; sat, silently looking over the edge of the launch, watching the flying spray as she cut her way out in the direction of Bear Island.

There was silence for a long time ; then Guelvada said quietly : " Why not stop here ? How deep is it ? "

Jacques shrugged his shoulders. " Not so deep.

Yo're shallow for a long way here. Yo' don' go deep until you get out a long way farther. It's about twenty feet here—not more."

Guelvada said : " Put out the hook. Let us stop here. Let us talk." He smiled at Jacques.

" Why not ? Yo're the boss, Mister Guelvada." Jacques left the wheel. He cut the engine ; went forrard.

Guelvada heard the sound as the anchor went over. After a minute Jacques came back ; jumped into the cockpit.

Guelvada said : " Sit down, my friend—over there opposite me. Here's your drink. Would you like a cigarette ? "

" Ah'd sure like one of dem cigarettes of yo's, Mister Guelvada," said Jacques. " They are pretty good. Ah think yo're a pretty kind sorta gentleman—a good sort, yo' know." He sat down ; took the drink, the proffered cigarette.

Guelvada said wryly : " I can afford to be kind. You know it is a tradition with certain people that somebody who is about to die should have everything they want."

" Yeah ? " Jacques laughed. His laugh was musical. " What's that got to do with me, Mister Guelvada ? "

Guelvada said, with an almost charming smile : " You are about to die, Jacques." He took his hand from the pocket of his jacket. Lying on the palm Jacques saw the black shadow of the automatic.

He said : " Look, Mister Guelvada. Yo're a joke. Yo're playin' some game——"

Guelvada said : " I'm not playing any game. Drink your drink. Light your cigarette. I'm going to talk to you, Jacques. You're going to find it very interesting. Tell me something. When you hook a shark you play him till he's tired, don't you ? That takes a long time, my near-ebony friend, doesn't it ? But eventually he

171

gets very tired. You get him alongside or against the stern. Then what do you do ? "

Jacques looked bewildered. He said : " Then you kill him."

" Precisely," said Guelvada. " When you get one alongside how do you kill him ? "

" Why yo' take a gun on him—a heavy gun—a .45. Yo' give him four five bullets out of a .45."

" Exactly." Guelvada's voice was almost casual. " I suppose you'd never use a .45 on anything else except a shark. You'd never use that gun you keep aboard for killing sharks on a human being, I suppose?"

Jacques said : " Look, Mister Guelvada, what the hell—— ! "

" Keep quiet," said Guelvada. " Talking is not going to help you. Now, tell me something. . . ." He settled himself comfortably in his seat. He went on : " You remember Mr. Julian Isles, don't you—the man who ran away from the island—the Englishman who forced you to take him to Miami because he had got himself implicated in some killing—the killing of a man called Gelert ? "

" Sure thing, ah remember. But what's that to me ? He got aboard this boat an' held a gun on me same way as yo're holdin' one now. He made me take him to Miami——"

Guelvada said : " I know all that. But what did you do when you got to Miami, Jacques ? Shall I tell you what you did ? " He leaned back ; drew on his cigarette. He was obviously enjoying himself. " I'll tell you what you did. You were supposed to refuel your tanks with gasolene and come back. No one would imagine that you would take a further interest in Mr. Isles. But you did. You landed at Miami. You went to an individual named Jake Carno—a private detective. You told Mr. Carno that a certain person living in Miami—a lady by the name of Mrs. Thelma

Lyon—would be very interested in the fact that Isles had landed. You knew that Mrs. Lyon was in Miami. You knew where she lived. You knew quite a lot about her. So Carno got in touch with Mrs. Lyon and you went back to Dark Bahama. You thought that that would be the end of Mr. Isles ; that Carno would take care of him ; that Mrs. Lyon would want him out of the way because it might interfere with her plans if he was suspected of murder on the island. And when you'd seen Carno you came back here."

Jacques said : " Ah don't know what yo're talkin' about, Mister Guelvada."

Guelvada smiled. " Oh, yes, you do, my friend. You know all sorts of things. You knew what Mrs. Lyon arrived on Dark Bahama for originally, or at least if you didn't know, the people you're working for did know."

Jacques said : " Ah don' know nothin' . . . ah don' know nothin'. . . ."

Guelvada shrugged. He drank a little more whisky. " My friend, I don't expect you to agree with *everything* I say. There's something else I want to talk to you about. Do you remember the night you went shark fishing with Mr. Sandford—the night he unfortunately went overboard—the night the shark got him ? That was a nasty accident, wasn't it, Jacques ? Very bad. You didn't like that, did you ? "

Jacques said : " No, sir . . . but ah couldn't help it."

" You're a damned liar," said Guelvada cheerfully. " You murdered Sandford. When Sandford came aboard this boat he was half-drugged. You put him in a seat with the straps cut through. When the shark took the line and Mellin, your mate, was forrard and couldn't see, you helped Sandford over the stern. You killed him. Do you know why ? "

Jacques said nothing. He sat looking at Guelvada

with dull eyes, his hands, lean palms uppermost, on his knees."

Guelvada continued. There was the same pleasant note in his voice. " You had instructions to dispose of Sandford, because he was an *agent*. You knew he was an *agent* and you knew for whom he was working. He had to be got out of the way. Perhaps he discovered a little too much. Perhaps he knew a little too much about Miss Steyning. Hey, my good Jacques? Your instructions were to get rid of him somehow. You chose an opportune moment." He leaned forward a little. " My friend, my considered belief is that Sandford had elected that night to get away from the island ; to get over to the mainland ; possibly to get in touch with the F.B.I. or to talk to Mrs. Lyon, who was living in Miami ; to discover all he wanted to know. On the island he had come to the conclusion that it was time he did something about it. Somebody had tried to stop that. They had tried to stop it by doping Sandford's drink. Well, he was too good for the dope. He got down to the boat and you finished him."

Jacques said : " Yo' listen to me, Mister Guelvada. Yo' can't go talkin' like that to me. Yo're accusin' me of murder. Yo've got to prove murder. Yo' heard what ah said. . . ." His voice was shaking. " Yo've got to prove it."

Guelvada laughed. " I can always prove what I say, my dark friend. You forget your mate Mellin. Mellin has made a deposition. He confirms everything I say. Believe it or not, as Sandford went over the stern, Mellin was about to come aft. He saw you push him over."

Jacques said : " That goddam liar ! "

Guelvada spread his hands. " Maybe," he said. " But he is going to swear to that. In any event, even if you got away with that one, which you couldn't possibly do, you wouldn't get away with the second one."

Jacques asked : " What do yo' mean ? What's got into yo', Mister Guelvada ? What do yo' mean—the second one ? "

Guelvada said almost cheerfully : " You killed Gelert. Figure it out for yourself, my friend. You have disposed of Sandford. Some time afterwards another stranger appears on the island. This time a Mr. Julian Isles. You know quite a little about Mr. Isles, because someone either in Miami or on the island, has told you about him—someone who got at Miss Steyning's maid—someone who knew that Miss Steyning's maid expected a gentleman to arrive—a gentleman to whom she was to telephone so that he could meet her mistress, Viola Steyning ; so that he might look after Miss Steyning or possibly get her away from the island—a process which would have annoyed your friends very much. Am I making sense ? "

Jacques said nothing.

Guelvada went on : " So a telephone call was put through to Mr. Isles. It was put through to him at a call-box near the Leonard Hotel. But it wasn't Miss Steyning's maid who made that call. Shall I tell you who made that call ? *You did.*"

Jacques said in a high voice : " Yo' goddam white man——"

" Keep quiet," said Guelvada. " That's the voice you used, isn't it ? The voice you use when you're excited—a high falsetto that might belong to a man or a woman. You rang through to the call-box and told Isles to go up to Evansley—the house where you'd just killed Gelert. You shot Gelert with the .45 pistol that you use for killing sharks, and when you'd shot him you rang through to Isles and got him up to the house. He was to be the fall guy. By going up there, which you knew he would do, he implicated himself in that murder and as a suspect he was going to be in a tough spot."

Guelvada laughed happily. "Immediately you'd made the telephone call you came back to your boat. That was where you were supposed to have been all the time preparing for Colonel MacPherson's fishing party which was to take place that night." He laughed again. "You must have been very amused when Isles came down to your boat and told you that Colonel MacPherson's fishing trip was cancelled, and forced you to take him over to Miami."

He held up a finger. "But the joke is, my friend, that now you will laugh on the other side of your face. That is my case against you. You killed Sandford. You gave him to a shark. You killed Gelert. You killed them both for the same reason."

Jacques said slowly : " Yo're talkin' nonsense. Yo' can't prove anythin' about me. Yo' don' know anythin'."

Guelvada said : " Don't I ? Shall I tell you what happened on that night ? Somebody had been working on Miss Steyning's maid. They were very interested in the whereabouts of a package Miss Steyning had. It is my belief that you telephoned Miss Steyning and asked her to meet a gentleman at Evansley—someone whom she must see—someone who had something important to say to her about her brother who was dead. I think that is about the only thing that would have had any effect on that drunken young woman.

" So she went, but because she was a little uneasy, a little frightened, shall we say, she did what any young woman would do in the circumstances. She sent a message to her friend Hubert Gelert and asked him to be there also. It is my belief," said Guelvada, " that you kept the appointment with her at that house. You told her what you wanted. She refused to play. She wouldn't give you the package. She wouldn't tell you where it is."

Guelvada yawned. " I imagine you were going to get a little tough with her," he went on, " when Gelert arrived. Gelert told her to go home. Maybe she took his car. Maybe she was sober enough for once to drive it. Then Gelert had a showdown with you and you killed him."

Jacques said : " Yo' can talk a lot, Mister Guelvada. Yo' can't prove nothin'."

" No ? Shall I tell you something ? I went walking about that house looking for things ; about the grounds. What do you think I found, Jacques ? I found the cap that you were wearing that night when you went there —a facsimile of the one you have on your head. It has your initials in the lining. I found it where you dropped it in a slimy puddle near the water culvert on the other side of the pathway in the coppice."

Jacques said : " You goddam liar. Ah never had no cap that night."

Guelvada said : " Maybe. But the cap's there. *I put it there.* When we go back, my friend, I am going to see the Commissioner of Police. I am taking Mellin with me. Mellin will make a deposition as to your deliberate murder of Sandford. I shall tell Major Falstead my story. They will search the grounds ; they will find your cap. What do you think they are going to do with you, Jacques ? They'll hang you by the neck until you are dead, and you know it. Your murder of Sandford was obvious. You thought Mellin would never talk. You thought he'd be too scared to talk. Unfortunately for you, he's been too scared *not* to talk."

He picked up the whisky ; finished the drink. His eyes never left Jacques's face. He said : " Pick up the hook, Jacques. We're going back to Dark Bahama. I'm going to leave you in your boat. I'm going to leave you to think over what I've said, just for five minutes. Then you're going to tell me something. You're going to tell me the names of the people who employ you. You're going to tell me the names and whereabouts of the people who employed you to kill Sandford ; to try and get the packet from Miss Steyning ; the people for whom you killed Gelert."

His voice changed. He said : " That is going to be very difficult for you, Jacques, because I imagine these people are very terrible people ; they do very terrible things. And you know that when you give them away they'll do something very bad to you. If you don't give them away "—he shrugged his shoulders—" I'm going to do something bad to you." He smiled. " You make your choice. You thought you were safe when you killed Sandford. You knew what Sandford was doing, but you forgot one thing, Jacques. In our peculiar and somewhat mysterious service, whoever you may kill, someone else will come to take his place. Tell your friends that, if you ever see them. Tell them that I, Guelvada, am here to take Sandford's place. Let them get me as they got him, if they can. Take up the anchor. Be quick. Start the engine. We are going back to Dark Bahama. If you hesitate for as much as a second I shall kill you as I would a dog. Maybe there's a shark waiting for *you* in the bay to-night."

Jacques got up. He stood there, his shoulders slumped, his eyes wide with fright. He scrambled forward, Guelvada watching him. Then he came back ; started the engine. He turned the boat ; headed the launch back towards Dark Bahama.

Twenty minutes later Jacques tied the boat up at the jetty. Guelvada got out. He lighted a cigarette.

He said : " Go and sit down, my friend, and think out your little problem. Sit down in the stern and don't move. What are you going to do ? Are you going to answer my questions? Are you going to tell me who employed you, or do I go to the Commissioner?"

Jacques said from the shadows of the stern sheet: "Ah'm not sayin' nothin'." His voice was almost hysterical. "Ah'm not sayin' nothin' to you. Ah don' know nothin'."

Guelvada said: "Very well. They'll come for you in the morning. Good night, Jacques. Good hunting to you."

He walked down the jetty.

In the shadow of the palm trees he stopped; turned; watched the boat for five minutes. He could see the mast of the launch with its riding light showing against the quay. Suddenly it moved; then with the engine all out, gathering speed, it shot away from the quayside out into the waters of the bay. From where he stood Guelvada could see the white spume flying as the fast launch cut its way through the waters, out in the direction of Bear Island.

Guelvada smiled to himself. He lighted another cigarette; began to walk back towards his apartment, whistling softly to himself.

CHAPTER TEN

THE SMALL ivory clock on the mantelpiece in Guelvada's apartment struck one as he entered the room. He switched on the lights ; put his hat on a chair ; went out on to the veranda. He stood looking over the moonlit waters of the quiet sea, wondering exactly where Mervyn Jacques was at the moment ; what his eventual destination was to be. He shrugged his shoulders. Not far away, the dance orchestra at the Leonard Hotel was playing. The throbbing metre of the rumba music entranced Guelvada.

Guelvada thought he liked music a great deal because there was something in it akin to life. Goddam it, he thought, music is exactly like life. It can be quiet or solemn, or gay and amusing or, in the hands of the right composer, it can embrace all the attributes of life.

The orchestra stopped ; then began to play a samba. An interesting tune—quiet, almost soulful, with a throbbing undercurrent of sound produced by someone beating a tropical gourd and the occasional click of castanets. With sambas, pondered Guelvada, you had a little difficulty, because you never knew how they were going to end. You could never determine what was to happen next. Sambas—like life—were almost inconsequential and often written as if the composer were not quite certain how he was going to finish.

In this respect, thought Guelvada, they were something like his life and his profession. You started something but you were never quite certain as to how it was going to end. You followed your nose and you hoped. But certainly you *hoped*.

The music changed its *tempo*. He stood listening, smiling—entirely detached from the serious business of the day—thinking only of the music. He shrugged his shoulders again ; went into the drawing-room ; passed through into the bedroom ; took off his clothes ; lay down on the bed.

He was satisfied—as satisfied as he could be up to the moment. He had started something—something which must finish soon and which he was determined should finish his way. He relaxed on the bed, his hands clasped loosely across his stomach, his eyes closed. A small, almost cherubic smile played about his mouth. He lay there, dozing, waiting.

．　　　．　　　．　　　．　　　．　　　．

At two o'clock in the morning Isles swung his car off the main road on to the dirt track that led to Mellin's shack. Beside him in the passenger seat, silent, almost gloomy, sat Mellin. Isles stopped the car.

He said : " Well, here we are. Pleasant dreams, Mellin."

Mellin got out of the car. He said : " I hope they're gonna be pleasant. An' I hope he's gonna be satisfied. I don't like this goddam business. I don't——"

Isles interrupted. " Who cares what you like or what you don't like, Mellin." He smiled. " All we have to do is what we're told to do. Besides, I don't think you have anything to worry about. Perhaps for the first time in your life you are on the side of law and order—or are you ? " He looked at Mellin sideways. " A nice change for you."

Mellin said : " O.K. . . . O.K. . . . Well, I hope you're right, Mr. Isles. An' what's the next thing gonna be ? "

Isles shrugged his shoulders. " You know as much as I do. I expect if there *is* a next thing you'll hear about it. If I were you I'd go inside, give yourself a drink and go to bed. Sleep the sleep of the just." He grinned cynically. " Good night, Mellin."

He turned the car ; drove back on to the main road. He settled down behind the wheel ; pushed the car up to fifty.

When he arrived at the Leonard Hotel he left the automobile in the palm-fringed courtyard ; walked through the main entrance out to the back of the hotel. The back lawn, partly covered with a dancing floor, was a glamorous scene of light and colour. Multi-coloured electric lights glimmered and sparkled in the palm trees. In the corner, under a striped awning, a negro band played Spanish and Mexican music. Sixty or seventy couples—the women in light evening frocks, the men in white tuxedos—danced or drank at small tables set beneath the palms. Isles thought it was a nice sight. He thought it was a sight one would remember. He thought, maybe at some other time when he was not feeling so good he would like to remember it then.

He skirted the dance floor ; went into the back entrance of the hotel ; made his way to the long bar. The place was crowded. Isles ordered a large iced whisky and soda ; took it to a solitary table at the far end of the bar. He sat down. He thought that, like Mellin, he wondered what the next move would be. Then he thought that curiosity killed the cat. He was in this thing and all he could do was to go on with it ; to do what the rather peculiar and fascinating Guelvada told him to do. Yet, in spite of a cautious and somewhat cynical nature, Isles found that he had a rather extraordinary trust in Mr. Guelvada—a trust amounting almost to a peculiar faith in this Anglo-Belgian who treated life and death with an air of superb lightness, whose strange conversation showed little of the seriousness of the matters which he was handling. Isles sighed. He lighted a cigarette. He began to think about Thelma Lyon.

A voice behind him said : " Well ... my good friend Julian ? And how do things march with Julian ? To me, my friend, you look a little reminiscent. Maybe you are indulging in memories of the past. But I assure you, goddam it, that that is a process which seldom pays dividends. Better to look forward to the joys of the future, my Julian, or could it be . . ." said Guelvada, drawing up a chair, planting it on the other side of the table and sitting down, " that your mind was concerned with the delicate beauty of a lady who is known to both of us ? "

Isles looked at him. Guelvada sat there, easy and relaxed, grinning at him like an imp.

" You are a good guesser, Ernie. I *was* thinking about her." Isles leaned forward. " You know, I think she's a rather wonderful woman."

" But, of course," said Guelvada. " And what you are trying to tell me, my friend, without putting it into so many words, is that you are in love with her. Englishmen," he continued, " find the greatest difficulty in talking about being in love. It is a word which they endeavour to avoid. Being the most superb artistes in under-statement, they find it almost impossible to allow themselves to indulge in any enthusiasm what-soever, even about a *grand passion*. In which they are stupid."

He shrugged his shoulders. " Women should be made love to with a complete enthusiasm—almost a ferocity. Women will forgive anything—even the utmost in-fidelity—providing the man is prepared to love like a tiger and lie like a trooper. Goddam it ... love should be like a thunderstorm, not an April shower. It should be exhausting, devastating and utterly impossible. I, Guelvada, say so, and, goddam it, I ought to know."

Isles grinned. " I suppose you've been in love a

thousand times. Each time more sincerely and ferociously than the last."

"Probably...." Guelvada spread his hands. "But always I am in love with my work which, believe me, my friend, possesses some of the attributes of a most perfect passion. In love, it is necessary to believe in oneself and not to be surprised if one is discovered in a ditch with a knife in one's back. An angry woman can kick back at a man with the same *esprit* as an outraged enemy. A woman can adore you and still take delight in your downfall, in the same way as an enemy may admire your technique and personality and still plot your death. Love is interesting, but so is life, with the exception that one may seduce countless women, but one cannot seduce life—not often—because life, unlike a woman, strikes back at one logically. But it has always been obvious to me that you, my Julian, are what is called crazy about Mrs. Lyon. I guessed it from the start.

"And of course she's a wonderful woman. One of these fine days, my friend, you will realise that the people who work for my esteemed employer are all rather wonderful people. In addition to which," he continued, "our Thelma has beauty—an attribute which I, Guelvada, have not. Looks, yes ... courage, yes ... cunning, amounting to that of the snake, yes ... Guelvada has all these things, but he has never deluded himself that he is beautiful."

Isles said : "Really ? Thank God there's something you haven't got, Ernest."

Guelvada produced his ornate cigarette case ; lighted a cigarette. He said : "Now, tell me about our friend Jacques. I am intrigued with Jacques. After we landed at the quay I talked to him and left him in the boat. And then I walked down the quay wondering whether he had enough guts to shoot me in the back. He had not. From the shadow of the palms

184

I watched him. He started the engine and took the
boat out to sea as if the devil were after him. He
seemed to be making straight for Bear Island. Did
you pick him up ? "

Isles nodded. " Mellin knew his stuff. After all, he's
been working with Jacques for years. We were lying
off the far end of Bear Island. Beyond it, off to the
left, is a little group of small islands—cays they call
them. Mellin said they were uninhabited. Jacques
made for one of them. It couldn't have been more than
three-quarters of a mile long and about half a mile wide.
He ran the boat in close. There's a shelving beach
there, Mellin said. Jacques anchored the boat about
fifty or sixty yards from the cay beach. There's not
much water there. He went overboard ; swam for ten
or fifteen yards ; then waded ashore."

Guelvada said : " Excellent. Where did he go to ? "

Isles shrugged his shoulders. " We couldn't see.
The place was thick with trees, foliage and undergrowth all over the place. We saw him go up the
beach ; then he disappeared."

Guelvada asked : " And Mellin told you that there
were no people living on the cay ? "

Isles shook his head. " He said he didn't think
there was anyone on any of the cays. He thought
occasionally fisherman used the place. Sometimes
people stayed there for a few weeks and then moved
on. Mellin said he didn't know that cay. He couldn't
say for certain if there was anyone there."

Guelvada nodded. " So what did you do about our
Mr. Jacques ? " he asked.

Isles grinned. " We fixed him. He's stuck there on
the cay and he can't get off. I should think the place
was about three or four miles from Dark Bahama. We
took Mellin's boat alongside Jacques's launch. He
knows the boat, you understand ? There's a sea-cock
forrard. He opened it. She was on the bottom within

about twenty minutes. Jacques will have a hell of a job before he gets that boat afloat again."

Guelvada smiled approvingly. " Excellent. So as far as we know Mr. Jacques is on this tiny uninhabited island with no boat in which to remove himself. I think we might leave him there for the moment."

There was a silence ; then Isles said : " I don't want to appear curious, but could I ask what is the next dish on the menu—this rather extraordinary and exciting menu ? "

" My friend," said Guelvada, " you may ask anything you like. If I wish to give you the answer I will do so. In this case it suits me to do so. I will tell you what the next dish is." He looked at his watch. " It is now half-past two. You will finish your drink, after which you will get into your motor car and you will drive out to the unhappy Mellin once again. Probably," said Guelvada, with a smile, " he will not be overjoyed to see you. This Mellin, you understand, is a peculiar person. Nothing makes him happy. Always he looks at life through spectacles which are tinted, I think, with particularly gloomy tints. You will put him in your car. You will take him back to the quay. You will tell him to get his boat in readiness ; see that there is gasolene in the tank, and you will wait. Sometime —I cannot tell you exactly what the time will be—I shall be with you. You understand ? "

" I understand." Isles leaned back in his chair. " You know, Ernie, believe it or not, I am beginning to enjoy working with you. I don't know how this thing is going to end or whether I am going to find myself inside a gaol before I've finished, but I think it's a lot of fun."

An expression of surprise came over Guelvada's face. " But of course ! . . . How can there be any doubt about that ? " He leaned forward. " To work with an artist like Guelvada must be fun. Why, goddam it, sometimes I think it's fun myself—very funny ! Remember . . . have the boat ready in an hour. Stand by till I come to you. *Au revoir*, my friend." He got up. He disappeared through the door at the other end of the bar.

·   ·   ·   ·   ·   ·

Major Falstead, the Commissioner of Police, found sleep a little difficult sometimes. Very often he wished that he was back at his old job as an assistant magistrate in India. That life he had found more simple, less involved, than the processes which surrounded him at the moment. First of all he was worried about the Gelert murder. Nothing had emerged. Isles had returned to the island and as far as the Commissioner could see, beyond the fact that he had discovered the body, there was nothing to link him to the murder. He thought, looking through the darkness at the ceiling above him, that the life of a police commissioner on Dark Bahama was not all cake. He thought there were too many flies on it. Already people were asking questions. Already people were suggesting that some murdering maniac was wandering about the island ready to shoot someone else.

Falstead sighed again. He leaned out of bed; switched on the electric light; took a cigarette from his bedside table and lighted it. Then the telephone rang.

The voice of Guelvada came softly over the telephone on Falstead's ears. It said : " Good morning, Mr. Commissioner. May I have the pleasure of introducing myself to you ? My name is Ernest Guelvada. I assure you I am not an unimportant person. Also it is necessary that I see you immediately."

The Commissioner said : " Of course." He had seen Guelvada's name on the list of visitors to the island—

the list which was brought to him daily. He had noticed it. That was all. He said : " I take it that your business is of the utmost urgency, Mr. Guelvada? "

" You're telling me," said Guelvada. " I assure you, Major, you don't know the half of it. Goddam it, I am going to surprise you. I would like to see you about two murders."

Falstead raised his eyebrows. He said : " *Two* murders ? "

" Precisely," said Guelvada. " You have had two murders on this island within the last six months. *You* think you have had one. I'm going to produce another one. So as to save time, my dear Commissioner, I am going to suggest that you make an immediate telephone call. I suggest that you get a Government urgent priority telephone call through to Miami. You will ask to be connected to Mr. Willy Frim, who you will find is the Federal Bureau of Investigation field agent stationed at Miami—one of Mr. Hoover's young men. You will talk to him. You will ask him about Mr. Ernest Guelvada. You will tell him that I am seeing you on an important matter. I think you will find," Guelvada continued pleasantly, " that Mr. Frim will assure you that I am a person of responsibility who may be believed ; that it might be a good thing for you to take such action as I advise."

The Commissioner felt a little bewildered. He said : " Very well, Mr. Guelvada, if you wish it. May I ask exactly what is your official position in these matters ? "

Guelvada said cheerfully : " Goddam it . . . no ! . . . I suggest that after you have talked to Mr. Frim you will consider the question unnecessary."

" Very well," said Falstead coldly. " And when may I expect to see you ? "

" Commissioner, I shall be with you in ten minutes," said Guelvada. " Have no diffidence about seeing me in your pyjamas. I think they are the most comfortable form of clothing. I often see my best friends in pyjamas. They find the process sometimes very entertaining. *Au revoir.*"

The Commissioner put the receiver back in its cradle. He sighed. He said to himself : " Well, I'm damned . . .! "

He considered dressing. Then he thought that this might be unnecessary. After all, the Guelvada person had said he did not mind pyjamas. He picked up his uniform cap which was on top of his neatly-folded uniform on the *chaise longue* at the bottom of the bed. It was a nice, dark-blue, peaked cap, silver laced and almost new. He put it on and looked at himself in the glass. He thought he looked damned funny. The uniform cap with sky-blue pyjamas, frogged with darker blue fastenings, just didn't go.

He sat down on the bed and picked up the telephone. He called the Inspector on duty at the Police Barracks.

He said : " Is that you, Bonaventura ? Listen to me. Call Miami. You want to speak personally to the United States Marshal. Get the call through in a hurry. Urgent. . . . Government. . . . Priority. See ? When you get the United States Marshal check that the Field Agent of the F.B.I. in Miami is a gentleman called Willy Frim. Have the Marshal get a cut-out connection with Frim, and put him through to me here, as soon as possible. Have you got that ? "

The Inspector, who was coloured, said in a gentle and soothing voice : " Yeah, Commissioner. Ah got it. Yes, sir. An urgent government priority call to the U.S. Marshal, Miami. Check on Mr. Frim—Mr. Willy Frim on the F.B.I. Field Office, Miami. Then Mr. Frim makes a direct cut-out call to you at yo' house, sir. Ah got it, sir."

The Commissioner sighed. He replaced the receiver. He walked over to the mirror and looked at himself again. He thought he looked damned silly. He threw the uniform hat into the corner of the room and put on a dressing-gown.

Then he went to the dining-room and poured himself an outsize whisky and soda, and cursed because there was no ice.

He sat down ; waited for Guelvada.

It was three-thirty when Guelvada followed the Commissioner of Police into the dining-room. He sat down ; took the whisky and soda that was offered him ; drank a little ; lighted a cigarette.

He said : " Major . . . here's to your health. I am delighted to meet you. I am more than delighted to bring a little excitement and happiness into your— what is the word—prosaic existence. Yes, goddam it. You will agree with me that there is nothing like a couple of murders to stir the blood of a Police Commissioner at three-thirty in the morning. Have you spoken to Mr. Frim yet ? "

Falstead shook his head. " Not yet. He'll probably be through at any moment now. We have a very quick telephonic tie-up with Miami."

" Good," said Guelvada. " Excellent. Now I have some news for you "—he was grinning like a mischievous child—" because I have to tell you that on this island there is a young lady called Miss Viola Steyning who is beautiful and charming and very cockeyed all the time. Goddam it, she is permanently drunk and looks as if she is going to continue that way. Well . . . I regret to tell you that she has contracted an appalling disease which she has also communicated to her native maid—a particularly unintelligent negress. These two people—for the safety of the other residents on this island—must immediately be removed to an isolation hospital. Your official doctor must see them immediately and order them away to the hospital. You understand, Commissioner ? "

" My God ! " said Falstead. " I understand all

right. But what the devil has this to do with the murders you spoke of? I don't understand. I——"

The telephone rang. Falstead went to the instrument. He said : " This should be the Miami call."

Guelvada got up. " Superb. . . . Everything works like clockwork. Behind everything can be seen the most superb organisation of Guelvada. If that's Frim, when you have finished I want to talk to him."

Falstead took the call. After a few minutes he said : " All right, Mr. Guelvada. That's good enough for me. Now . . . will you talk to him ? "

Guelvada moved over to the telephone. He drew up a chair ; sat down. For five minutes he talked softly, quickly. Watching him, Falstead thought that wonders would never cease ; that anything could happen, even in a quiet place like Dark Bahama.

Guelvada put the receiver back in its cradle. He got up ; sat down by the Commissioner.

He said : " Now, listen, my friend. Now that you know about me—now that you understand a little of the very arduous work which confronts me—I will be grateful if you will listen attentively. First of all let us consider the murder of the man Sandford. Mervyn Jacques, the skipper of the boat, was employed by some not-very-nice people who wished Sandford out of the way. So Jacques helped him overboard and a shark got him. And that was that ! Just another fishing accident. Such things have been known to happen before."

" So that was the story ? " The Commissioner shrugged his shoulders. " No one would ever have suspected that. Jacques has been here for years. He has a very good reputation, but——"

Guelvada interrupted. " Every man has a good reputation until he starts to lose it. This man Jacques, I think, is a vain man—very vain. I imagine he likes money. Men will do all sorts of things for money, especially if they are also scared of the people who employ them. The point is," continued Guelvada, "Sandford was an operative employed by the same organisation for which I work. His business on this island was to keep an eye on Miss Steyning, because the drunken Miss Steyning has some very important documents which she received from her brother just before he died. It is necessary that these documents fall into the right hands. You understand, Commissioner? That is "—he smiled—" into my hands.

" Now let us consider the second murder—the murder of the young man Gelert. You know what goes on on this island. It is your business to know. And, therefore, you will understand that there had been some sort of, shall we say, flirtation between Miss Steyning and the young man Gelert—that is before she got so frightened that she took badly to liquor. It is my belief that an appointment was made by Jacques to meet Miss Steyning at the house Evansley. He had a message for her. I imagine he lured her there under the pretence that he had some information about her dead brother. Actually, it is my opinion that he was endeavouring to force from her information of the whereabouts of this packet she had received from her brother. But I do not think she liked the idea of going to this place alone, so she telephoned Gelert.

" She asked him to go quickly to Evansley. He was probably in the middle of shaving at the time and hurriedly put on his collar and tie and his jacket, and went. Which would account for the fact that only half of his face was shaved when he was killed.

" Well, there was a showdown between the three of them at Evansley; then I think the girl left and went back to her home. Then probably Gelert threatened that he would take action against Jacques ; that he would report the matter to the police. So Jacques killed him."

Guelvada got up; lighted a cigarette; began to walk about the room. He went on : " Of course one has no direct evidence to this effect, Major, but when I was there wandering around the grounds of this house, searching vainly for some indication which might put me on the right track, I found something. I found a red and blue fishing cap that belonged to Jacques. His initials were in the lining. I found it in a coppice immediately opposite the french window—the window through which the murderer made his escape after he had killed Gelert.

" Now," said Guelvada, " about the *first* murder. There is evidence. I have talked to the mate who was on the boat the night that Sandford died—the man Mellin—a white man. Mellin is prepared to make a deposition. He is prepared to inform you officially that he saw Jacques push Sandford out of the boat after the shark had struck."

The Commissioner said : " That's good enough for me, Mr. Guelvada. We'll have Jacques brought in now."

Guelvada put up his hand. " I'm afraid not. You see, I did not want Jacques to be arrested. I have been out in his boat with him to-night. I have been talking to him. Goddam it, we had a most interesting conversation ! I made him an offer. I told him that if he agreed to give me the names of the people who were employing him I might be a little merciful, but if he did not I should come straight to you. When we returned I left him in his boat at the quay to think things over. A few minutes afterwards he took the boat out to sea. I do not think you will be troubled with Mr. Jacques any more. And I do not think if I were you I should worry much about him. I have an idea," said Guelvada cheerfully, " that we shall have news of him soon,"

The Commissioner said : " I see. . . . Well, Mr.

Guelvada, after my conversation with Frim I believe the least I can do is to give you your head for a day or two. Now, what is all this business about Miss Steyning's illness ? "

Guelvada smiled. " This is a little fable concocted by me. The story is that your medical officer here has reason to believe she has contracted some dangerous disease ; also her maid. I would be grateful if you would get him out of bed immediately. He should be instructed to call on Miss Steyning. He will find that he believes her to be suffering from some disease. I have no doubt he can select a good one. Immediately, he orders that she and her maid be taken away and isolated in some hospital, or some place where they will both be safe from interference. Perhaps you will be good enough to have a police officer stationed there with them."

The Commissioner nodded. " I can arrange that."

" In two or three days' time, when the situation is a little clearer," continued Guelvada, " your good doctor can find he has made a mistake. He can discover that his diagnosis is wrong, and they can be released."

Falstead said : " Very well. I don't think we can do much harm in doing that."

" There is one other thing," said Guelvada. " The doctor must go to the house immediately." He looked at his watch. " It's getting very late—or very early, whichever you prefer—and I have a great deal to do. Immediately these two are taken away—and understand that Miss Steyning must not be allowed to pack anything, or leave the room once the doctor is there— immediately they have been taken away perhaps you will lend me two or three of your very efficient policemen."

Falstead said : " You're going to search the house ? "

Guelvada nodded. " I'm going through it with a fine tooth comb. It is my belief that the documents are

194

there. With Miss Steyning out of the way we have a chance to find them."

Falstead said : "Very well." He went to the telephone. As he picked up the receiver he looked over his shoulder. "You were perfectly right when you told me you were bringing a little excitement here." He smiled. "I don't know that I mind. I find it rather interesting."

He began to talk into the telephone.

.   .   .   .   .   .

At four-fifteen in the morning a native policeman named Dalaras, searching in a dress cupboard in Viola Steyning's bedroom, found beneath a pile of soiled linen a large, sealed and taped envelope. He took it to Guelvada.

Guelvada held it in his hands ; read the address ; examined it. He smiled.

He said : "My friends, our task is over. Put everything back as you found it, and go home to bed. Good night to you."

He went out of the house, down the pathway to the gate, the envelope held under his arm beneath his coat. He walked quickly to his apartment ; switched on the lights ; put the packet on the table. He stood for a few moments looking at it. Then he mixed himself a drink. Then he sat down. He began to open the packet.

.   .   .   .   .   .

It was almost daylight when Guelvada left his apartment. He had shaved, bathed, changed his clothes. He looked immaculate as if he had just risen from a long sleep ; also he looked extremely pleased with himself. He walked quickly down to the quay. Isles was walking up and down. Moored at the end of the jetty was Mellin's boat, with Mellin smoking in the stern.

Guelvada said : " Good morning, my friend. Everything marches. Everything goes extremely well. I am beginning," he went on, " to be very interested in life which, when you come to consider it, or even if you don't, is always refreshingly amusing. Let us go."

He got into the boat. Isles followed him.

Guelvada said : " My good Mellin, take us out to this cay where Jacques landed. Show me where his boat was sunk."

Mellin said : " O.K. There's going to be a lot of trouble gettin' that boat up."

Guelvada said : " Maybe it will be worth your while to get it up, even if it costs a little money and some trouble. Has Jacques any relatives ? "

Mellin shook his head. " I wouldn't know."

Guelvada said : " Maybe one day the boat will be yours. Who knows ? "

Mellin said nothing. He started the engine. The boat began to move away from the jetty.

Forty minutes afterwards Mellin cut the engine. Now it was daylight. There was a hint of sunlight on the water. Guelvada, leaning over the side of the boat, could see, twenty feet below, Jacques's launch as she lay on her side on the sandy bottom. A fish swam out of the forrard cabin as he looked.

" Life," said Guelvada, " is amusing. One day a launch is a fishing boat—the next day a home for a very pleasant fish." He sat there admiring the iridescent colours of the fish as it swam gracefully away. Then he said : " Get in as near as you can. I'm going ashore."

Mellin said : " I can't take her any farther. I'm afraid you will have to get your feet wet."

" What can be nicer ? " said Guelvada. " Stay here. It will be pleasant in the sea." He said to Isles : " Do you like swimming ? "

Isles nodded.

" I suggest," said Guelvada, " we try it." He began to undress.

Ten minutes afterwards Guelvada and Isles came out of the water ; walked up the sandy, sloping beach. Thirty yards from the sea the cay was a mass of thick, tropical undergrowth and trees. Guelvada began to walk up and down the edge of it. Eventually, he stopped.

He said : " As you see, my friend, here is a path. Let us follow it and, who knows ? And I hope there are no snakes out this morning." He began to walk along the pathway, Isles following silently behind him.

They walked for a long while. The path twisted tortuously through the thick undergrowth. Then, suddenly, they came to a clearing. In the middle of the clearing was a shack—a well-built shack. Outside it were two or three packing-cases. A thin wisp of smoke emerged from the chimney.

Isles said : " It might not be so good if someone's inside—someone who doesn't like us, I mean. If I go into a scrap I like to have some clothes on."

Guelvada shrugged. " I don't think you need worry, my friend. In any event, it is as easy to fight without clothes as with them."

He walked across the clearing ; opened the door of the shack ; went inside. Isles, looking over his shoulder, stopped dead at the picture before him. The shack was divided into two rooms. They stood on the threshold of what had apparently been the living-room. There were shelves filled with tinned foods ; an open fireplace in which some embers still glowed.

There was a table in the middle of the room and across it lay the body of Jacques. He was slumped forward, half-sitting in a chair, his head and shoulders on the table, his left hand hanging grotesquely by his side. On the floor beneath the nerveless fingers was a dead, half-smoked cigarette. Jacques was not a pretty sight. He had been shot through the left eye at close range. It was as well that the good side of his face lay uppermost.

Guelvada sat down on a wooden chair. Isles thought he looked even more extraordinary without clothes than with them. Stripped, Guelvada, who was inclined to look plump when he was dressed, had not a particle of fat on him. He was all hard muscle and sinew. His skin, white as a woman's, glowed with health, and when he moved Isles could see the muscles ripple under his skin.

Guelvada said : " So you see, my friend, *this* was the end of Jacques. I knew it."

Isles said : " Not a good end."

" Consider to yourself," said Guelvada. " This man was a fool. He thought that the people who employed him would look after him, threatened as he was with arrest. So he came back to them for help. What a fool," he repeated. " Did he think that they would let him live knowing what he knew ? "

He walked across the room, past the table ; pushed open the door of the second room. It was a bedroom, roughly but comfortably furnished. Guelvada pointed to the corner. A wireless transmission set lay on the floor.

" It is quite simple," said Guelvada. " One man lived here. This was the person from whom Jacques received his instructions. An excellent hiding place. From here he could report to his principals on the mainland. He could know what was happening on Dark Bahama through Jacques. With Jacques dead, his murderer makes a getaway. I wonder where he's gone. Maybe I can guess."

Isles said : " There must have been another boat."

" Of course," said Guelvada. " Of course there was

another boat." He went back into the living-room. He regarded what remained of Mervyn Jacques.

He said quietly : " You will now have a long time to consider, my friend Jacques, how particularly stupid you were." He turned to Isles. " Let us go. There is nothing to do here. I prefer the sunshine outside to this. He went out of the shack.

.   .   .   .   .   .

It was twelve o'clock. Guelvada finished his second cup of coffee. He got up ; walked to the window ; looked out across the sunlit sea. Then he went into the bedroom. When he returned, Isles saw that he held in his hands the package.

Guelvada said : " My friend, this is the cause of all the trouble. These documents ! " He held up the package. " For these, men have lived and worked and died. Sacrificed for these things have been young Steyning's life, his sister's health, Gelert, and our friend Mr. Jacques, who lies so uncomfortably across a table somewhere out there." He looked at his strap-watch. " The afternoon plane goes at two-thirty. You will be on that plane. Return to your hotel ; pack your things ; eat some lunch. You will be in Miami soon after three o'clock. Take these documents ; give them to Mrs. Lyon. Tell her to keep them in safety until she receives an instruction as to their disposal. I shall stay here."

Isles asked : " Will you be coming over to Miami ? "

Guelvada nodded. " In two or three days' time. I have one or two matters to clear up here. I must attend to the disposal of our friend Jacques. I must see the Commissioner. But I shall be with you . . . perhaps to-morrow, perhaps the next day. *Au revoir*, my friend. And good luck to you." He threw the package on the table. Isles picked it up.

He said : " All right. I shall be on the two-thirty plane."

Guelvada said archly : " It will be very nice to see Mrs. Lyon again, don't you think ? I shall think of you to-night. I expect you will be dining with her in that charming dining-room of hers with french windows looking out on to the lawn."

Guelvada yawned artistically. " Consider what a time you can have on the airplane. Your trip takes just over half an hour—long enough for you to plan your attack on the delightful and charming Thelma. Consider your position. You arrive at her apartment a hero—or almost a hero. You have the documents and her job has been successfully completed for her. No longer need she worry about the possible criticism of her employer. She will be happy. More, she should be well disposed to you."

" I hope you're right." Isles smiled. " I think I'd like it a lot if I felt that she was well disposed to me."

Guelvada smiled mischievously. " Be wise. On your journey think out every honeyed phrase possible. Refurbish your technique of love-making. Be ferocious and interesting, subtle and alarming in your approach." He sighed. " I wish I were you, my friend." He sighed again. " You should be delightfully happy."

Isles grinned. " Why not ? "

Guelvada said : " Precisely ! And in the meantime you will take good care of that package. You wouldn't lose it, would you ? "

Isles said : " No. That I promise you. Well, I'll be seeing you, Ernie."

" You may rely on that," said Guelvada.

Isles went away.

Guelvada stood by the table until he heard the front door close behind Isles. Then he went to the sideboard and mixed himself a drink. He came back to the table, sat down, put his feet on the table and gave himself up to thought.

He thought he liked Isles. The Englishman was an admirable character. Even if he was young in the mind he was still an admirable character and eventually life and this and that would give him added mental years. Guelvada visualised Isles on the airplane, working out his plan of attack on Thelma, polishing the phrases with which he would make his approach.

Such nonsense . . . Guelvada thought. The trouble with Anglo-Saxons was that they tried to play a woman in very much the same way as they played a game of golf—with a carefully thought-out technique for each shot—with force on the fairway and suavity on the putting green.

He got up ; stretched. He felt a little tired. He yawned and went over to the telephone. He asked the operator for the Commissioner of Police.

.   .   .   .   .   .

Guelvada stood on the edge of the sun-baked airfield waiting for the two-thirty plane for Miami to leave. He stood in the shadow of a palm tree from which position of vantage he could see the Customs office, the waiting-room and the strip of shrub-bordered promenade where passengers, having cleared through the Customs office, stood about in small groups waiting for the plane.

At the end of the promenade, leaning against the white wall of the waiting-room, stood Isles. Guelvada thought that he looked immaculate in his tan gaberdine coat and slacks, with a cream silk shirt and a white-spotted brown tie. His document case was in his left hand ; an iced rum drink, generously laid on by the Clipper services, in his right hand.

Guelvada sighed. He thought that Isles would be

happy, or at least contented. His work, he thought, was over. The excitement of his short stay on Dark Bahama was already becoming a memory and he was looking forward to Miami and his next meeting with Thelma Lyon.

Guelvada grinned. He thought to himself, with a wry twist of the lips, that people—even quick-brained and clever people like Isles were, occasionally, very simple. When they wanted to reduce life to plain and simple terms—because that is how they wanted life at the moment—they invariably managed to talk or to think themselves into the appropriate frame of mind.

Guelvada shrugged. That, he supposed, was human nature. At the moment Isles believed that he had materially assisted in the work which had originally brought Thelma Lyon to Dark Bahama. He believed that she would be grateful. He already saw himself, in spite of his own natural cynicism, something of a hero in her eyes. He probably visualised the scene in her apartment after his arrival when she would endeavour to make him aware of her gratitude.

Guelvada grinned again. Very few people, he thought, were wise to Thelma Lyon. Very few people —except those who, like himself, had an acute perception of what went on inside the minds of some types of women—realised that she was brilliant and clever and tough and ruthless. Otherwise she would never have been able to stand the years with Quayle—the war years—when she, like Guelvada, had taken her life in her hands on half a dozen occasions merely in order to carry out a job for which, at the end, there would be little material gain, no bouquets and, if lucky, a mere commendation given almost grudgingly by Quayle.

Isles, said Guelvada to himself, had a great deal to learn, but if, in the meantime, he wished to enjoy a suggestion of a fool's paradise—well, why not?

The Clipper, her wings gleaming in the sun, taxied down the runway ; turned in front of the airport buildings ; stopped. The pilot, co-pilot and a slim dark-haired hostess, descended. The passengers began to go aboard. Isles, his document case under his arm, was the last passenger to mount the steps that led into the plane.

The pilot and co-pilot went aboard. The plane began to move down the runway ; then, at the end, like a great silver bird, suddenly she was airborne ; began to climb rapidly.

Guelvada turned away. He thought to himself : Well . . . good luck, Isles . . . my romantic friend.

He began to walk towards the spot where he had left his car.

He wondered if he would ever see Isles again.

It was three o'clock when he stopped the car outside the gates of the Police Barracks. He went in ; crossed the sun-baked square ; entered the building on the other side. He knocked at the door of the Commissioner's office ; went inside.

Falstead, in a white uniform, a white topee on the back of his head, sat at the desk in the cool office.

He said : " Good afternoon, Guelvada. What's the newest excitement ? "

Guelvada helped himself to a cigarette from the box on the desk. He said : " The excitement is coming to a close, I think, my dear Major. Isles has just left for Miami. He has flown into the blue. Goddam it . . . sometimes I wish I were Julian Isles. But only for a moment. By and large—and I don't mean maybe— I prefer to be Ernest Guelvada.

Falstead said : " Yes ? Well . . . life must be any-thing but boring for you. Yours is a strange job." He paused for a moment ; then : " I suppose you'll think I'm damned curious, but I'm wondering just how you got into it ? "

Guelvada grinned. " I'll tell you. Once upon a time
—believe it or not—I was what you call a very nice
little boy. I lived in a small town in Belgium. A place
called Ellezelles. Then the first war came. And the
Germans. I was fourteen when they shot my father for
killing a German who assaulted my mother. After that
I wasn't quite so nice. I used to spend my time
planning how to kill Germans and I became most
proficient at it. I learned to throw a knife very
adequately—I'm telling you ! Then I contacted some
British secret agents and began to supply them with
information. It was easy. I could go anywhere and I
could look very innocent. No one ever suspected me,
and people—especially when they had drunk too much
—were not afraid of talking in front of a boy. And so
one thing led to another, and I progressed from one
stage to another, until here I am to-day. Still doing
the same things, being the same sort of person. Simple
. . . isn't it ? "

Falstead asked : " D'you like it ? "

Guelvada smiled. " Why not ? It's amusing. The
time passes quickly. There isn't enough of it for one
to spend too much time thinking about oneself. Also
. . . there is a certain excitement. Besides which, it suits
me, and," he added modestly, " I'm damned good at
it . . . goddam it, I am a master of my profession ! "

Falstead smiled. " I think you're an amusing person.
An amusing person with one hell of a nerve.

Guelvada stubbed out his cigarette. " I have come
to say *au revoir*," he said. " I am leaving on the nine
o'clock plane to-night. I do not know how long I
shall be in Miami or where I shall go when I leave
there." He grinned. " Maybe I'll come back here.
In the meantime there are one or two little points.
The first one is Jacques. Jacques, our not-so-clever
friend, is dead. His body is on the cay beyond Bear
Island. He went there when he took a run-out on us

204

yesterday. He went to see his boss; to tell him that you were going to get after Jacques on a murder charge. He thought his boss would help him."

Falstead said : " I see. . . ."

"Jacques, of course, was a fool," Guelvada continued. " But he was very scared and he did what he thought best—at the moment. His boss helped him a lot. He shot him. An obvious course, because Jacques, in your hands, could have been very inconvenient. He could have talked quite a lot in an endeavour to save his skin—or his neck."

Falstead said : " All right. We'll clean that up. I'll send out to-morrow and pick up the body. We'll keep it as quiet as possible. I suppose you'd like that ? "

" Candidly, my friend, I don't care," said Guelvada. " But there is one little thing which you must do for me. Here is a list. This afternoon, telephone through to Frim and read it to him. He will understand exactly what you mean."

Falstead took the half-sheet of paper. He read it. It said :

> " *The Altermeyer Hotel,*
> *Orchid Beach.*
> *Ferenzy's Bar.*
> *The Altermeyer Hotel.*"

" All right," said Falstead. " I'll get through immediately."

" Excellent," said Guelvada. " And perhaps you'll make a reservation for me on to-night's plane ? "

Falstead nodded. " I'll do that."

Guelvada went to the door. " I have come to the conclusion that I am tired. I shall sleep . . . the sleep of the happy, contented and very just man. So long, Falstead. I'll be seeing you . . . maybe ! "

He went out.

Falstead picked up the telephone.

He said to himself : " An amazin' feller ! A damned amazin' feller ! "

. . . . . .

It was soon after four o'clock when Isles pressed the door-bell at the Lyon apartment. He waited with a pleasurable sense of anticipation. Outside, the afternoon sun was shining on the shrubs and flowers in the *patio*, but here it was cool.

The negro maid opened the door. She said : " Good afternoon, Mistah Isles. Ah'm glad to see you again."

Isles said : " I'm glad to be here again. Is Mrs. Lyon in ? "

The maid shook her head. " She's been out since dis morning, Mistah Isles. She said she'd be back for dinner."

Isles felt disappointed. He had a sense of something like an anti-climax. He said : " I see. . . ."

She said : " You sure do look tired, Mistah Isles."

" I am tired," said Isles. " I've been missing on my sleep lately. Mary Ann, is my room unlocked ? "

" No, Mistah Isles. Ah got the key. Heah it is—all ready for you." She produced the key from a pocket in her apron.

Isles took it. " All right. I'm going to have a bath and get some sleep. If Mrs. Lyon comes in tell her I'll see her at half-past eight to-night."

She said : " Ah'll tell her."

Isles walked down the long corridor ; opened the door of his bedroom ; went in. He put the document case under the mattress of the bed ; unpacked his grip ; undressed ; got into pyjamas ; lay on the bed.

He was thinking about his meeting with Thelma ; what he was going to do or say. He began to think

about himself; that it was time he settled down to
some regular profession—some routine of life—something in which there would be a future. He grinned
wryly. He could not quite see that. All his life he had
adventured and he supposed if you were built like that
you went on being like it. He lay there, his hands
behind his head, looking at the ceiling, thinking of the
past, considering the present, wondering about the
future. He went to sleep.

It was eight o'clock when he awoke. He got up;
took a shower; dressed; walked down the corridor.
The Lyon apartment door was open. Isles walked
across the hall into the drawing-room.

She was mixing cocktails. She wore a camellia-pink
dinner-gown with a gold lace scarf.

Isles said : " I think you look simply terrific."

She smiled at him. " I'm glad you like it. But what
are you doing here ? I didn't expect you to be back so
soon."

He held up the document case. " Here it is. I didn't
expect to be back so soon either. But Ernie Guelvada
is a fast worker . . . I'll say . . . ! "

She said : " So you have the Steyning documents—
the cause of all the trouble ? "

He nodded. " You know . . . it's odd, but this afternoon when I arrived here I had a peculiar sense of
anti-climax."

She came towards him ; handed him a Martini. She
asked : " Exactly what does that mean, Julian ? Does
it mean that you are a little sorry now that you think
the excitement might be over ? "

He said : " Might be ? It *is* over. This looks like
the end of the story, and I don't know that I'm too
pleased with it being the end."

She laughed. " Why ? " she asked.

He shrugged his shoulders. " I'm not quite certain.
I suppose, during the last few days, I've been living in

a sort of strange dream world ; doing the most extraordinary things without quite knowing why, but
enjoying it. I suppose the excitement appealed to me.
Now it's over, and what happens? Nothing . . .
unless . . ."

She sat down opposite him. She asked : " Unless
what, Julian ? "

He said : " You know, I'm never sure whether to
take you seriously or not."

She laughed again. " Very often I don't know
whether I take myself seriously. But exactly what do
you mean ? "

He finished the Martini ; put the glass down. He
asked : " Do you remember that little scene in the
Hyde Park Hotel on the night that you and I first
met ? I have a vague idea that you told me that when
this job came to an end I might find you not ungrateful.
I've often wondered what you meant—if you meant
anything at all."

She smiled. " I always mean what I say when I *say*
it, Julian. But haven't you forgotten something?
When we met in the Hyde Park Hotel I was your
client—giving you a definite commission. That commission was that you got Viola Steyning away from
Dark Bahama. That was the job in those days. *That*
was the idea. Well, she's still there, isn't she ? "

Isles said : " You're hedging. You knew perfectly
well at the time that that story wasn't true, any more
than the second story you told me, about your black-
mailing friend on the island, and your indiscreet letters,
was true."

She shrugged her shoulders. " What else was I to
do, Julian. I couldn't very well tell you what I was
really trying to do or what my job was. But if you
want me to tell you that I am very grateful for what
you've done, all right . . . I'm telling you that now."

Isles grinned wryly. " You know, while I was on

208

Dark Bahama I thought a great deal about you. I indulged in all sorts of day dreams."

" I hope they were pleasant ones, Julian." She moved over to the french windows ; drew the curtains. She turned on an additional light—a rose-shaded standard lamp. Isles thought that the room looked delightful—a perfect setting for her.

He said : " They were pleasant enough, but of course they were day dreams. I don't suppose there's very much chance of their coming true."

" Day dreams seldom do. But what were they, since they gave you so much pleasure ? "

He said : " Mainly they concerned you and me. I wondered if there might be any possible future for us."

She laughed. " Disabuse your mind quickly, Julian. However could there be any future for me with anyone ? "

" Why not ? " asked Isles.

She shrugged her shoulders. " Really," she said, " there isn't a great deal of future for anybody who is doing my sort of work. It is a thing one doesn't consider. But if you're thinking about marriage, Julian, get it out of your mind. I'm not that sort of a woman."

He said, with a smile : " You mean you're wedded to your job ? "

" If you like," he said.

There was a long silence ; then he said : " Well, that's that. I wonder what the next move in the game is going to be."

" Didn't Ernest Guelvada tell you ? " she asked. " He's usually quite definite about what he wants."

Isles said : " His instructions to me were to bring these documents to you. Well, here they are. I suppose you understand what you have to do with them. Guelvada said he'd be over here soon."

She asked : " When ? "

" I don't know. He said within two or three days. Until then I imagine we just wait."

She was silent.

Isles said : " You don't seem very happy about something."

She moved across to him ; picked up his glass ; took it to the sideboard ; refilled it. She said : " I'm just wondering what Guelvada is playing at. He's an interesting type, but in the long run I think he's usually right."

" You don't mean to say there are going to be some more ramifications ? " Isles voice was almost hopeful.

She said : " You'd like that, Julian, wouldn't you ? This business is an adventure to you—a not unpleasant one. You'd like it to go on for ever."

He asked : " Why not ? It's been amusing. But I don't understand why you seem to be unhappy."

She said shortly : " I tell you I'm not unhappy. I'm just wondering. Are you certain that Guelvada gave you no other message for me ? "

He shook his head. " That was all. He told me I was to bring the documents to you. Here they are. He said he would be over some time—in two or three days. He seemed quite happy about everything."

She nodded. She smiled wryly. " I believe Ernest Guelvada is always happy. I'm told that he possesses an almost eternal youth—a complete faith in himself. I wonder what he'd look like if he *were* unhappy. However, these questions will probably answer themselves in due course. Now I suggest we eat. I was delighted to hear from Mary Ann that you'd arrived back. She's promised to prepare a special dinner for you."

She rang the bell.

Isles drank his second cocktail. There was a long pause. She stood in front of the french windows, waiting. Isles thought there was an unusual expression on her face.

After a minute she said : " It's funny she doesn't answer." She went out of the room.

Isles stood there, wondering what it was all about. He thought women were strange things. You expected them to be pleased ; they weren't pleased. He wondered what was in her mind.

The door opened. She came back into the room. She looked at him. There was a peculiar smile on her face. Isles opened his mouth to speak and then stopped. A man followed her into the room.

He was thin ; well dressed in a tan gaberdine suit. He wore a fawn fedora over his left eye. He was swarthy, with a small black moustache and gleaming teeth. He was smiling. In his right hand, which was hanging down by his side, Isles saw the Mauser automatic.

The man said, with an Italian accent : " You take it easy, kids. It ees notta going to do nobody any good making a noise. It ees all over." He dug Thelma Lyon in the back with the muzzle of the gun. " You go and sit on da settee with your boy friend. And don' start nothin'."

She said : " Well, Julian, here it is. We'd better do as we're told." She walked across to the settee against the opposite wall. She sat down. Isles sat beside her.

She said to the man : " What have you done with my maid ? "

He said : " Looka, baby, you don' ask no question . . . you don' get no lies. Jus' taka eet easy." He moved across the room ; drew back the curtains before the french windows ; unlatched the windows.

Two other men came into the room. One was short and stout ; the other of middle height. Isles thought they both looked very unprepossessing.

He said : " Listen, what is this ? "

The short man spoke. " It's easy, bud. All we want is that document case. Well, it looks as if we've got it, don't it ? The second thing we want is that you behave yourself an' do as you're told. If you don't you're gonna get hurt. So's your girl friend. You gotta understand we don't stand no nonsense from nobody."

Isles shrugged his shoulders.

The short man picked up the document case. He undid the straps. He took out the taped, sealed packet ; looked at it ; examined the address on the envelope. He said : " It looks as if it's all right this time, boys." He walked across to the settee ; stood looking down at them. He said : " I reckon it's tough bein' you. I wonder what's gonna happen to you two mugs. Maybe we'll know soon."

He went on : " Mrs. Lyon, you and your boy friend are going for a little ride. Maybe you'd like to put a coat on. It gets plenty cold sometimes at night when the wind comes up."

She said : " My coat is in my bedroom."

" O.K.," said the man. " Julio, take baby-girl along. She wantsta put her coat on."

She got up ; went out of the room. The man in the tan suit followed her.

Isles stood there twiddling his thumbs. Then he took a sudden dive at the short man. The man, very agile for his weight, took a step backwards and kicked Isles in the stomach. Isles fell against a chair ; knocked it over. He lay on the floor gasping.

The short man said : " I toldya to behave yourself, bud. The next time you try something like that I'm gonna hurt you but good. Get up, you bastard . . . an' relax ! "

Thelma Lyon came back into the room. She had on a light fur coat.

The man in the tan suit stood just behind her. He said : " For crissasake ! . . . So da boy friend tried to be tough ! " He looked at Isles, who was leaning against the wall holding his stomach.

The short man said : " Yeah . . . baby-boy's a scrapper ! He wantsta fight. He's a tough guy, see ? "

Julio said : " For me I'd like to taka care of him. I'd like to maka him squeal good."

The short man said : " What's eatin' you—gettin' bloodthirsty again ? Come on." He said to Thelma Lyon : " We're going out through the french windows. We gotta car outside. You're going in it. You're gonna keep nice an' quiet. If anybody tries somethin' they're gonna get a slug where it'll hurt most, see ? Here we go. . . ."

He stood to one side.

Thelma Lyon said to Isles : " It's no good trying to do anything about it." She smiled. " I hope they didn't hurt you too much."

She went out through the french windows. Isles and the three men followed.

CHAPTER ELEVEN

At nine thirty-five the Clipper landed at Miami airport. Guelvada took a taxicab; drove straight to the Altermeyer Hotel—a quiet residential hotel, which lay back away from the beach.

Arrived there, he paid off his cab; arranged for a hired car to be brought round; went to his room. He bathed; shaved; dressed himself; rang down for a shaker of Martinis. When it was brought he sat on the bed, drinking Martinis, smoking cigarettes, wondering.

Guelvada, who had spent quite a lot of his time thinking about people, had come to the conclusion after a great deal of experience that in the long run they always ran true to form. You met people, you watched them, you endeavoured to become acquainted with their habits, their method of thought, but once you had put your finger on that method it was not difficult to guess what their course of conduct would be in most circumstances. In this case, he thought, everybody had run true to form—even Miss Steyning.

Casually, Guelvada wondered—if there had been no documents, if her brother had not died, if none of these things had happened, whether or not Viola Steyning would have finished as a young woman who was too fond of hard liquor. He thought so. Fear, excitement, anger jealousy, hatred—all these things accentuated the weak points in the characters of people. They did not change character. They did not create new desires, new feelings, new attributes; they simply pinpointed what was already there.

The telephone rang. It was the desk downstairs, telling him that his car had arrived. Guelvada looked at his watch. It was ten-thirty. It was a lovely night with a full moon. He thought that a quiet drive along the shore might intrigue him. He grinned to himself.

He finished the Martini ; went downstairs ; got into his car. He began to drive towards Orlando Beach. He drove unhurriedly, leaning back in his seat in the car, steering it with his finger-tips. Past him came the evening traffic towards Miami. Ornate cars flashed by filled with young men, gaily-dressed women, bound for the hundred points of gaiety and excitement in Miami. Guelvada smiled to himself. He thought that for a little excitement now and again they should have his job, which was much more exciting, and with an excitement that was much more lasting.

It was nearly eleven o'clock when he stopped the car on the palm-bordered boulevard opposite the Orchid House Apartment. Guelvada got out ; walked slowly across the boulevard, his hands in his pockets, a cigarette hanging languidly from the corner of his mouth.

He began to think about the reception committee. He wondered what it would be like. Would it be Thelma, exquisitely dressed, with Isles smiling and contented in the background, with long drinks and cigarettes, and mutual congratulations ?

He rang the front-door bell. He stood there waiting patiently. Nothing happened. After a while he walked out into the *patio* ; walked the length of the block ; turned through the side gate along the path across the lawn to the french windows which gave excess to the drawing-room in Thelma Lyon's flat. One half of the window was open. Beyond lay darkness.

Guelvada sighed. He threw away his cigarette stub ; put his foot on the glowing butt. He stepped through the window into the room. He stood there for a moment, sniffing like a dog. There was a vague aroma of cigarette smoke. He walked across the room ;

found the electric light switch. He turned on the lights. In the middle of the floor was an overturned chair. Guelvada thought that the overturned chair created a strange atmosphere ; it spoiled the picture. There was something grotesque—something macabre about the chair. He began to whistle softly to himself. Then he went through the apartment. It was empty. The kitchen door was open. There was no maid—nothing. Only a peculiar, brooding silence.

Guelvada went into the bedroom ; switched on the lights. The bed was undisturbed. There was a faint suggestion of perfume in the room. He shrugged his shoulders. He thought to himself once more that people always ran true to form.

He went back to the drawing-room ; crossed to the sideboard ; mixed himself a drink. Once again he had a vague sense of annoyance at the sight of the over-turned chair. He walked across the room and set it up on its feet. Then he sat down in one of the armchairs with his drink.

He was thinking about Isles. He was wondering how sensible Isles was—whether he was as cool, cynical, as detached when things came to a head, and did not look quite so good, as he was normally. Guelvada thought that this was one of those questions that only time could answer. He finished the drink. He went through the french window, closing it carefully behind him ; walked across the lawn, through the *patio*, out at the main entrance. He got into his car. He drove back to Miami.

Ferenzy's bar is like or unlike many places in Miami. You pay your money and you take your choice ! It had good liquor, lots of music and a floor show, featuring many pretty girls, which began at midnight. It was crowded. The long bar, with its six bar-tenders in their resplendent white jackets, echoed with a buzz of conversation. Opposite the bar, set against the wall, were tables, comfortable chairs. But few people sat at the tables. They preferred the bar.

Guelvada ordered a highball. He took it to a table in the corner of the room ; sat down. He leaned back in his chair ; lighted a cigarette. His eyes, half-concealed by their eyelids, wandered round the room. At the end of the bar nearest the door was a tall, thin man. He had a pencil-line moustache. His face was thin and the cheek-bones stood out. Just beneath them, accentuating the unhealthy pallor of his face, was a slight flush—almost the flush of a consumptive. He played with a drink, but now and again his eyes sought the table where Guelvada sat.

Guelvada finished his drink. He got up. He walked past the tall, thin man out into the street. He turned left. He began to walk slowly up the long, narrow side street leading to the interior of the town. Now and again he stopped ; looked into one of the brilliantly lighted windows. Behind him, some way down the street, he could see the tall figure keeping its distance, moving when he moved, stopping when he stopped.

Guelvada shrugged to himself. He thought there was nothing so stupid as a shadower who allowed himself to be shadowed by his prey.

Guelvada moved on a little ; stopped again outside a man's store. He stood, looking at the ties with admiration. He waited there some time until he heard the car turn at the bottom of the intersection ; drive slowly up the street. Guelvada turned away from the window ; began to retrace his steps. He began to walk towards the sea front. He passed the thin man looking into a tobacconist's shop.

Guelvada said to him : " Good evening, my friend. I do not think you are very expert at your job, but maybe your boss is not rich enough to employ an expensive staff."

The man said : " Say, buddy, what the hell d'you think you're talkin' about ? "

" Of course you wouldn't know," said Guelvada.

Now the car came to a halt at the edge of the pavement. Two men got out. One said : " Hallo ! Mr. Guelvada ? "

Guelvada said : " Good evening. This is my friend." He indicated the tall, thin man. " I don't know what his name is, but take him away. He has begun to annoy me."

One of the men said to the thin man : " Come on, buddy. You come and take a ride with us. We wanta talk to you."

The thin man said : " What the hell is this ? "

The man who had got out of the car said : " F.B.I. An' we never like arguments. Get inside."

Guelvada waited until the car had driven away. Then he walked back towards Ferenzy's bar ; found his car where he had parked it ; drove back to the Altermeyer Hotel.

He went up to his room ; opened an attaché case. He took out the Swedish sailor's knife ; put it into his trouser pocket. He put a short-barrelled Luger pistol in a holster under his left arm. Then he went out.

He drove off; stopped outside the Greenacre building. He consulted the indicator in the hallway ; went up in the lift. When he opened the outer door of the office the man who was sitting at the desk looked up quickly.

He said : " Yeah ? What can we do for you ? "

Guelvada said : " My friend, I doubt if you can do anything for me. I have some particularly urgent business with your boss, Mr. Carno."

The man said : " He ain't in."

Guelvada raised his eyebrows. " But you're expecting him ? "

The man said : " Yeah. The thing is, is he expectin' *you* ? "

" No. . . ." Guelvada smiled pleasantly. " I assure you, my friend, that I am the last person in the world that he expects."

The man said : " So what ? " He looked bad-tempered.

Guelvada said : " So nothing. I'm just waiting." He took the pistol out of the holster. " I'm very good with this. Practically, I am one of the best shots in Europe. Also it would mean nothing at all to me to put a bullet through your head or somewhere where it might hurt even more."

The man said slowly : " For crissake ! . . . I believe you mean it."

Guelvada said : " Take your hat off the hook and go away. My advice to you, my friend, is to go away and stay away." His voice was terrible. " Because I think it might be very unpleasant for you if you stay."

The man got up. " Look . . . I'm not arguin'. I just do a job here on the night staff." He grinned. " I *am* the night staff. But I don't want to be no corpse."

" I think you are very sensible," said Guelvada.

The man put on his hat ; passed Gulevada. He opened the door.

Guelvada said over his shoulder : " If I were you I'd go straight home. I wouldn't even try to find Jake. You understand ? "

The man said : " Look, mister, I got medals for keepin' my nose clean."

Guelvada heard his steps echoing down the passage-way.

He moved over ; sat behind the desk. He sat there smoking a cigarette, the pistol lying on the blotter in front of him. Twenty minutes went past slowly. The door opened. Carno came into the room. He stood

219

in the doorway, big, burly, aggressive, looking at Guelvada, looking at the pistol.

Guelvada smiled cheerfully. He said: "Good evening, Jake. This, I think, is an historic occasion. Keep your hands just where they are and precede me into your private office. You and I have some business to discuss."

"Say, listen," said Carno. "What is this? What the hell do you think you're playin' at? Do you think you can get away with this Red Indian stuff around here?"

Guelvada picked up the pistol. He threw it in Carno's face. When it struck it made a noise like a mallet striking wood. Guelvada followed it like a streak. His hands shot out. Carno described almost a semi-circle; finished on his neck near the door of his own office. Guelvada kicked him in the stomach.

He said almost casually: "I think it is better to get the preliminaries over quickly. Goddam it, it makes things so much easier, don't you think?" He kicked Carno again. Then he picked up the pistol. He said in an icy voice: "Go into your room and sit down."

Carno picked himself up. His face was covered with blood. One tooth was missing. Guelvada followed him into the room. Carno sat at his desk. He held his handkerchief to his face. He was breathing heavily. Guelvada drew up the chair opposite the desk; sat down.

He said: "You are filth! In my life I have met many really bad men, but you stink. Men may murder and still have souls. They may cheat, lie, rob, and still be men. But a man who is prepared to sell his country is the filthiest cur in the world."

Carno said: "What the hell is all this in aid of? D'you think you are gonna get away with this? What goes on?"

Guelvada said: "I shall get away with it. I assure you of this." He was smiling almost pleasantly.

" Maybe, Jake, you have heard of Alcatraz—that island prison where Federal prisoners go ; where the electric light is always on in the cell. The place where most inmates would prefer to die than to go on living there. That is where you are going." He continued : " Like most inefficient stooges you over-played your hand, Jake. When Julian Isles arrived in Miami on Mervyn Jacques's boat, Jacques came to you because you are working for the same people as he was. And I said *was*. He told you about Isles. He told you about Isles's escape from the island. So you telephoned Mrs. Lyon. You knew all about her, but she knew nothing of you. I can imagine, my friend, what you told her. You told her that you had heard from the police here in Miami that they were looking for an escaped suspected murderer from Dark Bahama. You told her that the escaped suspected murderer, Julian Isles, had been landed by Mervyn Jacques from his fishing launch early that morning. You told her that for a consideration you would straighten things out ; that you would get Isles away from Miami to New York and thence to England where he would be safe."

Guelvada spread his hands and grinned. He threw the pistol on the desk in front of him with a careless gesture. He asked ; " What could she do ? She knew she had got Isles into this jam by sending him to Dark Bahama. She thought you were telling the truth. She *hoped* you were telling the truth, so she gave you a thousand dollars and told you to get Isles out of the way. I'm guessing pretty well, aren't I, my friend ? "

Carno said nothing.

Guelvada went on : " Unfortunately for you, Julian Isles was not so easily intimidated. At this moment he was not quite sure of Mrs. Lyon himself. He had an idea that you were employed by her. Anyway, he took a chance and went to see her. Some time afterwards she telephoned you and told you not to worry ; that she was satisfied with the situation."

Guelvada sighed. " How happy your employers must have been. Here they were—Mrs. Thelma Lyon and Mr. Julian Isles—stuck here in Miami right under their noses in a place where they could watch every movement they made. Unfortunately they—and you —did not reckon on one thing—that thing being Mr. Guelvada ! Well . . . ? "

Carno said nothing. He sat looking at the desk in front of him, dabbing at his face with a blood-stained handkerchief.

Guelvada said : " You are small fry. You are nothing. You are a hewer of wood—a drawer of water. You are like a cheap messenger employed to do the dirty work. The unfortunate Jacques is dead. He left Dark Bahama to report to his chief on the cay behind Bear Island. He was shot—a fitting end for such an indifferent person. And his boss made a getaway. His boss came to Miami. He is still here. He will remain here until this little affair is brought to an adequate conclusion. I suggest that you take me to see him."

Carno said : " What the hell do you mean ? I——"

Guelvada said : " Look . . . which you like. . . . In any event, you are going to prison for a long time . . . the Federal prison at Alcatraz. How long you stay there ; what eventually happens to you depends on how you behave to-night. Make your choice. You will take me to see the man who has employed you here, or you can go round to the F.B.I. Field Office now. Think it over."

Guelvada got up. He did not even bother to pick up the pistol. He lighted a cigarette ; stood leaning against the wall, looking at Carno.

After a while Carno said : " You win. But this might be tough."

Guelvada said : " Nothing will be tough. Go and

put some water on your face. Pull yourself together. Then we will go, my friend."

Carno went behind the screen in the corner of the office. Guelvada, comfortable in his chair, lighted a cigarette. He listened to the sound of Carno splashing about in the wash-bowl. After a minute he came out, dabbing his nose.

He said : " Look, mister, maybe you're gonna believe me an' maybe you're not, but I don't get all this. What was all that stuff about being a Federal rap ? Nobody ain't taken anybody outa this State yet."

Guelvada asked pleasantly : " What exactly do you mean by that, my tender-nosed friend ? " He leaned forward. " Goddam it, Carno, you're not trying to tell me that you don't know what you've been doing, are you ? Tell me, what do you *think* you've been doing."

Carno said : " I thought that it was some kidnap rap . . . this dame Lyon. I was told to keep an eye on her. I was told she got plenty of jack—a rich woman, see ? An' if anything happened to her her friends would pay plenty. I was supposed to keep an eye on her."

Guelvada said : " I see. So, according to you, the idea was to . . . snatch, do you call it . . . Mrs. Lyon and hold her to ransom ? Is that what your principals told you ? "

" That's the idea," said Carno. " That's what I thought. When this guy Isles landed at Miami from Dark Bahama, Jacques came to me like you said. Jacques was working for the mob too. He was keepin' an eye on the Lyon dame when she was on the island. He told me that this guy Isles had something to do with her. Maybe he was a bodyguard or something. But he'd got himself mixed up in a murder rap— see ? "

Guelvada said : " I see. . . ."

Carno dabbed his nose with his handkerchief ; then

he took out a cigarette pack ; began to smoke. He said : " Here's where I thought I could get myself a bit on the side. I thought maybe she'd pay some dough for gettin' this guy Isles out of it. I thought he was in trouble, see ? I thought I might do a little private business, so I telephoned her. She came round to see me and she gave me a thousand bucks to get him out of it. Like you said."

Guelvada said : " So that's why you had that very inefficient tail on me to-night. If what you say is true ; if you thought this business was just a kidnap plot, why did you put that not-very-good-looking friend of yours to follow me to-night ? "

Carno shrugged his shoulders. " I don't know anything. I do what I'm told. I heard that maybe you'd be coming over here from the island ; that if you came I was to keep an eye on you."

Guelvada said : " If what you say is true, my burly and unintelligent friend, maybe I shouldn't have been quite so tough with you. Supposing I were to tell you that the kidnap part of this scheme is just nothing at all—merely an incident—merely an incident in a greater scheme on the part of some enemies of your country to become possessed of certain documents ? "

Carno said : " For crissake ! . . . Look, I'm tellin' you I didn't know anything about that. I thought this was a big snatch, but I wasn't havin' anythin' to do with takin' anybody outa this State, see ? That's what would make it a Federal rap. I was gonna finish before then—take my dough an' finish. An' that's the truth."

Guelvada said : " The joke is I don't disbelieve you. Well, now you know. My advice to you, my friend, is to make yourself useful. Do I take it that the individual through whom you have been obtaining your in-structions has only recently arrived in Miami ? "

Carno nodded. " Yea . . . that's right. I had a phone call. I had a phone call that said he was to be the boss from now on. I was told where he was. When the guy I'd put on to you reported back to-night I was supposed to go an' see him. I was to telephone him."

Guelvada said : " An admirable arrangement. Well, what's stopping you ? I suggest you get on the telephone, my friend. Tell your principal that you are coming round to see him. Then we will both go and see him."

Carno said : " That's O.K. by me. But ain't you takin' a bit of a chance ? "

" Life is a matter of taking chances," said Guelvada. He pointed to the telephone.

Carno picked it up. He began to talk into the transmitter.

.   .   .   .   .   .

The house was a one-storey, stucco building—a large-sized cottage, surrounded by a lawn with a white paling. It was a pleasant-looking place—a mixture of Spanish and Colonial architecture. There were flowers in the garden. Guelvada thought it looked delightful and charming—the sort of residence that a rich denizen of Miami would keep for week-ending. It stood back from the main road between Orlando Beach and Miami.

Carno pushed open the wrought-iron gates. He said : " Look, have you got a gun ? "

" No," said Guelvada. " I left mine in your office. Have you ? "

Carno shook his head. " It might not be so easy."

Guelvada smiled. " On the contrary, we have now arrived at a stage in these proceedings when firearms are, I think, of little use." He led the way up the gravel path ; went up the portico steps ; pressed the door-bell. Carno, his hands in his pockets, stood close behind him.

The door opened. Inside, in the half-light, Guelvada could see the squat figure of an Asiatic house-boy. The man was well dressed, neat.

Guelvada said : " Mr. Carno has an appointment with your master."

The servant nodded. " You come this way, please."

They followed him across the hallway down the short passage. He opened the door at the end. They went in. Guelvada heard the door close softly behind them.

The room was large, with big windows looking out on to a garden at the back of the house. It was well furnished. There was a desk in the corner with a shaded light on it. Behind it sat a man.

He was tall, thin and distinguished looking. He had a small beard. He was smiling. He seemed a pleasant sort of individual.

He said : " Good evening, gentlemen. I'm doubly honoured. I expected only Mr. Carno."

" I am glad you are pleased," said Guelvada. " My name is Ernest Guelvada. Maybe at some time, in some place, you have heard of it."

The man smiled. He got up. Guelvada saw that he was almost elegantly dressed.

He said : " I am glad to meet you, Mr. Guelvada. I have heard of you a long time ago in circumstances which were perhaps as difficult as these are. My name is Voisana."

" I don't suppose it is," said Guelvada ; " but it will do."

Voisana shrugged his shoulders. " Won't you be seated ? "

Guelvada sat down. Carno moved to the fireplace ; stood, his back to it, his legs wide apart.

He said : " Listen, there's just one thing I want to talk to you about before he starts in." He indicated Guelvada with his thumb. " Right from the first I thought this business was a snatch job and I thought the idea was to snatch Lyon ; that all I had to do was to keep my eye on her until the time came. Then I was to take my dough and get out. I didn't know anything else about this, an' I don't like it. Maybe I've been goddam crooked in my life, but I've never got myself in a job against this country. I'm sorta fond of it."

Voisana said : " I cannot be blamed, Mr. Carno, for your supreme unintelligence. Also it has never been my policy to inform underlings exactly what they are doing."

Carno said to Guelvada : " So that lets me out. Now you know I was tellin' the truth."

Guelvada said : " I'm glad to hear it." He faced Voisana. " Mr. Voisana, the situation is rather unfortunate for you. In the language of the romantic I think the game is up."

Voisana said : " Is it ? Is that what you think, Mr. Guelvada ? "

Guelvada smiled. " I don't think. I know. Consider your position, my friend. For some time you have been living on that solitary island three or four miles from Dark Bahama. Carno was your contact here—an unwitting one possibly, who did not know what the real game was. His business was to look after Mrs. Lyon ; to report when she left Miami for Dark Bahama. On the island, Jacques was your agent. He worked for you. It was on your instructions he killed Sandford. And when he came to see you last, to report that his arrest on the island was imminent, you killed him."

Voisana said gently : " I always thought that Mervyn Jacques was a stupid individual. I overestimated his intelligence."

Guelvada said : " Maybe. Well, what do you propose to do now ? "

Voisana shrugged his shoulders. " I don't propose

to do anything. My business is finished. I think I may say that this little affair has come to a successful conclusion for us. What you say or do now means nothing."

Guelvada grinned. " In other words you are a philosopher, Voisana ? "

" Why not ? " said Voisana. " This is one of those moments when philosophy is a good friend. Whatever happens to me I shall have the pleasure of knowing that we succeeded."

Guelvada said : " That remains to be seen. I take it that somewhere or other you have Mrs. Lyon and Julian Isles ? Do you think I should consent to use them as a base for bargaining ? "

" I don't even mind," said Voisana. " I'm not interested."

Guelvada asked : " Where are they ? "

Voisana laughed. " You must think our organisation is a very stupid one, Mr. Guelvada. I have not the remotest idea where they are. Our little society is what you call watertight. We each do our own job. We know enough to do our job. It is not part of my business to know where the estimable Mrs. Lyon or the doubtless gallant Mr. Isles are at this moment. It is a matter of indifference to me what happens to them. I should think it might easily be the worst. That is my attitude. Do you understand ? "

Guelvada nodded. " In other words you have the courage of your convictions. The only point is that I think your convictions are lousy."

He got up. He asked : " Would you like to get a hat, Voisana ? There is quite a breeze to-night. Or perhaps you like to feel it on your hair."

Voisana said : " Why should I worry about a hat ? "

Guelvada smiled. " I think you are right. I should not even worry about your head or your neck if I were you. And don't think you are going to have

228

a heroic trial. The charge will be murder. I don't know what they do in this State. I think they might save the Dark Bahama authorities the trouble. I have an idea they'll deal with you here. I don't know whether it is hanging, electrocution or the gas chamber. I suppose you don't even mind about that."

Voisana said smilingly : " Not very much. I have served my purpose."

Guelvada said : " Take him away, Carno. Walk down the road towards Miami. There will be a car not far away from here. Take him to police head-quarters. They'll know what to do with him." He turned to Voisana. " It may seem to you that your departure is heroic. To me it is merely rather sordid. I have no doubt you profess yourself to be full of ideals for the salvation of the world. To me you appear merely as a cheap and inefficient killer."

Voisana raised his eyebrows. " Inefficient ? "

Guelvada grinned wickedly. " Inefficient. Because, before you die, my friend, you will realise that you have failed."

Carno said : " Come on, Tutz ! "

Voisana got up. He came round the desk. He said :

" Good night, Mr. Guelvada." He went out of the room with Carno on his heels.

Guelvada lighted a cigarette. He began to walk up and down the room. He looked at his strap-watch. He walked out through the french window on to the lawn ; followed the path round the side of the house on to the main road. Fifty yards in front of him, in the moonlight, he saw the car draw up. Carno and Voisana got in. The car made a " U " turn ; drove away.

Guelvada walked down the side of the road, smoking his cigarette, crooning softly to himself.

After a hundred yards a dirt road led off to the

right. Just down it he saw the second car. He walked over to it. Frim got out.

He said : " Good evening, Guelvada. How's it with you ? "

Guelvada said : " Not at all bad."

" We've been on your tail to-night," said Frim. " I've had some good men on Isles and Mrs. Lyon from the time he arrived."

Guelvada asked : " Where are they ? "

" They're in a house on the other side of Orlando Beach—a big place. It's called Maple Glade."

Guelvada said : " What does the situation look like there ? Does it look as if it might be what you call tough ? "

Frim said : " You know as much as I do, but we don't even mind if it is tough. I've got six cars out there all round the house. They've got smoke bombs, machine guns, everything. We're gonna get those boys dead or alive."

" It's much more amusing to get them alive," said Guelvada. " I'd hate them to get very angry at this moment."

" You're thinking of Mrs. Lyon and Isles ? " queried Frim.

Guelvada said : " Yes, but only so much. If it is necessary they'll have to die. But I think it might not be."

Frim asked : " How do you want to play this ? "

Guelvada said : " For me I think I'll do a little talking. Give me twenty minutes. Lend me a car. Give me twenty minutes in the house. If I don't come out you'd better move in. You spoke to the Police Commissioner on Dark Bahama ? "

Frim said : " Yes, I told him all about it. Everything's laid on from that end. Two men are flying over from there to-night."

Guelvada said : " Good. I'll be on my way."

" You'd better take this car," said Frim. " I'll tell you where the place is. Don't go in by the front entrance. We've got men there in the driveway. Go down the side road. You'll find a side door. I hope you get a nice reception."

Guelvada smiled. " This is one of those things."

Frim said : " What are you doing this for ? Why don't you let me play it my way ? I suppose it's Mrs. Lyon ? "

Guelvada said : " Not only Mrs. Lyon, but also the unfortunate Isles. He is what I regard as an enthusiastic amateur."

Frim grinned. " You got your nerve, buddy ! Well, have it your way and if you don't come out we'll come in. I'll tell you the way to go."

The two men inside the car got out.

Frim asked : " Would you feel happier with a tommy gun ? "

Guelvada shook his head. " Those weapons are extremely attractive at the right moment, but they make too much noise, my friend. Sometimes they give me a headache."

Frim told him the way. Guelvada got into the car ; let in the clutch ; took the main road towards Orlando Beach.

CHAPTER TWELVE

GUELVADA STOOD on the grass verge that bounded the dirt road. On the other side of the road, set in the high wall, were tall, wrought-iron gates. Through them, in the pale moonlight, he could see the wide drive, curving through the wooded park, leading, he imagined, towards the house. He smiled gently to himself. He thought that the residences of the people who worked for the other side were romantic and aristocratic. The idea amused him.

He looked back towards the coppice where he had hidden the car. It was well concealed ; could not be seen from either side of the road. Guelvada walked down the grass verge, keeping in the shadow of the trees, away from the iron gates, following the curve of the high wall.

He walked for some minutes before he saw the smaller wooden gate that led into the estate. He crossed the road. The gate was locked. Guelvada walked away from it ; took a quick run ; jumped for the top of the gate ; drew himself up and over. He dropped on to the grass on the other side.

Some distance away, through the trees, he could see the house. It was large and imposing. And it was in darkness except for one small window, right at the top—an attic window, he thought—which showed a light.

He began to walk across the well-kept grassland, through the trees, avoiding the narrow, gravel paths that bisected the grounds.

After a while, he stopped walking. He was within two hundred yards of the house, and the trees began to thin out. Here and there he could see where they had been cut down to give a vista from the house windows. But on the left and right sides of the house were thick shrubberies with narrow gravel paths leading to the back of the building.

Guelvada moved to the right, keeping in the shadow of the trees ; then, arrived at the shrubbery, he began to work his way round the side of the house, stopping now and then to listen.

He had arrived at the thickest part of the shrubbery when he heard the voice. It said in a thick, guttural tone :

" Put up your hands and keep them up. If you don't I shoot you ! "

Guelvada put up his hands. He turned. A few yards away was the tall figure of a man. He was dressed in a uniform which Guelvada guessed was that of a house guard—an unofficial corps supplied no doubt by one of the Miami organisations for the protection of estates in the neighbourhood.

The man came towards Guelvada. He carried a short automatic rifle, and there was an automatic pistol in the holster at his belt.

He said : " Well . . . what is it ? " He spoke slowly and with a foreign accent.

Guelvada took a chance. He replied in Polish. He said : " Don't be foolish. I am expected. I have a pass. Weren't you told about me ? "

The man said in the same language : " Show me the pass."

" Certainly," said Guelvada. He put his hand into the inside breast pocket of his coat. As he did so he took a step towards the guard. Then, as his hand came out of the pocket, it flashed forward and upward. He struck the guard with a ju-jitsu neck clip, delivered with the edge of the hand immediately under the Adam's apple. The man staggered backward under the force of the blow, gasping for breath. The rifle dropped from his fingers.

Guelvada sprang forward like a tiger. With one hand after the other he flung two of the *atimi* attack blows at the face before him. First a cut under the jaw bone with the left hand ; then a right-handed downward cut on to the muscle at the side of the neck.

The guard dropped like a stone, unconscious.

Guelvada dragged the prostrate body into the shadow of the shrubbery. Then, with a half-formed idea in his head, he picked up the automatic rifle, carried it twenty yards towards the tree-dotted parkland ; threw it under a bush. He went back, past the prone figure of the guard, on to the gravel path. He followed it round to the back of the house.

Standing there in the shadow of the shrubbery, Guelvada could see the light from an open french window facing on to the lawn at the back of the house. He came out of the shadows ; walked across the lawn to the french window. Behind it, the curtains were drawn and he could see into the interior of the room.

It was a large room, furnished as a study. Bookshelves lined the walls, and the antique tables set about the room were littered with books and documents. On one side of the room was a large mahogany desk, clear except for two telephones, a cigarette box and the usual writing set.

Guelvada stepped into the room. He lighted a cigarette ; walked across to the desk ; sat down. Three bell pushes were fitted on the left-hand side of the desk. Guelvada, with a grin, rang them all.

He sat back, drawing on his cigarette, waiting.

He heard the hurried steps outside the room ; then the door opened. A man stood in the open doorway, looking at Guelvada with eyes wide with astonishment.

Guelvada said : " Good evening, my young friend. Come in. Make yourself at home ! "

The man came into the room. He was young—
about twenty-five years of age, Guelvada thought. He
was dressed in a blue gaberdine suit, with a shot-
silk bow over a pale-green, silk shirt. He had a pale,
effeminate face, a cruel tight mouth, and hard eyes.

Guelvada said, with a small smile : " I take it that
you are a secretary—of sorts. I suggest you go and
find your employer and tell him that Mr. Guelvada is
here—Mr. Ernest Guelvada. I have no doubt he has
heard the name at some time or other."

The young man said : " You tell me how you get
in. How you get in here ? "

Guelvada looked at him with contempt. " Do not
be a greater fool than God made you," he said im-
pertinently. " Do as I tell you. Otherwise I'll deal
with you. I don't like you. You look like some sort of
bad-tempered fish. Get out and bring your boss here.
And be quick about it ; otherwise I'll have the whole
damned lot of you thrown into the local hoosegow.
Goddam it, don't stand there looking stupid. Go
away ! "

The young man said something unintelligible in a
foreign tongue. He went away, leaving the door open.

Guelvada lighted a fresh cigarette. Already his
volatile mind was playing with the passing idea which
had come to him during his encounter with the guard
in the grounds of the house. The idea, he thought,
might sound sufficiently reasonable to get by. He
shrugged his shoulders. This was a case, he thought,
when one was entitled to take a chance.

Two men came through the door. One was the
young secretary. From behind him came a man of
middle height, with long, carefully-groomed, grey hair.
His face was oval and good complexioned. He was
well dressed, his linen spotless, his hands mani-
cured. Guelvada noticed his eyes. Eyes that, behind
the horn-rimmed spectacles, were long, almost Asiatic.

They shone with what seemed to be a malicious humour. Guelvada thought they were spiteful eyes.

The man said to the younger man : "It's all right, Petrof. You may go . . . have no fear. . . . I am sure Mr. Guelvada will do us no harm." He smiled at Guelvada, exuding venomous humour.

Petrof went off, shutting the door behind him. Guelvada, smoking casually, kept his seat behind the desk.

The man in the horn rims pulled up a chair. He sat in the middle of the room, looking at Guelvada.

He said : " Mr. Guelvada, permit me to introduce myself. I am Kyria Karolov. Once upon a time, during the war, I nearly had the pleasure of meeting you in Riga. But you were a little too quick for me. I must congratulate you on that escape. But, of course, then I was not Karolov. I think my name was Vastov —Sergei Vastov—in those amusing days."

Guelvada grinned mischievously. " Perhaps it is as well for me that we did not meet."

Karolov smiled. " Those far-off days. . . ." He sighed pleasantly. " However . . . now we meet on what we might call neutral ground. Actually, I am not surprised to see you. I have of course noticed the activity round this house to-day—ever since last night, in fact. In spite of the elaborate precautions which your good friend Mr. William Frim—the Field Agent of the F.B.I. . . . I am sure he *is* your good friend . . . has taken, it was not possible for us *not* to be aware of what was going on. My servants tell me that it is practically impossible to move about the surrounding roads owing to the heavy traffic of F.B.I. cars, Miami State Police Troopers and, of course, the local Miami Police. . . . A most interesting situation ! "

Guelvada nodded. " Of course. . . . I think, Mr. Karolov, that things have moved a little too quickly for both you and me. That is why I thought it better

if we met and talked a little business—discussed this
thing as between ... what shall I call us ... professional
operators in a big way ... and tried to come to some
sort of terms ? Incidentally, in order to arrive here, I
had to be a little rough with one of your guards out
in the grounds."

"Think nothing of it," said Karolov. "I was just
talking to him. Beyond the fact that he seems to have
a permanent crick in the neck he seems quite well.
Please tell me what is in your mind."

Guelvada stubbed out his cigarette end in the ash-
tray. He began to lie glibly.

"Of course I should have guessed that when Julian
Isles arrived in Miami with the Steyning Formula
documents, that stupid Jake Carno would be aware of
the fact. He was of course watching the airport. I
was very foolish not to have considered this fact. Carno
reported to Voisana, your deputy, and you took care
of Isles and Mrs. Lyon *and* the documents almost as
soon as Isles delivered them."

Karolov nodded. "But of course, my friend. And
the documents are safe. They left by plane some time
ago. I am afraid you must say good-bye to them."

"As I thought," said Guelvada. "I must tell you
that I have, in my mind, very regretfully already said
farewell to the invaluable Steyning Formula. I must
congratulate you on the possession of those documents.
But it is not of that part of the business that I wish to
speak. I wish to make a deal with you, if possible, for
the return, *in good health,* of Mrs. Lyon and Mr. Isles.
Mrs. Lyon is, of course, a most valuable *agent.* She is
very useful to us, whilst the unfortunate Julian Isles is
merely an amateur who was caught up in this business
almost by accident."

Karolov said : "I shall like to accommodate you,
if possible, Mr. Guelvada." His eyes gleamed. "I have,
as you know, the greatest admiration for your technique.

By the way, supposing I were to consider the release of Mrs. Lyon and Mr. Isles, in good order and unhurt, what would you be prepared to offer me ? "

" I will tell you," said Guelvada. He helped himself to a cigarette from a box on the table ; lighted it carefully. " Your friend Voisana has been a little stupid. Before he left his lonely little island near Dark Bahama he found it necessary to kill a negro fishing skipper—a person of little consequence called Mervyn Jacques. We found his body on the island. This, of course, is murder and, as Voisana is, at the moment, under arrest in Miami, you will appreciate the position."

Karolov nodded. " I think I understand. Please go on."

Guelvada continued : " If you agree to release Lyon and Isles, in good order and unhurt as you so kindly put it, then I shall be perfectly prepared to undertake that Voisana is merely tried and executed on a charge or murder—the murder of Jacques. No other implications will be brought into the trial. If, on the other hand, your attitude is unsatisfactory about Mrs. Lyon and Mr. Isles, then I shall make it my business to turn this murder charge into a Federal charge of espionage and murder. This will bring you into the business. The story of your organisation here, of the murder of the agent Sandford, as well as your schemes about the Steyning Formula, will be made public. I do not think you would like that. It would mean that you would be arrested and probably finish up in Alcatraz."

" I see," said Karolov. " And, I suppose, most of my associates ? "

" Precisely," said Guelvada, with a pleasant smile.

" And the alternative ? " asked Karolov.

Guelvada got up. He began to walk about the room. " If you hand over Mrs. Lyon and Isles, you can make a getaway. You have the Steyning Formula and I do not hope, at this time, to recover it.

"Here is my offer. Voisana will be charged with simple murder. He will not talk about you and we shall not talk about you. You will leave this place to-night at an agreed time. You will be allowed to proceed out of this State and out of the United States. The F.B.I. and the State police will see you over the State line to-night. But Mrs. Lyon and Isles must be handed over."

"I am inclined to agree," said Karolov. "But there is one small point on which you must concur. You see, my dear Mr. Guelvada, I do not trust you. I know you to be a cunning, resolute and extremely clever person. I do not propose to play into your hands. Therefore I must stipulate that I shall not release Mrs. Lyon and the man Isles until I and my associates, who are now preparing to leave, are well away from here and over the State line. Then, and only then, will I release them. Mrs. Lyon and Isles can make their way back here as best they can when I feel that I am in a position of comparative safety."

"Very well," said Guelvada. "Then I suggest that you will approve this arrangement. You and your party will leave this house at, say, three o'clock this morning. When you are out of this State you will release Mrs. Lyon and Isles."

Karolov said : "That is so. We will leave at that time. There will be two cars. I and my associates will be in the first limousine. In the second limousine, which will be driven by one of my men, with an armed guard, will be Mrs. Lyon and Isles. If we are allowed to proceed unmolested out of the State, Mrs. Lyon and Isles will be released. You, on your part, will charge Voisana with a simple charge of murder and nothing else."

Guelvada nodded. "Agreed. I will now go straight

to Frim and inform him of the decision. You will realise that on your way out of the State you will be under the supervision of F.B.I. and State police cars. But you will be unmolested . . . that is unless," said Guelvada, with a smile, " you open fire on any of the U.S. cars. So, if you have any friends with uneasy trigger fingers, you had better warn them."

" I understand that," said Karolov. " I shall warn them. There will be no incident."

Guelvada walked to the french window. " Good night, Karolov, *alias* Vastov, *alias* Heaven-knows-what. . . . One day I hope to meet you again."

" I hope so too," said Karolov. " *Au revoir*, my friend."

He smiled cynically as Guelvada passed through the french windows.

Outside, Guelvada turned right. He walked quickly along the narrow, gravel path leading round the left-hand side of the house. Once in the shrubbery on the other side, he began to run. In a minute he found the spot where he had hidden the guard's automatic rifle. He picked it up ; ran swiftly through the trees ; climbed the gate ; went back to the spot where he had left the car. He threw the automatic rifle into the back of the car. Then he began to walk down the road away from the house.

At the end of the estate wall at the inter-section of the State road, Guelvada found Frim and the F.B.I. radio car. Frim came to meet him.

He said : " Well, I'm glad to see you in one piece. What do we do now ? "

Guelvada said : " My friend, I will tell you. Things may easily go wrong, but we must take a chance. I have made a deal with Karolov."

Frim raised his eyebrows. " Was it necessary ? " he asked.

Guelvada shrugged. " You know these people. They

are desperate, and Karolov is courageous. Satisfied
with having the Steyning Formula, he now proposes to
save himself and his people if possible. He is holding
Mrs. Lyon and Isles as hostages. He knows that your
cars are all round the place. He wants to make a
getaway."

Guelvada smiled. He went on : " Well, let him
make it. This is the deal I have concluded with him.
Goddam it, I think it is a nice deal. Karolov and his
party leave at three o'clock in two limousines. In the
first car will be Karolov and his *aides*. In the second
car, a driver, an armed guard and Mrs. Lyon and
Isles. Karolov says that provided he is allowed to get
over the Miami State line he will release Mrs. Lyon
and Isles and allow them to make their way back as
they wish. But if he is interfered with by you or the
State Troopers "—Guelvada shrugged his shoulders
again—" I think it will not be very good for those two."

Frim nodded.

" I have also agreed," said Guelvada, " that when
Voisana is tried this story shall not be made public.
He is to be tried for murder—the murder of Mervyn
Jacques. Do we agree ? You will extradite him back
to Dark Bahama. He will be tried and hanged."

Frim said bitterly : " So Karolov gets away with
it ? He's got the Steyning Formula and he's gonna get
out of here to do more plottin', more schemin'. . . ."

Guelvada interrupted. " My dear Frim, some enter-
prising Scotsman once said that the best laid plans of
mice and men sometimes do not come off. I have
another idea."

Frim said : " Yeah ? You're full of ideas, Ernie,
aren't you ? "

Guelvada smiled. " Very often. I made a second
stipulation with Karolov. Quite obviously, he trusts
me as much as I trust him. He knows that if it were
necessary for me to lie to him I should lie. Therefore,

PETER CHEYNEY

you may take it that all his people will be armed. I
warned him to be careful of some of his henchmen
with trembling trigger fingers. I told him that he
would receive no interference from the F.B.I. or State
cars which would see him over the State line, but that
if any of his people fired a shot I could not be responsible
for what happened."

Frim said : " Well, they're not going to fire a shot,
are they ? They don't have to. All they do is just
waltz out of this State an' make a getaway."

Guelvada held up his hand. " Let us see. . . ." He
went on : " I suppose there are police cars along all
the side roads ? "

Frim nodded.

Guelvada said : " My friend, I must leave you now.
I have no doubt I shall see you soon—in any event,
to-morrow morning there are one or two things we
shall have to arrange. In the meantime, *au revoir.*"
He turned ; began to walk down the road in the
direction of his car.

    .   .   .   .   .   .

Guelvada sat in his car in the shadows. The automatic rifle lay on the seat beside him. He picked it
up. Under the dashboard light he examined the
mechanism. It was a two-way weapon. It could be
fired either as a single-shot rifle or, by pulling down the
automatic catch, as a sub-machine-gun. Guelvada
thought it was a nice job. He put it down against the
passenger seat. He looked at his watch. It was twenty
minutes to three.

He started up the engine ; drove down the road for
half a mile. Then he came to a side road. At the
entrance was an automobile notice saying that the road
led on to the main State highway. Guelvada turned
down the road. He drove half-way down ; parked his

242

car on the grass verge in the shadow of some trees ; turned out the lights ; picked up the rifle ; got out of the car ; locked it. He turned into the thick woods on the left-hand side of the road ; began to make his way through the trees, walking parallel with the road.

In ten minutes he arrived at the apex of the two roads. Immediately in front of him was the broad State highway. Twenty yards to his right, parked in the middle of the side road, was a State Trooper's car. By the light of the dashboard Guelvada could see two men seated in the car . . . nearest to him the driver and on the right in the passenger seat a State Trooper with a sub-machine-gun on his knees.

Guelvada turned off to the left. He took up a position just inside the trees verging the main road, where he could watch both the main road and the State car. He examined the automatic rifle, made certain that the catch was in position for a single shot ; then he sat down on the damp grass, waiting.

A quarter of an hour went by. Then, from somewhere down the road, from the direction of the Karolov house, he could hear the sound of automobiles. He moved towards the edge of the road. Away down the road he could see the headlights of two limousines. They were driving slowly at about thirty miles an hour.

Guelvada, just inside the edge of the wood, lay flat on his stomach, the rifle cuddled into his shoulder, pointing in the direction of the State Troopers' car. He waited. Now the leading limousine was about a hundred yards behind him. Guelvada took a sight on the rifle. He aimed at the window of the police car. He took a short, careful aim ; squeezed the trigger. Almost simultaneously with the shot, the window of the State Troopers' car was shattered. Guelvada could see that, as he had intended, he had put the bullet clean through the window in front of the two State Troopers in the car.

He saw the Trooper with the sub-machine-gun bring it to his shoulder. There was a chatter of bullets as he opened fire on the leading limousine. There was an answering shot from the car ; another hail of bullets from the State Troopers' car. Then the limousine heeled over ; turned into the ditch on the side of the road.

Guelvada swung round as the second car, its brakes screeching, stopped almost opposite him. He snapped down the catch on the automatic rifle ; sprayed the front windows of the second car with bullets. The car stopped. Guelvada dashed into the road ; arriving simultaneously with the two State Troopers from the police car. He opened the door of the second car. On the floor were Isles and Thelma Lyon.

Guelvada said : " Good morning. I hope you are both well ? "

Isles said : " My God ! . . . So it's you, Ernie. What's happened ? "

Guelvada shrugged his shoulders. " Somebody fired at a State Troopers' car. It must have been one of Karolov's men. They opened fire on his car. By the amount of bullets they put into it I should think no one was alive. Then somebody shot your driver and the guard. I consider it most appropriate. One might almost describe it . . . goddam it . . . as a happy ending."

Thelma Lyon said : " Maybe. But I wish whoever it was did the shooting had concentrated a little more on the driver. Believe it or not, I think I'm hit in the arm."

Guelvada said : " Let me look. . . ." He threw back the shoulder of her fur cloak ; tore open the flimsy silk of her frock.

He said : " My dear, it is nothing. Just a little scratch on the fleshy part of the upper arm. I promise you that if it is properly attended to there will not even be a mark."

A car, its brakes screeching, pulled up beside them. Frim got out.

Guelvada said : " *Au revoir*, you two. Get back as quickly as you can to Thelma's apartment."

He went over to meet Frim.

Frim said : " So what, Ernie . . . ! "

Guelvada said : " It was most unfortunate. Somebody fired at the police car in the side road. They opened fire on the leading car ; then somebody put some bullets through the front windows of this car. You will find that the driver and his colleague are both dead. Mrs. Lyon and Isles are all right."

Frim looked at him and grinned. He said : " For crissake, Ernie ! . . . Are you some baby or are you . . . ? "

Guelvada smiled. " Remember, my friend, I told you the best laid plans of mice and men . . . You will also remember that it was Karolov's car that fired the first shot."

Frim nodded. " Yeah. . . . I'll remember that ! "

Guelvada said : " Get Mrs. Lyon and Isles back to her apartment. I'll come and see you in the morning, Willie."

He turned back into the woods. He came out on the side road ; began to walk towards his car. He thought the moonlight was beautiful on the road. He felt happy.

He began to croon to himself an old Spanish love song.

CHAPTER THIRTEEN

ISLES WAS standing at the french windows, looking over the sun-flooded lawn, when Guelvada turned the corner from the *patio*. He was wearing a tussore silk suit, a white, soft hat and brown and white suede shoes. Isles though he looked almost too well dressed to be true.

He turned and went back into the cool drawing-room. He began to mix himself a drink at the side-board.

Guelvada stepped through the windows. He said : " Good morning, my friend. How do you find yourself after all your adventures ? And how is Thelma this morning ? "

Isles said : " She's all right. As you said, it was the merest flesh wound. So that's that. Except that the fact that she wasn't seriously hurt—or even killed—wasn't *your* fault."

Guelvada said : " Perhaps you will mix me a brandy and soda—with ice. Also, my delightful Julian, you should remember that it is impossible to make omelettes without breaking eggs."

Isles said shortly : " Even if the egg is a woman ? " He began to mix Guelvada's drink."

Guelvada shrugged.

Thelma Lyon came into the room. She was wearing a white shark-skin coat and skirt. One arm was in a sling made from a matching silk handkerchief.

Isles said, as he handed Guelvada the drink : " So this is the end of the adventure. I think it's a great pity that after all this effort the documents have been lost. Are you pleased with *that*, Ernest ? "

Thelma looked at Guelvada. " Have they been lost, Ernest ? "

" Of course not," he said. " The Steyning Formula is on its way to F.B.I. Headquarters in Washington." He looked at his strap-watch. " That is if it has not already arrived." He sipped his brandy and soda. He continued : " Surely, Julian, you did not expect that I would trust *you* with those documents ? " He was smiling pleasantly.

Isles said : " I see. So I was merely a stooge."

" No, Julian," said Thelma. " Not quite that. You will remember that when you arrived here with what you thought were the documents I was a little dubious. I couldn't believe that Ernest had handed them over to you."

Guelvada sat down ; adjusted the crease in his immaculate trousers. He said : " Steyning was clever. Unfortunately—or fortunately—his sister was stupid and careless. For me, from the start I never believed that he would despatch such important documents through the post to a sister who was foolish and too fond of drink. I was right. He did not do that."

" What did he do ? " asked Isles.

" He wrote his sister and told her that he was sending her the documents. He allowed someone to see that letter. Then he despatched a series of documents which purported to be the scientific work on the Steyning Formula, on which he had been working during the previous six months. He enclosed a note to his sister informing her that the real documents had been despatched under separate cover to the post office in Dark Bahama to await collection by her."

Guelvada sighed. " When she received the fake documents she did not even bother to look through them or to read his note which was attached to the last page. She was probably tight—and scared. She re-taped the package and hid it under a pile of linen, where I found it with the note. This was the package

I gave you, Julian. The other package—the real one —was retrieved by the Police Commissioner on Dark Bahama and handed over to the F.B.I. agents sent over by Frim."

Guelvada smiled. " I was delighted with the situation. You will realise, my friend, that I did not know what agents Karolov had on the island or in Miami. It was important that I should. I knew that after my conversation with Mervyn Jacques he would go straight to his boss and tell him what had happened. I knew that our enemies here, in Miami, would watch every movement from the island. I knew also that when you landed with the fake documents they would come out into the open ; that Carno was watching Thelma ; that immediately you arrived they would strike. Well . . . they did. They did what I expected them to do. They abducted the documents and you and Thelma. They had to. And the results, as you have seen, are admirable. The U.S.A. Government has the documents. Voisana will be charged and hanged. Karolov is dead. What more do you want ? "

Thelma asked : " What now, Ernest ? "

Guelvada smiled. " Our work is finished for the moment. Goddam it . . . we have all done a very good job. I am delighted with everyone. I am also very pleased with myself ! "

He walked across to the sideboard ; mixed a drink ; brought it to Thelma Lyon. He said : " It is unfortunate that *you* should be our only casualty. But it is an honourable wound."

He went back to his chair. He said : " Julian . . . in a few days you will wish to return to England. I expect your Mr. Vallon will want you to report on your successful case for his client." He grinned at Thelma Lyon. " Thelma . . . you may do as you wish. You may remain here, at your apartment, for a holiday, until our chief wishes you to report back to him. Or you may return to England with Julian . . . if you wish to do so."

She asked : " And you, Ernest . . . what are you going to do ? "

He smiled at her. " I am returning to Dark Bahama. Goddam it . . . I like the place. I am going to swim and laze in the sun. I am going to fish for sharks and barracuda. I am going to walk and ride and drink a little in the evening. I am going to be very happy. . . ."

He got up. " I have to see Frim. And then, for the moment, my work is done. I have already hired a fishing launch. After lunch I shall set out for Dark Bahama. I shall arrive there this evening."

He picked up his hat ; moved to the french windows.

" *Au revoir*, my friends. As you know, I am a great reader of people's minds. I know exactly what you two are going to do. . . ."

She asked : " What *are* we going to do, Ernest ? "

He grinned at her. " You will stay here for a few days. You will walk and talk and amuse yourselves. Then, when you are bored with Miami, you will begin to think of England and the delights of the voyage home. You will return to England together and all the while Julian, who is charming, will make delightful love to you, my Thelma."

Isles began to speak. Guelvada held up his hand.

" Do not argue, my friend," he said. " Always I have had the ability to read the future. *Au revoir*, my delightful, my brave companions. Guelvada thanks you from the bottom of his large heart."

They watched him walk across the lawn.

Isles said regretfully : " There goes a hell of a man. . . ."

.   .   .   .   .   .

It was two-thirty when Guelvada walked down the

wooden jetty on the water-front and jumped into the cockpit of the thirty-foot motor launch.

He lighted a cigarette ; relaxed on the cushioned seat.

He said to the skipper : " Warm up your engines. We shall leave very soon."

The skipper started the engine. Guelvada got up ; leaned over the stern ; stood, watching the jetty.

He smiled as Thelma Lyon came into sight. She wore a white skirt and a blue jumper with a smart blue beret set jauntily on her black hair. Behind her came a negro porter carrying two suitcases.

Guelvada jumped on to the jetty. He said : " I am delighted that you have come to see me off. I think that is charming of you, my Thelma. But then you are a charming and delightful person."

She smiled at him. " I'm not seeing you off, Ernest. I'm coming with you. I, too, am fascinated by Dark Bahama."

Guelvada said nothing. He helped her into the boat. The negro porter handed over the suitcases. Guelvada tipped him and the man went away.

Guelvada said : " Cast off, skipper. Goddam it ... this is going to be my favourite holiday ! "

The launch began to move out towards the open, sunlit sea.

Thelma Lyon said : " There's one snag, Ernest. I haven't a reservation at the hotel on the island. I hadn't time."

Guelvada smiled at her. " Don't worry, my sweet ... I made a reservation for you at the Leonard Hotel before I came to see you this morning ... ! "

THE END

>>> If you've enjoyed this book and would like to discover more great vintage crime and thriller titles, as well as the most exciting crime and thriller authors writing today, visit: >>>

The Murder Room
Where Criminal Minds Meet

themurderroom.com